SCARLET WHITE

Jody Marie White

SCARLET WHITE

a novel

TATE PUBLISHING & *Enterprises*

Published by Tate Publishing & Enterprises, LLC
127 E. Trade Center Terrace | Mustang, Oklahoma 73064 USA
1.888.361.9473 | www.tatepublishing.com

Tate Publishing is committed to excellence in the publishing industry. The company reflects the philosophy established by the founders, based on Psalm 68:11,
"The Lord gave the word and great was the company of those who published it."

Published in the United States of America

ISBN: 978-1-61739-154-5
1. Fiction, Historical
2. Fiction, Romance, Historical
10.10.07

This book is dedicated in loving memory to Brandon White, loving husband and father.

CHAPTER 1

"God, please don't let there have been an accident. I need him home this week." She glanced out the front window for the hundredth time. The train was late. She was beginning to worry.

"Hurry, Hannah, he should be here any minute," Elizabeth Wyley shouted as she ran into the expansive kitchen where Hannah was making a peach pie.

"I'm goin' as fas' as I can, Miss Lizzy. I don' think he'll be wantin' anythin' 'mediately after he gets here anyway," Hannah called after Elizabeth with a smile, as she reached for one of the jars of canned peaches.

"I know, Hannah," Lizzy said as she grabbed a slice of peach from the canning jar. "I just want everything to be perfect. Things have changed so much around here since he last left, and I want at least your peach pies to be as perfect as they were when he had them last year."

"Flatterin' me, child, will get me no faster." Hannah giggled.

Lizzy smiled after her and flew out the kitchen door and up the servants' staircase to make sure Charles' room was in perfect order. "It looks great in here, Rosie. Just like he left it."

"I'm glad I can help make somethin' like dat, Miss 'Lizbeth," Rosie said with a sad smile.

Lizzy smiled back and left the room, slower this time. Things had changed so much since Charles had been home last Christmas. Before then, life was as it had been for the nineteen years of Elizabeth Wyley's life. The Wyley's were prominent and respected in Atlanta and for a large part of Georgia, as they had been for generations past due to the success of the cotton plantation. Their plantation flourished. They'd had a constant flow of visitors for teas, parties, and hunts. Each year, Mrs. Wyley threw a Christmas ball and a harvest ball. These were attended by nearly everyone of prominence from the city.

As for the family, Mother and Father were the head of the house. As such, they were obeyed and respected. Mother and Father were kind, though strict, and did not show love outwardly. Lizzy felt she needed to always do something to make them proud of her and love her though; since they never praised her, she never knew if she succeeded.

Edward, four years older, was the big, strong oldest brother. He was popular. Unfortunately, this popularity caused discomfort for Lizzy. Edward wanted to be powerful among the other plantation owners and their sons, therefore, he rubbed shoulders with them and adopted many of their ideals. Lizzy did not know what he did exactly with their field slaves, but if the harsh, controlling, sinister look she saw daily on his face was any indication, she decided she did not want to know.

Charles, two years older than Lizzy, was the smart one off to business school in Boston. He was Lizzy's best friend. They shared many of the same ideals. They had been inseparable from an early age.

Lizzy was the youngest who attended all of the social events with her friends, like a good southern belle was expected. She did not enjoy the social events, yet she tolerated them, knowing it made her mother happy. She truly wanted to please her mother. She had three close friends and preferred to spend her time with them. These three were her brother Charles; his best friend, Tyler; and their neighbor, Maggie.

Now, everything was different, socially and personally, for the whole family. Last Christmas, Lizzy's mother, Martha Wyley, had been struck ill with a fever. She survived it but was left in her own world. She was not herself anymore. Or, rather, she was more herself than before. She had always been a proud woman. She was a social woman. Her parties were second to none. She brought her children up to be fine, upstanding southern citizens. She was a typical southern belle. She owned slaves and always treated them as though they were no more than slaves. This was the aspect of their mother's personality that came out most after the fever.

Lizzy no longer attended the social events. She had stopped accepting invitations early in the last year and eventually the invitations slowed to a trickle. She didn't mind not going to the social events, in fact, she almost welcomed it. She never did care for all of the gossip and backbiting the girls seemed to do at all of these events. Most of her acquaintances were married or engaged now anyway, and she just didn't fit in.

Lizzy's father, Major Samuel Wyley, couldn't handle his wife's illness. He had been so scared during the time of the illness, he took early retirement from the army to stay home with his wife. He alternated between staying by her side for days and too scared something would happen that he remained busy with plantation work and didn't see her at all for other days. This lasted for a month.

Soon, he became emotionally distant and heavier handed with the family and the household help. He barked orders now, as he had during his days in the army. There was no softness toward his children or his slaves. He did show a tender heart with his wife. He tried to be kind and loving toward her to ease her life. He had always been softer with his wife. The children knew they loved each other. They had grown up childhood sweethearts, married at a young age, and, together, enjoyed their status as two of Atlanta's elite plantation owners.

Lizzy's oldest brother, Edward, tried to emulate his father. He followed the major around and learned the ways of the plantation according to his father. Soon, he was more heavy-handed than the major.

Charles had left to finish his third year of business school in Boston while their mother had still been ill. It was a hard decision for him, but Lizzy insisted that he go. This left Lizzy in charge of the household. She didn't mind, "It's a great opportunity for me to learn how to run my own household should the time come," she would always tell Charles when he wrote his thoughts about leaving Boston and coming home.

"Where's my favorite sister?" came the call from the front hall that jerked Lizzy out of her musings over the past. It was Charles. He was home at last. She hiked up her skirts and flew down the curved staircase to embrace her big brother. "Whoa, there," Charles said, almost falling over. "I think you knocked the wind out of me."

"You've always been weaker than me," teased Lizzy.

"Weaker than I," scolded Charles teasingly.

"And you've always been smarter than I—I mean me," Lizzy finished dramatically. "Let me help you with your bags, and then we'll go into the kitchen for some of Hannah's famous peach pie."

"All right, they're in the carriage with Bartholomew," Charles said. "I asked him to wait while I came in to tell you I was here."

They walked arm in arm outside to where Hannah's husband, Bartholomew, was unloading the carriage. "Bartholomew," Charles said, "I told you not to lift a finger with those bags. Lizzy and I will get them."

"I know, Missuh Charles," Bartholomew said, looking around nervously. "But if Misus Wyley saw me jus' standin' here wi' these bags in de carriage, she'd have my hide."

Charles and Lizzy frowned. They knew his statement was true. "Please, Bartholomew," Lizzy said, "don't worry about it. She's sleeping in her room and won't be up for hours. Please let us get them."

"At least let me carry somethin,' Miss Lizzy," Bartholomew pleaded. "On a day like today with Missuh Charles comin' home, I don' wanna take a chance."

Charles and Lizzy exchanged glances, but finally agreed to let Bartholomew help with the bags. The three of them marched up the stairs to Charles' room. "Thanks, Bartholomew," Charles said. "I want to unpack, and then we'll be down to see you and everyone else."

Bartholomew nodded and left the room.

"So," Lizzy started, as she relaxed on the window seat, "Tell me all about your year. How are John and Michael? Any girls yet?"

Charles smiled. "John and Michael are fine; they and Aunt Sally send their love. And no, there aren't any serious girls yet."

At the word "serious," Lizzy's head perked up. "Nothing serious, huh? But that means that there could be something not serious, right?"

"Well, there are some prospects, but I really want to finish my schooling and have a way to provide for a wife before I take one."

"I understand, but if you wait too long, all of the good ones will be gone," Lizzy teased.

"Well, it would be their loss then, wouldn't it?" Charles teased back.

Then, both fell into a comfortable silence as Charles finished unpacking. Charles and Lizzy had been very close throughout the years. They could sit in each other's company and not say anything for hours.

"It's nice to have you home again, Charley," Lizzy said melancholically.

"It's nice to be home," Charles matched her tone.

They both knew home wasn't home anymore.

The hardest part for Lizzy and Charley was the way their parents treated the slaves. They did not believe the same as their mother and father on slavery. They grew up on the plantation and were taught their parent's beliefs but had never felt very comfortable with it. When Charley went to school in the north, he connected with many Northerners who were against slavery. He became close with them and shared their ideas with Lizzy. He didn't share his ideas with their brother Edward, because Edward vehemently shared the beliefs of their parents.

"How's Mother?" Charley asked.

"The same," Lizzy answered sadly. "It's so hard to see her like this. It hurts so much to see her treat the slaves like she does too. They're all so scared. I'm scared."

Charley crossed to look out the window where his sister was sitting. He gazed at the trees lining the river on the east side of his family's property. His eyes fell on his sister's favorite willow tree.

"Lizzy, I have to tell you something," Charley said hesitantly.

"What is it? Are you all right?" She grasped his arm. She searched his profile for any hint of what he was about to say. He was working his square jaw, as he often did when he was nervous.

He turned his ocean blue eyes on her. "I'm fine," he said reassuringly. "I have to tell you though …I'm not going back to school."

"What do you mean?" Lizzy asked cautiously, as her hand dropped to her lap, her gaze never leaving his.

He ran his hands through his brown hair making it stand on end as he dropped to the window seat next to her. "After Christmas, when I go back north …I'm joining the United States Army."

Lizzy was quiet for a while. Charley searched her face. "Lizzy, aren't you going to say anything?" he asked.

Lizzy smiled a sad but loving smile. "I can't say that I'm surprised."

"Really?" Charley asked.

"Really," Lizzy replied. "I guess I'm more surprised that it took you so long."

"What do you mean?" Charley asked.

"Well, you've been writing a lot about your views on the slavery issue and the issue of the states separation. Then there's South Carolina actually seceding from the Union. I guess I've just been waiting for this to happen."

"So what do you think about it?" Charley asked, seeking her approval.

"Well, a lot of things," Lizzy answered. "Obviously, I'm sad and scared at the prospect of you not coming back. But more than that, I'm proud."

"Really?"

"Of course. You're doing something that you believe in. You know the repercussions of what you're doing with our family, as well as the dangers you'll face, but you're doing it anyway. You're following your convictions. I'm proud of you."

Charley came and sat by Lizzy and put his arm around her shoulders. "Are you just a little bit jealous too?"

Lizzy looked up at him. "You know me too well."

"Why are you jealous?"

"You know why," Lizzy answered, a little exasperated at her brother. "You get to do something with your life that you believe in. What do I get to do? I have to stay here attending parties, trying to find a husband that I don't want among the stuffy, slave driving Southerners! Of course I'm jealous of you. When is it going to be my turn?" she finished quietly. Lizzy had always wanted to be allowed to do what her brothers were able to do. She wanted the same education, independence, and opportunities. Now, she wanted to fight in the war as well.

"Just be patient, little sister. Your time will come."

"Obviously you don't know me well enough if you're telling me to be patient." Lizzy smiled.

"On the contrary." Charley smiled back. "I know you too well, as you stated before. I also happen to know the One who created you, and He has more patience than either of us. Just tap in to that. Your time will come. I can feel it."

"I hope so," Lizzy answered. "Charley?"

"Yes?"

"Do me a favor, will you?"

"Depends on what it is." He smiled.

Lizzy didn't match his smile. "Don't tell anyone until after the party."

"After the party? But that's in two days."

"I know, but it's our Christmas party and your coming home party. Please…" She looked at him imploringly. "Mother's been planning this party for a while now. She's almost to her old self when she plans it. Things have been almost pleasant around here with this for her to place her focus. Father's been somewhat kinder as well. Please."

Charley paused and looked at her imploring face. "All right, I'll wait. I guess it will give us more time to plan on how to tell them anyway, huh?" They both smiled at each other.

A soft knock came at the door. "Come in," Charley said. Robert, one of the new household help, entered.

"Master Charles, Miss 'Lizabeth, Major Wyley requests yo' presence in his study, soon's yo' able."

"Thanks, Robert," Lizzy answered. "We'll be right down."

Robert left to tell Major Wyley their answer. "Well, I guess we'd better get this over with," Charley said. "I was hoping for some of Hannah's pie before going into the lion's den, but I guess it will be a nice treat after coming out." Charley and Lizzy smiled at each other and left to go to their father's study.

As Lizzy and Charley entered their father's study, they surveyed the room. Major Wyley sat in his high, straight-backed chair that the two secretly called his "throne." Their father always sat in this chair during family meetings. The ornate carvings indeed made the chair look like a throne. Edward sat on a smaller straight-backed chair near the major. Martha lounged on a chaise on the opposite side of the room. Sarah, Martha's personal maid, sat trying to be invisible in a straight-backed chair in the corner of the room near Martha. Lizzy and Charley came in and sat together on a love seat in the middle of the group.

They felt their father's and brother's eyes on them as they came to sit down. "Welcome home, Charles," Major Wyley said stoically.

"Thank you, Father," Charley answered, "it's good to be home."

"Charles!" Martha squealed. "So nice of you to join us. We've missed you." She didn't get up from her perch on the chaise.

"Thank you, Mother," Charles answered. "It's good to see you."

Edward simply nodded his greeting. Charles nodded back.

"Let's begin the meeting," Major Wyley started. "The purpose of this meeting is to welcome Charles back, of course," he nodded toward Charley, who nodded his reply, "and to give assignments for the upcoming party. As you all know, in two days we will be hosting our annual Christmas party. It will be our usual large ball with all of the most prominent people in Atlanta present. I hope to make it a huge success for your mother." Martha beamed and blew a kiss to her husband who, embarrassed, ignored the gesture.

"In order to accomplish this," Major Wyley went on, "we must give assignments to help the party run smoothly. First, Elizabeth, you will help your mother with everything in the house. I expect you to know everything that is going on, from the food to the house cleaning, and I expect it done well. Anything your mother wishes will be done. Understood?"

"Yes, Father," Lizzy answered. She understood this too well. She had been playing this role the entire year before. Basically, she was in charge of the house. Her mother announced her desires and Lizzy was to make them happen, unless they were too outlandish. If that were the case, Lizzy was usually able to assess the situation and make it so her mother wouldn't remember giving the order.

"Charles," Major Wyley continued, "you are in charge of the stables. I want to make sure our stables are the cleanest they have ever been. I want no carriage in those stables unless they are spotless. Understood?"

"Yes, Father," Charley answered, not relishing this detail. Edward gave Charley a smug look of satisfaction, which Charles ignored.

Edward's look went unnoticed by Major Wyley as he prepared to give Edward his assignment. "Edward, I want you in charge of the grounds. Every tree must be trimmed, every bush shaped to perfection. Every corner of the porch and pathways swept. Understood?"

"Yes, sir!" Edward answered.

"Now, for the actual party, Charles and Edward, you will be free to mingle with the guests. If they have any need that you see is going unmet, make sure to get it met. Elizabeth, you will stand with your mother and I at the receiving line for the beginning as your dance card is being filled, and then you will be free to dance with the guests."

Martha looked incredulous. "But, Samuel," she cried, "Elizabeth should not be with us at the receiving line. She should be mingling with the prospective, available young men!"

"My dear," Major Wyley soothed, "She will mingle with the young men, but what better place for the men to see her than the receiving line? Then, after greeting her, they can go straight to her dance card."

Martha softened at that idea. "We may find you a husband soon, my dear," she cooed at Lizzy. Lizzy just smiled and nodded her acknowledgment, not wanting to be the center of attention at this party.

"Are there any questions about assignments for this party?" Major Wyley asked. No one raised any questions. "Well, if that's it, then—"

"Father," Edward interrupted, "I don't have a question, but I do have an announcement."

"By all means, Edward, what is it?"

"Well, I wanted to announce to my family first that I am engaged to be married to Alice Mayer. We have just begun talks of our wedding."

"Wedding? Married?" Martha's head shot up. These were the only words she heard from her son. "You're married? Why didn't you tell us? Why didn't you invite us to your wedding? Edward, what did we do to you to deserve this?"

"No, dear, he's engaged to be married," Major Wyley tried to explain to his near-hysterical wife. "He's not married yet."

Martha heard none of this. She continued her wailing. Sarah instantly stood up along with Lizzy to try to coax her mistress out of the room. "Come now, Missus Wyley. Let's go lay down. I'll fix you a nice cup of hot tea."

"Get your black hands off me, girl!" Martha shot at Sarah. "Can't you see I'm upset? My son has gotten married, and I didn't know anything about it."

"Mother," Lizzy tried, "Please, go lie down. We'll talk with Edward and get this all straightened out."

Martha got up, still complaining, though quieter now and, slapping her hands, led Sarah out of the room. Lizzy tried to go out, but Sarah stopped her, sensing that there was more to the family meeting.

"I'd better go see to her," Major Wyley said, as he pushed up from his chair. Stopping at the door next to Lizzy, he said, "Before I go, Elizabeth, I want you to know that having you as a part of the receiving line is more of a help with your mother. Should she need to leave, Sarah will be around to take her for some help with the kitchen or something. You will then take your mother's place at my side. But," his gaze hardened, "if you do not find a suitor during this party, someone to bring a good name to this family, it will not be my fault. Understood?"

"Understood, Father" Lizzy answered coolly.

As Major Wyley left the room, Charley and Lizzy turned hard looks at Edward.

"What?" he asked uncaringly as he cleaned the dirt from his fingernails.

"Don't play stupid," Lizzy said as she crossed to him with clenched fists. Charley jumped up and put a steadying hand on her shoulder. She stopped and shook Charley's hand off. "You know what you did. How could you bring up something like that without bringing it to me beforehand? You know how Mother only hears certain parts of conversations and how she blows things out of proportion!"

"There just wasn't a good time to do that," Edward challenged smugly, as he jumped up to his full height, more than a head taller than his younger sister. "Anyway, what's done is done. I will announce my engagement at the party. There, I've given you fair warning, do what you need to do with that." He then strode out the door without another word.

"I can't believe he did that!" Lizzy said through clenched teeth. "He's so insensitive. Now, we have to try to fix this and prepare Mother for his announcement at the party. What a—"

"Lizzy," Charley steadied her again with his hand on her shoulder. "What's done is done. We'll work through this. We always do. Now, let's go get some of Hannah's pie and get calmed down from this, all right?"

Lizzy worked her jaw in anger as her brother had earlier in nervousness. "All right." Lizzy resigned.

The next morning, the preparations for the party started off without a hitch. Everyone worked together to accomplish their assignments. The stables were the cleanest stables in town. The house was immaculate—
—mirrors and brass fixtures sparkled, floors were waxed till shining.

The decorations in the house were second to none. Garland raced up the front pillars to the roof. Holly berries chased each other along the garland to the top. Iron lanterns adorned with red bows lined the winding, tree-lined driveway, as well as the garden maze behind the house. In the house, the staircase in the foyer wrapped around a large Christmas tree decorated with white candles and silver ornaments. A smaller tree stood sweetly in the ballroom, decorated with red and green bows and white candles.

Smells from the kitchen made everyone's mouth water throughout the house. Pies, cakes, cookies, and other pastries were flowing into the dining room.

Not only did the house look splendid, but everyone caught the spirit of the party. Everyone wanted to do their part to make this the best party ever. In the back of their minds was the thought that this might be the last of the Wyley Christmas parties, though not a word was said of the fact. No one knew what might happen with Mrs. Wyley's health and, with the conflicts between the North and South looming over the country, no one knew what might happen with the men of the family.

Everyone worked hard through the morning. A light brunch was prepared in a corner of the kitchen so as not to take away from the preparations for the party. A late lunch was taken after noon, and then work resumed. Everyone was still in high spirits, though they were beginning to become tired. It was this tiredness that hit Mrs. Wyley the most.

Toward late afternoon, the kitchen workers were busy making their treats. Lizzy and Sarah were working together to make an apple pie. They were quite intent on their work and their conversation that their attention was not as close on Mrs. Wyley as it should have been. Lizzy and Sarah were brought out of their conversation by the frantic screaming of Mrs. Wyley and Dolly, one of the kitchen helpers.

Dolly was mixing cookie dough for her final batch of the day. She had dipped her spoon into the batter to taste the consistency. Mrs. Wyley saw her tasting the dough and mistook her taste testing for stealing food. She immediately railed on the girl.

"What do you think you're doing?" she screamed. "Stealing food? Don't we feed you enough? You'd steal from your mistress right in front of her? You little ingrate. How dare you! I'll teach you to steal from me!"

Mrs. Wyley yanked the wooden spoon out of Dolly's hand and began beating her with it. All the while, Dolly was trying to explain her actions amid the blows from the spoon.

When Lizzy and Sarah came to their senses after the initial shock of the outburst, they ran to Dolly's rescue. They were too little too late though. Dolly's face was bleeding, and she had welts all over her back from the blows. Lizzy and Sarah were able to remove Mrs. Wyley from Dolly as some of the other help guided Dolly away, though the two sustained some blows from Mrs. Wyley as well. Lizzy was struck on both hands and Sarah on the back of her head, a bump immediately rising.

After the initial blows, they were able to restrain Mrs. Wyley and remove her from the kitchen. They took her to her room and laid her on her bed. She was spent. Warm water was brought up to them, and they placed warm, wet cloths on her forehead. Soon after, she fell asleep.

When they were sure Mrs. Wyley was asleep, Lizzy and Sarah left the room. Once in the hallway, Lizzy's tears began to flow.

"I should have been more attentive," she began. "I should have been closer. I knew the work might get to her, but I didn't pay close enough attention. Poor Dolly. I can't believe I allowed that to happen."

"Now, now, Miss Lizzy," Sarah comforted, "you didn't 'low nothin.' These things jes' happen. If I blamed myself for everythin' yo' mama did, I'd be beatin' myself up every day. I did that in the beginnin,' but I realized it's not my fault. I do what I can, but in the end, it's her. I know it's not really her, but I can't blame myself for it. You got to do the same. You hear? We got to get through this party. Two more days, and it'll be over. The stress is just gettin' to us all. We'll jes' be on the lookout more. All right?"

"I guess so," Lizzy answered. "It's just so hard to see her like this. I mean, where did this come from? Father has never condoned violence in this house, no matter how mad he got. I've never seen anyone strike anyone in this house before. If she did this today, what's to say she won't do it again, or worse, later?"

"We jes' got to pray, Miss Lizzy. We jes' got to pray."

The rest of the day went by quietly. Everyone finished their jobs, cleaned up, and went to their own quarters for the evening. Lizzy was in her room getting her clothes to air them out for the party, when a soft, urgent knock came to her door.

"Miss 'Lizbeth, Miss 'Lizbeth," came Sarah's urgent call.

Lizzy dropped the stockings she was deciding between and rushed to let Sarah in. "Come in, Sarah. What is it?"

"Come with me an' see, Miss Lizzy, please."

"Is Mother all right?"

"She's fine," Sarah reassured, "but please, come with me. She airing her dress. I think she plans to wear it."

The words sunk in and Lizzy let herself be led to her mother's room. The dress Sarah was referring to had been a controversy between Lizzy, Sarah, and Mrs. Wyley. Mrs. Wyley had made it with the purpose of wearing it to the party. It was a beautiful dress. Made of light champagne colored satin, it had three-quarter length sleeves with lace finishing to the sleeves, a lace high collar, and lace trimming the bottom hem. It was very elegant. Mrs. Wyley had done a stunning job. There was one major problem though. The lace around the bottom hem of the dress was two inches too long. The satin hem came to the floor as it was, but the lace came two inches farther than that. Sarah and Lizzy had tried to convince Mrs. Wyley several times to fix the dress, but she couldn't understand what was wrong. The two were extremely afraid that she would trip on the hem and either severely hurt herself or, at the very least, embarrass herself, both of which would be detrimental to her fragile state of mind.

Sarah and Lizzy had even tried to hide the dress and sneak it out to fix it themselves. Both solutions resulted in the loud, frantic search for the dress and, finally, a severe yelling at both ladies when the dress was returned. Mrs. Wyley had even gone so far as to throw a vase against the wall, narrowly missing Sarah, but a shattered piece bounced off the wall and cut Lizzy's cheek. Mrs. Wyley was mortified more at the sight of blood—she had always had a weak stomach—than at the fact that she'd hurt her daughter. She laid herself down in bed for two days. As for Lizzy, the doctor had been called, and he stitched up her cheek. That was almost a month ago, and Lizzy still had a pink scar on her right cheekbone.

As for the dress, Mrs. Wyley did forget about it for a few days—usually when it was hidden. Lizzy hoped they could pull it off again. She had gone out and bought her mother a dress of similar color, though a bit darker and similar style, hoping she might not know the difference.

The two worked quickly and quietly, since Mrs. Wyley was sleeping in the next room. They brought out the new dress and hung it to air out where the old dress was. They made sure all of the accessories matched this dress. They were about to leave the room and hide the old dress in Lizzy's room, when they heard Mrs. Wyley get up to come to where they were. Quickly, they threw the dress in a nearby trunk and pretended to be admiring Mrs. Wyley's "handiwork" on the new dress.

"Elizabeth, Sarah, what are you doing in here?" she questioned.

"Mother," Lizzy said, "we were just admiring your handiwork on this beautiful dress you made." She hoped the lie would work.

"Oh, thank you, dear." Mrs. Wyley beamed. "I worked very hard on it. It's of the latest fashion, you know. I want everyone to see me in my finest at the party."

"Indeed they will, Mother," Lizzy replied. "What are you doing awake? I thought you were tired."

"I'm rested up now, dear. I thought I'd sit in here and stitch a while, that is, if that old ninny Sarah would leave me alone." She cast a demeaning glare at Sarah. Sarah stood her ground and didn't shrink back at her mistress's words.

Lizzy was furious. She hated it when her mother talked like that. How awful! She cast an apologetic look to Sarah, who smiled her thanks. Fearing any more hurtful words from her mother, Lizzy simply said, "Enjoy your stitching, Mother. We're just leaving."

They left the room together as Mrs. Wyley picked up her stitching. "I'm so sorry, Sarah," Lizzy apologized for her mother's behavior.

"No mo' 'bout it, Miss Lizbeth. No mo' 'bout it." Sarah shrugged. "We jes' got to make shore yo' mama don' fin' that dress now."

"I'll check in periodically before the party to make sure," Lizzy offered. "Now, you go on to bed, Sarah, we've got a big day of finishing tomorrow. Thanks for coming to find me. Sleep well."

"You too, Miss Lizbeth. Thanks fo' yo' help."

Lizzy went back to her room and finished getting everything out to air for the party, and then she retired for the night.

The next day, Mrs. Wyley stayed in her room. The rest of the preparations went well, and everyone was more relaxed. There was a certain air of excitement as the day grew to a close and everyone retired for the evening, anticipating the party the next day.

As for the dress, Mrs. Wyley didn't suspect anything, and she came downstairs ready for the party in the darker champagne colored dress and told everyone who commented on it that she made it herself.

CHAPTER 2

The day of the party was uneventful. Last minute touches were made on decorations and house cleaning. The family took their time to get ready. Everything was perfect. When it came time for the party, the brothers took their places to receive guests in the ballroom, and Lizzy and their parents took their places in the foyer.

The first to arrive was the Thomas family. They were always the first to arrive to any social event. He was a judge and, therefore, very prominent in the community. They always wanted the prestige of being the first to arrive and see who else was invited, as well as pass on any information they deemed necessary about the guests. "Haughty gossips" is how Lizzy described them. She couldn't stand this family but was forced to be nice as the hostess.

They were polite enough as they passed through the line, giving bits and pieces of unnecessary gossip as they shook hands. Their son, Aaron, was right behind them, as haughty as ever. After the initial greeting, seeing no one else had arrived behind him, Aaron paused to talk with Lizzy.

"You look lovely this evening, Miss Wyley," he said, smoothing his already greased red hair.

Not wanting a prolonged conversation, Lizzy simply thanked him.

"I wonder if I might have access to your dance card," he continued. "I would like to reserve time with you."

Afraid this would happen, Lizzy had already put the dance card in Charley's hands. "You'll have to speak with my brother, Charles," she replied. "He is making sure all potential dance partners are worthy gentlemen."

"Well then," he answered smugly, stroking his clipped beard. "I'll have to go to him and assure him that I am a worthy suitor." He bowed slightly to her and left in search of Charley.

Lizzy was relieved he was gone and now turned her attention to the guests arriving. She immediately eased when her best friend Margaret Swanson, whom she affectionately called Maggie, passed through the line and told her she'd wait for her in the ballroom. The two girls had been close for as long as they could remember. Their families had neighboring plantations, therefore, their fathers often did business together. The Swanson's plantation was much smaller than the Wyley's. Mr. Swanson had inherited the plantation but had actually gone into the banking profession. Major Wyley helped him with the plantation, and Mr. Swanson helped the Wyley's with their banking.

Maggie had been born with her right foot turned inward at almost forty-five degrees, thus leaving her with a pronounced limp. She had a lovely, though plain, face and long, beautiful brown curls, but most people were unable to get past the limp to see her simple, attractive features and kind heart. Lizzy had always been protective of her friend for just that fact.

Maggie was a soft-hearted, sensitive person. Though she was used to people staring and even ridiculing her, Lizzy knew the comments and stares hurt her friend. She did anything she could to help ease the pain.

A steady stream of guests poured in over the next half hour. Lizzy's cheeks were growing tired from smiling. Mrs. Wyley was doing great. She seemed a little confused with the names of a few of the guests but otherwise performed well.

Lizzy smiled happily when Charley's friends Jackson Hill and Phillip Markley approached the line. They had always been kind to her, and she enjoyed dancing with them at the parties.

"Where is your dance card, Miss Elizabeth?" Jackson asked.

"I gave it to Charley for protection." She smiled conspiratorially.

"Good idea." He chuckled. "I will go find him and see if I pass the test."

"Please do," she said. "I would like to see his decision."

Jackson smiled and left to find Charley.

Finally, the stream of guests died down. About to ask her father if she could be excused to join Charley and Maggie, another hand was thrust in her direction and a voice stopped her.

"You aren't going to leave without greeting me, are you?"

Lizzy turned toward the voice. "Mr. Parker!" she cried and shook his hand. "I was wondering where you were."

Andrew Parker was a good friend of the Wyley family. Having known Major Wyley from a young age, their families continued a strong friendship through many years.

The Parker's owned the most successful of high society's tailor businesses in Atlanta. All of upper society went to his shop for the latest styles and greatest fashions. Lizzy had bought her mother's dress from him.

Ten years earlier, six months before his wife died, Andrew Parker freed all of the slaves working for him. Many of the slaves and their families had worked for his father. Not only did he free the slaves, he also hired any of those who were newly freed to work for him for comparable pay to many of the white tailors and seamstresses. Surprisingly, he did not lose as many of his white employees as he had feared. A few left, telling him exactly what they thought of his decision.

Judge Thomas actually tried to coerce other high society members to boycott Parker's business, to no avail. No matter Andrew Parker's views on slavery, he still produced the best, most fashionable quality clothes.

Major Wyley didn't agree with Andrew's decision, but their friendship stood the test of time and trial. The two simply never discussed the topic.

After Mrs. Parker's death, the Wyley's became second family to Parker's son, Tyler. He and Charley were already close friends, but their friendship strengthened as he spent weeks on end with the Wyley's while his father traveled overseas to study the latest European fashions, which he did about four months out of each year.

Now, ten years later, Lizzy, Charley, Tyler, and Maggie were nearly inseparable. Tyler was even in school up north with Charley.

"I was held up at the train station," Mr. Parker was saying.

"I didn't realize you were traveling," Lizzy said, somewhat confused, since she always knew the goings on of the Parker household.

"I wasn't," Mr. Parker said with a twinkle in his eye.

"He picked me up from the station," came another voice.

Lizzy's eyes lit up. "Tyler!" she practically squealed. "What are you doing here?" She ignored all propriety and gave Tyler a hug. Her father shot her a disapproving glance, which she wanted to ignore, but dutifully heeded and stepped away from Tyler.

"I wanted to come home for Christmas," he said simply.

"Charley said nothing about you coming home," she said.

"It's good to know he's a man of his word." Tyler smiled.

Lizzy turned to her father to gain permission to accompany Tyler to the ballroom. When it was granted, she turned to Mr. Parker, "It's great to see you. Thank you for bringing Tyler home." Then Lizzy and Tyler went in search of Charley and Maggie. Since Charley knew Tyler was to be there, he kept quiet until Maggie noticed the new arrival. Maggie, ever aware of social proprieties, was less vocal, but no less excited than Lizzy, to greet their friend.

"Tyler," she exclaimed, "What an exquisite surprise. To what do we owe this great pleasure?"

Tyler smiled in his reply. "I felt I was long overdue to spend Christmas with such good friends."

"I must say, it is a most wonderful surprise, if there ever was one." Maggie beamed.

"It's wonderful to know Charley is still a good man at keeping his word," Tyler said.

"Of course I am," Charley said in mock defense. "I have always been and always will be."

The evening passed comfortably with joyful conversation amid the intermittent dancing with the guests. All in all, they felt it was a good evening. Even Lizzy thought it wasn't a total loss dancing with Aaron Thomas, as, in her words, "Besides having a terrible personality, he is a fine dancer."

As the party wore on, the group became tired. Again it was Tyler's name on Lizzy's dance card. Noting the tired look on her face, Tyler suggested they take a break and get some fresh air on the veranda. The two were extremely close. They often shared secrets with each other that they didn't even share with Charley or Maggie.

The two walked out on to the back porch overlooking the rose gardens. It was a beautiful, clear night. The stars twinkled above them. They stood for a while in a comfortable silence, enjoying the night with the sounds of the party behind them. Then they decided to walk through the gardens as they talked.

Tyler broke the silence. "I've missed you while I've been gone, Lizzy."

"I've missed you too," Lizzy said lightheartedly. "Life's been really dull without you and Charley here to poke fun."

Tyler smiled. "I've really missed our talks. No one up north comes even close to knowing me like you do."

"Still haven't found a girl to pour your heart out to?" Lizzy teased.

"No."

"What's wrong with them?"

"They're not you."

"What?" Lizzy asked, confused.

Tyler didn't reply immediately but continued walking silently, as Lizzy's eyes searched him for an answer. Never needing small talk between them, Tyler dove in to what he wanted to say to his best friend.

"Whenever I thought of pursuing a relationship with a woman, I always found myself comparing her to you." He didn't look at her for her reaction, and she didn't respond.

"I would think, This one isn't as pretty as Lizzy. This one isn't as smart. None of them had your conviction. No one shared the same interests. I never felt that I could share my soul with any of them as I do with you. I constantly found myself wanting to share thoughts and experiences with you. Finally, I realized what I want," he paused to gather his courage, "is you." He finally looked at her for her reaction.

Lizzy stopped walking as her mind raced, unsure of what she had heard. This was her brother's best friend, her best friend. They had grown up together. They knew everything about each other but had always only been friends.

"Oh my," was all she could say.

"I know there was no way for you to be prepared for this," Tyler said, wringing his hands behind his back. "Has there ever been a time you thought of me as more than just a friend?"

"I—I don't know," Lizzy stammered. "We've known each other for so long. I think I've always thought of you as a brother, like Charley. I know I'm closer to you than anyone, even Maggie, but I honestly don't know that I've thought of you as more than that." She looked at him sadly, not wanting to hurt her best friend.

Tyler didn't say anything for a while. Lizzy knew him well enough not to say anything either. He started walking slowly. Finally, he spoke. "Have you ever thought of what your future husband would be like?"

"Yes," she said simply.

"What's he like?"

"Well, he's handsome." Lizzy tried to lighten the mood. "He loves God and me. He's kind, fun, has a good sense of humor. He's a hard worker. He's not intimidated by my desire to learn; he encourages it. He…" she looked more intently at him. "He has the same views as I do and …encourages me in them." She stopped short and drew in a sharp breath. "Oh Tyler, I've just described you, haven't I?"

"Have you?" he hoped.

She smiled. "Right down to being handsome."

His look told her he wasn't sure about that, but thanks.

"Oh," Lizzy said as she sat down on a nearby bench. "I did not think that would come."

"I hoped it would." Tyler smiled slyly.

"So, what now?" Lizzy asked, looking somewhat bewildered. She wasn't sure what to do. She'd just realized that she felt something more than friendship for a man she'd always considered just her best friend.

Tyler was silent for a while. Lizzy turned to look at him. They knew each other extremely well. They could often tell what the other was thinking. Lizzy felt this was one of those times. She looked hard at him, and then drew back sharply.

"Oh, Tyler," she cried, tears brimming her eyes. He turned to her. "Why did you do this?" she asked.

"Do what?" he asked, trying to put a comforting hand on her arm. He could tell she had become extremely shaken.

"Why did you help me realize my feelings only to go away, possibly to war?" she questioned.

"What do you mean?" Tyler said, though his face told her she was right.

"I know you, Ty. I can see it on your face. You didn't have to come home for Christmas. You don't usually. I should have seen it. Charley's going, of course you'd be going too. It was probably your idea. You wanted to come see us one more time before…" she drew a sharp breath and let it out slowly, "before you weren't sure if you'd be able to come home again."

"I'm sorry, Lizzy. I hope you'll forgive me," Tyler pleaded, giving her hand a gentle squeeze. "I wanted to tell you how I feel before I left. I wanted to know how you feel. I hope I'm not being too selfish."

"Of course not, Ty." She squeezed his hand in return. "I'm so glad you told me. I'm extremely sad you're going, but I'm so glad you told me." She paused, then asked again, "So what do we do now?"

He answered more quickly this time. "Lizzy, I won't ask you to make a decision now. If for no other reason than maybe you're caught up in the moment. I want more than anything to ask you to be my wife right now, but, as much as I don't want to think about what might happen, I won't allow for the possibility of you being a widow before you're a wife."

She drew her hand away to catch a gasp. He could see the pain in her eyes at that statement, though she didn't say anything. He continued. "What would probably be best would be for you to think about it and pray about it while I'm gone. Make sure this is really how you feel. If, while I'm away, you find someone who fits your desires better than I do, take him, marry him, and have a wonderfully happy life. But, when I get back, if I still fill your qualifications, maybe we'll talk more?"

"Of course, Tyler," she smiled through her watering eyes. "Thank you so much for understanding and being so sensitive to the situation. I will think about you constantly and pray for you every day."

He didn't miss the fact that she said she'd think about him, not just the situation. He smiled. "I will think about you and pray for you every day too. And, if it's all right with you, I'd like permission to write you while I'm away."

"I hoped you would," she answered.

They fell silent. He offered her his hand, helping her from the bench. They walked silently, arm in arm, back to the house. They saw Maggie waiting on the porch. Sensing their peaceful attitudes, she said simply, "It is a beautiful evening, isn't it?" They smiled at her, agreeing that it was.

"Charley suggested you step into the ballroom before your father questions your whereabouts," she said to Lizzy.

Knowing her father might make a scene, if not with guests present, then shortly after they left, Lizzy agreed, and they stepped inside. They met up with Charley, and he and Tyler went to get refreshments for the group. As Lizzy and Maggie talked, Aaron Thomas came to them.

"Miss Wyley," he announced without so much as a greeting to either woman, "I have taken the liberty of assessing your dance card. I have noticed that Tyler Parker has his name there several times. I would be more than willing to mention to your brother the possible ramifications with associating with someone of his social standing."

Lizzy bristled. She looked at him defiantly and responded, "Mr. Parker is a good family friend. I can tell you right now, I would not like to see that name changed."

Taken aback, he regained his composure quickly. "Of course. I'm sorry. I forgot." He did not sound the least bit apologetic. Changing the subject, he asked, "Could I bring you some refreshment?"

"Thank you, but no," Lizzy answered with a smugness to her voice. "Tyler has already seen to that." She emphasized the use of his familiar name as he approached with the refreshments.

Aaron nodded curtly to Tyler, and then turned to Lizzy, "I believe we are to dance in two more songs," he said almost coolly, then composed himself, "I'll return then." He bowed slightly and left the group.

Lizzy was livid. How she distained that man. When Aaron returned for her, she stiffly accepted his arm and went through the motions of the dance, quite relieved when it was over.

As she returned to the group, Maggie touched her arm and requested they move to Lizzy's room to freshen up.

When the two friends were behind closed doors, Maggie turned excited eyes to Lizzy. "What's going on?" she asked.

Lizzy looked confused, though she had a feeling she understood her friend perfectly. "What do you mean?"

"You and Tyler," she answered. "First, you two walk alone through the gardens. Now, I know that's nothing extremely new, but you have never done that in public before. And then when Aaron Thomas rudely expressed his opinion of Tyler, you answered a little more fiercely than normal." She cocked an eyebrow at her friend in anticipation of an answer.

Lizzy was too excited to play games, but she wasn't sure enough of the circumstances to let on her full excitement. She tried to remain calm as she gave her answer. "Well," she began slowly, "Tyler expressed that he has feelings for me."

Maggie's face lit into a big smile. "Are you serious?" she asked.

Lizzy simply nodded, but her eyes betrayed her excitement.

"How wonderful!" Maggie exclaimed. "You two would be perfect together. What did you say?"

"Well," Lizzy began again, not sure of what to say. She knew Maggie well enough to know that her friend would guess something was going on if she tried to hide anything, so she decided to let the conversation go where it wanted to. "We decided not to do anything official until he returns."

"School is over in May, that's not long at all."

Lizzy wasn't sure what to say.

Maggie looked long and hard at the person she knew better than anyone in the world. "What are you not telling me?" she asked, trying to mask the fear, concern, and anger all threatening to bubble over.

Lizzy took a deep breath and sighed. She knew she needed to plunge right in. "He's not going back to school," she said.

Maggie was silent, trying to figure the implications of the statement. "What is he doing?" she asked flatly.

Lizzy took another deep breath. "He's joining the U.S. Army," she answered as evenly as her nerves would allow her.

Maggie was speechless. She wasn't sure she understood what was happening. Seeing the utter confusion on her friend's face, Lizzy took her by the hand and led her to the settee to explain what she knew Maggie had knowledge of but did not comprehend.

"Hostilities are heating up between the North and the South," she began. "Soon, the southern states will try to break away. South Carolina already has. If the rest follow their example, there will be war. You know the boys want to preserve the Union. You know they want to put an end to slavery. They know this is the only way to make that happen." Lizzy fell quiet to let her words sink in.

Maggie's face went from blank, void of emotion, to registering shock, and finally anger. She jumped up and turned her emotional fury on her friend. "Why the army?" she railed. "They're not soldiers. Charley's a farmer. Tyler's a businessman. He sells clothes! Why did you let them do this? They're not fighters!"

Trying to remain calm with her friend's fury running barely checked at her, Lizzy remained seated, fingers clenching the blanket next to her. "Maggie, you know that's not true," she said as evenly as possible. "How many times did they fight for what Mr. Parker did and for the people he freed? How many times did they fight for us? Fight against the horrible things the other kids would say about your limp and our education and independence? They've always been fighters. They may never have had the guns to do it with, but they have always been fighters."

The two women stared each other in the eye, fighting for control of the situation, until Maggie conceded her friend was right and came back to sit down, defeated. She was not upset she had lost the argument. Having never been close with her father, she was afraid of losing the two most important men in her life. Maggie's father blamed her for her limp and never forgave her for that. He believed she would never secure a good match for marriage and continue on in the family plantation. She was an only child.

Lizzy was right. Like Lizzy, Maggie had always wanted more education. She had always wanted the same independence as men received. She never wanted to be treated differently for that or her disability. Tyler and Charley always supported her and encouraged her and Lizzy in their pursuits against what the rest of the world believed. They had stood up for her for as long as she could remember. They had fought for her. And she loved them for it.

Soon, true to her form, Maggie squared her shoulders and said, "They're doing what they believe in. They have a chance to make a difference. I will support them in every possible way. And I am extremely proud of them."

Lizzy knew she meant it truthfully. They were both extremely proud of the boys.

They sat in silence a few more minutes. Finally Maggie broke it, "We should probably return to the party. It's getting late. Guests will probably be leaving soon." She turned to Lizzy and added, "Thank you for telling me. We'll be here for each other while they're gone and pray it won't be long."

The two embraced in a sisterly, supporting hug. They knew they would need each other tremendously in the time to come.

They descended the stairs with a resolve to finish the party strongly. They danced the few remaining dances with friends and then said good night to the guests.

When all of the guests had left and only Tyler and Maggie remained, Major And Mrs. Wyley retired and Edward escorted his fiancée home.

The four made plans to meet in town for brunch the next day. Maggie gave the boys loving, supporting hugs and told them she was proud of them. Their eyes showed the appreciation that their voices couldn't.

Finally, Maggie and Tyler left, and Charley and Lizzy retired for the night.

CHAPTER 3

The day after the party started off quietly. The four had brunch together in town and discussed the events of the night before. They had a wonderful time together, laughing and getting acquainted again.

When they were finished, they parted ways, promising to get together again. Back at their house, Charley went for a ride on his horse and Lizzy went to her room to read.

A few hours later, Lizzy thought she heard some rustling outside her door. It was open, so she simply looked up to see what was in the hallway. She saw what looked like a shock of champagne colored satin. Just as quickly as she saw it, it was gone.

She sat there puzzled for a moment and thought she heard mumbling. She listened more intently. As she was putting her book down to rise and look in the hallway, she heard a muffled cry and several thuds, then immediately it stopped.

Still not sure what she'd heard, Lizzy rushed to her door to see if anyone was out there. No one was in the hallway. She moved to the stairs. As she started to descend, she saw at the bottom of the stairs a pile of wrinkled light champagne colored satin with lace around the bottom hem.

She screamed and ran down the stairs, careful not to meet the same fate she was afraid her mother had just met. She fell on the floor, throwing the fabric aside to find her mother's body. When she found it, she desperately tried to find some sign that her mother was alive and all right.

By this time, her screams had aroused everyone in the house. Charley had just returned from his ride and arrived at her side first, followed by Bartholomew and Hannah. Sarah was close behind almost in hysterics. Bartholomew ran outside to send Joseph for Major Wyley and Edward, then found Eli and sent him to town for Dr. Harrison.

The next few minutes were chaotic as Major Wyley ranted and raved hysterically trying to rouse his wife. Edward stood away, stunned. Charley and Lizzy, along with Bartholomew, tried to redirect the major.

Within ten minutes, Eli and Dr. Harrison came flying into the house. Dr. Harrison immediately took charge. Dropping his bag near Mr. Wyley, he sternly said, "Major, I need you to step back so I can examine your wife."

Stunned at the doctor's voice, yet relieved to have him near, Major Wyley allowed Charley and Lizzy to draw him a few steps away from his wife.

With Hannah helping to move the fabric out of the way, Dr. Harrison thoroughly examined Mrs. Wyley for any sign of a pulse or breathing. Finding no signs, he carefully examined her neck and back to confirm his suspicions.

Finally, with sad eyes, he looked to Major Wyley being supported by his son and daughter. "I'm sorry, Major," he said. "Your wife has broken her neck. She did not survive the fall."

Everyone was silent, anxiously anticipating the major's reaction. He simply stared at the doctor, seeming to will him to change the diagnosis. When the doctor remained silent, Major Wyley finally dropped his gaze to rest on his wife's lifeless form. When he spoke, it was so quiet that everyone had to strain to hear him.

"Take her," he said. "Please, just take her." Then, without waiting for a response, he turned and walked toward his study, closing the doors behind him. Edward soon followed suit and left to his room, leaving Charley and Lizzy in charge.

Charley spoke up, "What do we need to do, Dr. Harrison?" he asked.

"If you'd like," the doctor answered, "I'll take her and prepare her for burial."

"We'd appreciate that," Charley replied. "We'll make arrangements for the funeral and get word to you today of when it will be."

"That will be fine," Dr. Harrison said. Then he and Eli carried the body to his buggy and he left.

Everyone else dispersed quietly to their respective chores, leaving Charley, Lizzy, Hannah, and Bartholomew behind.

"We need to tell Tyler and Maggie," Charley said.

"I can do that fo' ya, suh, if you'd like it," Bartholomew said.

"Thank you," Charley replied. "I'd like to go too with you. Perhaps we can stop by the reverend's place on the way too." Then he turned to his sister, "Would you like to come too, Lizzy, or wait for us here?" he asked.

"I'll wait here, in case Father needs something," she said.

"We'll be back soon," Charley said and then turned to leave with Bartholomew.

Once the men were gone, Lizzy turned worried eyes to Hannah. "What are we going to do, Hannah?" she asked.

Hannah smiled lovingly at her mistress and friend. "We gonna to look to you, honey," she said.

Lizzy was startled. "To me?" she asked. "Why me?"

"You de one we been lookin' to fo' de past year," she answered. "Ever since yo' mama took sick. You been doin' a fine job too. You'll keep on doin' a fine job."

"That's a big weight to put on one girl's shoulders," Lizzy said.

"You got mighty strong shoulders, honey," Hannah said.

The two fell to a comfortable silence until Lizzy spoke. "Then, I guess we should get started planning the funeral." Hannah nodded and waited for her instructions.

"We'll need to wait to find out when the pastor can perform the service before we plan food," Lizzy said. "Why don't you get started making sure the main floor is clean for guests? I'll go pick out something for her to wear and get it to Dr. Harrison."

"Dat sounds fine," Hannah said and turned to leave.

"Thanks, Hannah," Lizzy said.

Her friend gave a reassuring smile in reply.

Lizzy headed upstairs to the unwelcome task of finding something for her mother to be buried in. When she reached her mother's room, she found Sarah inside and two dresses already on the bed.

She stood in the doorway. "Sarah?"

Sarah turned nervously toward the new mistress of the manor. She became easier when she saw the soft reassurance on Lizzy's face.

"I thought I'd pick out a few of yo' mama's favorite dresses," she explained, "so's you could choose which one she should wear."

Touched by the thought, Lizzy put a hand on Sarah's shoulder. "You pick it," she said. "You knew her best."

Sarah's eyes began watering. "De green one," she said softly. "Dat was her favorite."

"The green one it is," Lizzy said.

Then Sarah began sobbing. She sank to the floor with her head in her hands. Lizzy sat on the floor with her, not saying anything.

Finally, after a few minutes, Sarah coughed and sputtered, "You prob'ly think dis strange, me carryin' on such, de way yo' mama treated me."

Lizzy remained silent, unsure of what to say.

Sarah continued. "Sure yo' mama was out of sorts dis last year. But dat was de sickness, I know it wasn't her." She paused to sniffle, and then continued. "Before de sickness, yo' mama and I would talk. Sort of like you and Hannah," she smiled sweetly at the memories.

She began to pick at the fibers in the rug. "I would help her get ready in de mornin's or get her ready for bed in de evenin's. She would talk about her day or her thoughts and feelin's." She turned sad eyes to Lizzy. "She loved you—all of you. She wasn't no good at showin' it. She was proud of you too. She was proud of you and she loved you all. Remember dat, child."

"Thank you," Lizzy said softly as she sank down next to Sarah on the rug.

"I loved yo' mama too," Sarah said. "In de past, she was a good mistress. It hurt bad to see her like she was last year. Dat just wasn't her. Now wit her gone, I don't know what I'm gonna do. Please, Miss Lizzy, don't let yo' father send me out to the fields. I'm too old."

"I'll do my best, Sarah," Lizzy promised.

"Miss Lizzy," Sarah said hesitantly, "as much as I care fo' you and Master Charley, as good as you two are to me, I just don't know 'bout stayin' on here without yo' mama."

"Sarah, I wouldn't let Father sell you anywhere!" Lizzy said incredulously.

"I wouldn't want that either, Miss Lizzy," Sarah said. Then a knowing look passed between them.

Lizzy spoke up slowly and softly, "Sarah, please don't run away yet. Wait a bit. Let me sort things out and maybe I can help you. Please wait."

Sarah's look told her she was determined, but then her face softened. "All right, Miss Lizzy," she conceded. "I wait a few days. But please don't forget 'bout me."

"I won't, Sarah," Lizzy said. "Just give me some time."

The two stood up and began gathering jewelry to match the dress.

Lizzy and Charley, with Maggie and Tyler's help, put together all of the plans for the funeral. Everyone in the household, with the exception of Edward and Major Wyley, helped get the house and the food ready. Major Wyley stayed in his study most of the time. When he was seen, he walked as if in a stupor. Edward remained in his room. Lizzy and Charley tried to include them in the decisions. The major would turn and walk away when the subject of the funeral was brought up. Edward simply snapped, "It's not my job!"

The funeral was two days later. Rev. Adams did an excellent job, providing meaningful memories of Martha Wyley, as well as hope for future in Christ. The house looked great and everyone gathered together for food afterward.

Finally, the last guest left, leaving the four remaining Wyley's alone for the first time. They all sat quietly in the parlor near the warmth of the fire.

Major Wyley broke the silence as he stared into the fire. "I have decided to come out of retirement and offer my services to the Georgia Army. I report tomorrow. This is not an option up for discussion. I cannot remain here any longer. I will be gone before you rise in the morning."

Lizzy was stunned. Her father was leaving them? He knew Charley would be going back north, presumably to school. He would leave her here with Edward? She wanted to protest, but she knew he would not change his mind. When he said a topic was not open for discussion, he meant it.

Edward jumped in eagerly. "I will enlist also, Father," always wanting his father to think good of him. "I will pack my things, get word to my fiancée, and leave with you in the morning."

"Very well," Major Wyley said with little emotion.

Edward stood up and left. Charley and Lizzy sat in silence.

"Charles," Major Wyley said, still staring into the fire, "I suppose you'll be heading back up north."

Lizzy gave Charley a look pleading that he not say more than he needed to. "Yes, Father. I leave two days from now," was all he said.

"Very well," Major Wyley replied. "The care of the house then falls to you, Elizabeth." He finally looked up at her. "Everything you'll need can be found in my desk in the study. I've left plenty of money in the bank for you. The slaves know how to work the land. Keep an eye on them." He paused and looked at the floor.

Then he turned sad eyes back up to her. "I know you've practically been running the house for the past year, so I believe you'll do a fine job. Anything else you have questions about, talk to Mr. Parker or Mr. Swanson. They'll point you in the right direction."

Lizzy and Charley were too stunned to say anything. Feeling somewhat abandoned, they waited to see if their father had anything else to say. He did not. Finally, he stood up, looked each of them in the eye, and simply nodded. Then he left the room.

Still in shock, Lizzy and Charley remained silent for several minutes, lost in their own thoughts. Charley broke the silence. "I should tell him what I'm doing."

Lizzy's head snapped to look at him. "Please don't. Not yet."

"Why? He'll find out soon enough."

"Perhaps not."

"Lizzy, there's no way for him not to find out that his son is preparing to possibly fight against him. I do not want to meet him on a battlefield somewhere and tell him then."

"Surely there's some way we can keep it a secret," Lizzy said, hoping.

"There's not," Charley stated.

"Fine, perhaps not," she conceded. "Please, don't tell him yet though. He's been dealing with a lot lately. I don't want this to send him over the edge. Besides, I'm working on something that would need him not to know what you're doing."

"Elizabeth Marie," Charley said, afraid of what his sister might be scheming, "what are you working on?"

"Not yet, Charley," she said, with a hint of fear in her eyes. "I want to tell you and Tyler together. I'll need your help and support. Let's call him and Maggie over tomorrow, and I'll let you know. It will be better with Father and Edward out of the house."

Charley eyed her suspiciously but allowed her this time. "We'll bring them over tomorrow and discuss your scheme. In the meantime, get some sleep," his voice softened. "You've been going nonstop since mother passed. You need some rest."

"Thanks, Charley," Lizzy said. "I appreciate your willingness to hear me out. You get some rest too. You've been working hard as well." Then she got up to leave. "I'll see you in the morning. Good night."

"Good night."

The next morning, Lizzy woke just after dawn, hoping to at least catch a glimpse of her father and Edward before they left. She ran down the stairs to check her father's study. Then she ran to the stables. Their two horses were gone. True to his word, they were not there. Even though Lizzy had never been close to her father or her eldest brother, she still felt a profound sense of loss now that they, along with her mother, were gone.

She went to get breakfast in a very pensive mood, the weight of what she was determined to tell her brother and friends heavy on her shoulders. Charley found her sitting in the study staring into the fire, the tray of food untouched on the table next to her.

"Would you like to talk before I get the others?" he asked.

She smiled a sad smile at him. "I wish I could," she said. "However, I think it would be best to wait."

Charley nodded in understanding and turned to leave.

As important as she knew this was, Lizzy nonetheless did not relish what she knew would be their responses. She turned back to the fire and to pray.

An hour later, Charley returned with Tyler and Maggie in tow. They all had serious, almost scared looks on their faces, not knowing what their friend was about to say. They silently found seats together and waited, the look on Lizzy's face telling them that it might be extremely difficult for her to talk.

After a few moments of intense, yet oddly comfortable silence, Lizzy began. "I appreciate you all coming so quickly. I assure you there's nothing wrong. I am all right. I have come to a decision that I believe you all need to hear at least, if you can't directly be a part of." As she said this last part, her gaze fell on Maggie.

No one said anything. She did not expect them to. After a deep breath, Lizzy continued. "I have decided to offer this house as a station on the Underground Railroad. I want to be a part of helping slaves escape to freedom. I've already been able to make a few inquiries. Those I have talked with agree that it would be an almost ideal situation."

"I don't think so," Charley said in a voice shorter than anyone had ever heard him use, especially with his sister. He was shocked that she would do something so brazen in his eyes.

Equally shocked at his tone with her, Lizzy replied, "Excuse me?" her tone matched his. The other two wisely remained silent.

"I don't think it's a good idea," he said, almost laughing at the thought.

Lizzy had been prepared for him to say this. She tried to calm herself and evenly asked him, "Why?"

"It's too dangerous," he replied matter-of-factly.

"I am fully aware of the dangers," she retorted, a little miffed that he would think her so incompetent that she wasn't aware of the dangers.

"If you are, then you've greatly underestimated them," he shot back.

"Do you think I'm stupid?" she questioned angrily. This was something she felt a great passion for and here her brother, her best friend, wasn't even giving her a chance.

"No," he answered defensively, "I just don't think you've thought this through very well."

Lizzy became more and more upset. Charley knew as well as the others that Lizzy was not one to make rash decisions. She always thought things through and carefully prayed about them before deciding. Everyone, including Charley, knew his mistake at saying this. However, he was reluctant to retract his statement. They all sat in silence, unsure of how to proceed.

"I have thought this through extremely well," Lizzy said evenly. "I know that I disagree with slavery. I know it is still legal in this state. I know that the only way for slaves to reach freedom, if their masters don't set them free, is to run away. I know that safe houses are needed to hide the runaway slaves. With Mother gone, Father and Edward and you in the army, this house is empty. No one would think anything would be going on at this house with only a woman running things. They know Father and Edward are loyal to the South. They believe you and me to be as well. Believe me, Charles, I have thought this through."

Finally, Charley made a small concession. "What are the dangers you know of?" he asked as calmly as he could.

"I know if I'm caught, they would arrest me and try me as a traitor, possibly execute me," Lizzy answered.

"That's not enough to deter you from this?" Charley asked incredulously.

"No!" Lizzy jumped out of her chair. Showing every ounce of passion she felt for this cause, she said, "How can I sit here in comfort knowing there are people out there starving and dying unjustly when I finally have the opportunity to do something about it?"

"Why you though?" Charley asked almost frantically, as he too jumped out of his chair to face his sister almost nose-to-nose.

"Why not me?"

Tyler spoke up for the first time. "I think he perhaps means is there someone possibly more qualified or more experienced who could do this?"

Lizzy glared at him knowing full well he didn't mean someone with more experience; he meant a man. "Of course there are people more qualified," she emphasized the words, letting him know she knew exactly what he meant, "but they have cast their lot with the army, something I cannot do! If I could go about this in a more legal manner, you know I would, but this is the only option open to me."

"It's just so dangerous," Charley said worryingly.

Lizzy tried to soften her voice, but she was still upset, "I know it's dangerous, but it's no different than the danger you're asking me to worry about you with."

Charley didn't like that at all, "I believe there is a difference," he practically spat the words at her.

"There's no difference at all!" Lizzy shot back. "If I get caught, I'll be arrested. If you get caught, you're shot. If anything, you're asking me to live with more fear for your life than for mine."

"I think she's got a point," Tyler said quietly.

"I say you're crazy if you think that," Charley shouted.

"What's the difference you see, Charley?" Lizzy challenged, though she feared she already knew the answer.

Charley was so upset that he shouted his answer without thinking, "The difference is you're a woman!"

Dead silence. The silence was so heavy it almost crushed them. The hurt was so evident on Lizzy's face; she didn't have to say what she was thinking. But she did.

"How could you?" she asked in a hurt whisper. "You, of everyone in this household, have been the one person to always tell me to look past the fact that I'm a woman; to go for my dreams no matter what. Were you just patronizing me, or did you ever believe what you said?"

"Of course I believe what I said," Charley answered.

"Then why is this coming out now?" Lizzy asked pleadingly.

He looked her in the eye. "I'm sorry if I don't like the thought of my sister on the wrong side of prison bars or, worse yet, an executioner." He fell back into a chair, exhausted.

Lizzy went to him and knelt on the floor beside him. Putting a hand on his arm, she looked him in the eye and said intensely, "I don't want you to like it. Just like you don't want me to like the thought of my brother on the wrong end of a bayonet."

No one spoke or moved for several minutes. Finally, Charley addressed Tyler. "What do you say, Tyler?"

"I don't like the idea of Lizzy getting arrested or executed," he said.

Lizzy's heart sank. She needed their support.

Tyler went on, "But I tell you, I'll be mighty proud when she pulls it off."

Any relief Lizzy felt at Tyler's words was short-lived. Charley quietly, with a slight twinge of menace in his voice, confronted his friend, "So you're telling me you condone this? You're all right with her doing something that could potentially get her hurt, possibly killed? Who knows what rules are going to change once this thing blows up! I would have thought that after your conversation with her the other night, you'd be a little more protective of her."

Tyler knew that remark was supposed to cut, but it only made him more determined to support the woman he loved.

"No, Charley, I'm not all right with the possibility of Lizzy getting killed," he said, looking straight into the eyes of his friend. "But, especially thinking about the conversation we had the other night, I cannot tell her no. One of the aspects I love most about your sister is her determination to do what is right."

Then, turning to Lizzy, he said, "And I believe you are doing what is right. I don't like the danger. I don't like that you're going to have to lie. But I believe it is right to get these people out." He rose from his chair and knelt in front of hers. He grasped her hands in his. "Lizzy, I will support you with all that I am as long as you promise to be as safe and smart as humanly possible and rely on God for the rest."

"I will," she promised, almost unable to believe he had given his support.

"Think things through, and don't take any unnecessary chances," Tyler added.

"And, Maggie," he said, turning to the only one who had been silent throughout the meeting, "you keep an eye on her. However close you want, keep each other informed."

"I will," Maggie said, knowing he knew she would be as big a part of the operation as Lizzy would let her.

Then they all turned eyes to Charley. He was still sitting with a determined look on his face. They were all silent for a few moments waiting for him to speak. Finally, he looked at Lizzy, "I can see I'm not going to get my way on this," he attempted a small amount of humor. "Lizzy, I agree this is an extremely admirable thing to do. I too am proud. I'm still scared though. Please be smart about this. Please be safe. As long as he's here, allow Bartholomew to take care of you. If anything goes wrong, promise you'll at least consider abandoning the mission." He looked at her with pleading eyes.

"I'll consider it," she conceded. "Thank you all for supporting me in this. I will be safe and smart. I really believe this is the ideal situation," she repeated, "I'll be the only one of the family left here. Everyone knows Father is loyal to the South, therefore, they assume we are too. And no one is going to suspect a woman. This will be the one time I can use that to my advantage."

They all smiled, knowing how much she had never wanted to use her femininity as an advantage.

Tyler squeezed her hands again and rose to return to his chair.

"So," Charley said, "what's your plan going to be?"

Just then, before Lizzy could answer, a knock came on the study door. It was Bartholomew and Hannah. They entered without the need of being invited.

"Beggin' yo' pardons," Bartholomew said, nodding to all of them, "we were overhearin' yo' conversation, and I believe it should stop here." At everyone's confused looks, he continued, "It be best if y'all don't know Miss Lizzy's plans. Thataway, if you's questioned, you can honestly be sayin' you don' know."

"He's right," Lizzy agreed. "As much as I want you all in on this, unless you're going to be an active part," she again looked at Maggie, "you shouldn't know in case you're questioned. Besides, you'll be off north tomorrow anyway. You have enough to do."

The boys reluctantly agreed and decided to take their leave and finish preparations. They all made plans for a final dinner together that night. Maggie stayed behind as the boys left. The two friends sat in comfortable silence for a few moments. Maggie spoke first.

"Lizzy," she said, "you know I want to be a part of this with you, completely. Everything you do, I want to do. Everything you know, I want to know."

Lizzy smiled. "I had hoped for nothing less. What do you say, tomorrow, after we see the boys off, we come back here and check out the secrets of this old house?"

"Which secrets do you mean?" Maggie asked.

"I remember my grandfather saying a long time ago that his father built this house just before the Revolution," she explained. "He built it for the patriots. He hid many of them in secret passageways and secret rooms within the house."

"That would be perfect!" Maggie exclaimed. "Let's come back as soon as their train leaves."

CHAPTER 4

Later that evening, the four lifelong friends had a quiet, subdued dinner together in the Wyley's expansive dining room before they were to set out on their separate adventures. They tried small talk but couldn't think of much lighthearted conversation. They settled on bringing up memories and remembering happier times before facing what lay ahead. Finally, their dinner was over, and they went to the sitting room to finish their final evening together.

They sat in silence listening to the fire crackle. They had been friends for a long time. They had endured ridicule and hardship together. The hardship of the future, though different than any they had endured in the past, was not as daunting as the fact that they would be separated during the challenges. Maggie and Lizzy had always relied on Charley and Tyler for protection. Charley and Tyler had always relied on the women for comfort and sensitivity. Each pair would be lacking the other while facing the biggest challenges of their lives thus far. The fear each felt at this fact was almost chilling.

Maggie spoke up. "I know this sounds naïve, but I truly do hope that this entire scare will be for naught, and y'all won't actually have to fight a war."

Charley answered, "I appreciate the sentiment but, forgive me for being blunt, that is pretty naïve."

"I'm sorry, Maggie, but he's right," Tyler said. "With Mr. Lincoln winning the presidency, South Carolina has already seceded from the Union. Several states are sure to follow. Lincoln will never stand for a divided America. I'm sorry, Maggie, as awful as it is, there will be war."

Again there was silence. They all knew what would come. They all knew what they were called to do. Theirs was a friendship that had lasted through much adversity. They knew their bonds to each other were not easily broken. Still, they pondered the unknown. No one wanted to entertain thoughts of what if, but they all did. No one wanted to consider the possibility of one of them not returning, but consider it, they did.

Each mouth was silent, yet each mind was racing. There was so much to say, yet no one could bring themselves to utter a sound. There wasn't a need. Their four lives had been woven together so tightly, they could almost read each other's minds. It meant more to each one to sit in comfortable silence together than to ruin the moment with mere words.

The clock struck ten o'clock, and they knew their time together had come to an end. Charley offered to see Maggie home, leaving Tyler and Lizzy a few minutes alone.

They sat in comfortable silence a few more moments. Tyler was the first to speak. He rose and stood looking into in to the fire as he collected his thoughts.

"I have so much I want to say, but I don't want to cheapen our parting with simple words," he said finally, still gazing into in to the fire. "You know I've never been great at expressing myself though conversation." Tyler was a writer at heart and could truly express his feelings eloquently with pen and paper.

Lizzy remained silent, allowing him to collect his thoughts and continue. He was grateful for this.

He turned to her but remained by the fire. "Lizzy," he began slowly, "you know how I feel about you and that will never change. I do want more with you, but I won't pressure you in light of my situation. I would implore you, however, to please consider your feelings for me while I'm gone, and hopefully we can discuss it when I return."

"Tyler," she said quickly, before he could go any further, "I don't need to wait until you come home to tell you how I feel. I know my feelings now."

"Oh," he said, not sure what to expect. "How do you feel?"

"You are my best friend; that will never change," she said. "You have always believed in me—always thought the best of me. Because of that, I want more." His face lit up hopefully as she continued. "What I said the other night about the perfect husband was exactly true. I was describing you. As I've thought about it these past few days, I realized, as you did, that I've been comparing every gentleman who has come calling to you. I used to get so upset with God for not letting me marry when other girls my age were. Now I realize He was preparing me for you, and I could not have anyone better."

"I am so pleased to hear that," Tyler said, smiling, but remained where he was, sensing she had more to say.

"However much I want it though," she continued, "I agree that, in light of both of our situations, we should not act on our feelings right now. When you come home though, I want to do more than just talk about our feelings."

"I guess that's incentive for me to come home then," he said.

"And for me not to get caught," she replied.

Tyler's face turned sober, as if he had forgotten her plans.

"Tyler, please don't worry overmuch," Lizzy pleaded when she saw his face drop. "I'll be smart. I'll be safe. If it's not going well or something feels wrong, I'll stop. Please, don't ask me not to do this," she finished almost fearfully.

He crossed over to her and, squeezing her hand, smiled tenderly at her. "I would never do that. I know you'll be smart, and I'll continue to pray for your safety. Let's write as often as we can to update each other, all right?" he asked.

"I will," she said.

The clock struck ten thirty, and they knew they needed to part. Lizzy's eyes began to well with tears as she looked up at Tyler. "I don't know if I can bear to say good-bye again," she said.

"Then let's not," he comforted. "Let this be good night, and you don't need to see me to the station. I'd hate to have a hasty good-bye when we can say it here."

"Thank you for understanding," she said. Her tears were freely flowing now. She ignored propriety and flung her arms around him. "God protect him and bring him home," she prayed.

"And hold her safely in Your arms until I can come back and help You," he prayed, as he squeezed her in a loving, protective hug.

They both finished with a tear-filled "Amen." Then Tyler leaned down and kissed her cheek. "Good night, Lizzy," he said affectionately. "I'll be home soon." Then he turned and left the house, looking back once to smile and wave.

When he was gone, Lizzy sank down on the chair and let herself cry.

CHAPTER 5

The next morning, Lizzy woke early and made sure a hearty breakfast was in place for Charley. He attempted a brave smile as he came downstairs to eat. "Everything smells wonderful, Hannah," he said.

"Thank ya, suh," she said quietly and left the two to their last meal together for a while.

Charley noticed Lizzy's attire. She was wearing a house dress, not a traveling outfit as he'd expected. "You're not going to the station." It was more a statement than a question.

"I just can't," she said quietly. He knew she was fighting tears. "I said good-bye to Tyler last night, and I just can't bear to do it again. I was hoping you'd let me say good-bye to you here."

"Of course," he said sincerely. "It's much better to say it here than to risk it being cut short at the station."

"Thank you."

As they ate, their conversation stayed on trivial things, such as Charley's travel plans, where the books for the house were kept, and whether or not Charley had packed all he needed.

All too soon it was time for Charley to leave. Bartholomew had brought his luggage down, what little there was. He would have army issue for whatever he would need as he enlisted.

"I'll wait fo' ya outside, suh," Bartholomew said as he turned and left through the front door.

Charley looked at Lizzy. "I know I was difficult last night," he said. "I'm sorry. I do want you to know that I am so proud of you. I will pray for you every day. Be safe. Be smart. May God be with you." He hugged her.

She held on tight. "Be safe, Charley. May God go with you too," was all she could say.

"I love you, sis."

"I love you too." Then she drew herself up straight and said with as much bravery as she could muster, "And I'll see you soon."

He nodded, turned, and left the house.

Lizzy ran to the front parlor, threw open the curtains, and flung herself on the settee by the window, watching him leave through tear-filled eyes. Soon, exhausted from her tears, she fell asleep to the ticking of the clock in the now silent and empty house.

Lizzy woke to the sound of knocking on the front door. She looked at the clock and noticed that two hours had gone by. She felt a sharp wave of sadness. The boys would be gone now.

Hannah answered the door and soon Maggie, with red, tear-stained cheeks, came into the room. No words needed to be said. Maggie sat by her friend, and the two cried in each other's arms until there were no more tears to be shed.

"We leave them in God's hands," Lizzy said.

"As they do with us," Maggie agreed. Then, knowing neither one wanted to dwell on the issue, she changed the subject. "Shall we take a look at the secret rooms?" she asked.

"Great idea," Lizzy said.

"Do you know where they are?"

"Not really." Lizzy smiled. "I overheard my grandparents discussing it years ago but never was told where they were."

"I guess we go looking then." Maggie smiled back.

The two girls started wandering through the house, looking for anything that might lead to secret rooms. After about an hour of finding nothing, they were down but not ready to give up.

"I guess it's a good sign that we can't find it," Maggie said.

"It is more reassuring that others won't be able to find it," Lizzy agreed. "I just don't know how else to go about locating it."

"Miss Lizzy? Miss Maggie?" Hannah stood in the doorway of the room they were in. Sarah stood with her.

"Yes?" Lizzy answered.

"May I show ya somethin'?"

"Sure," they answered and followed her out of the room, down the hall. She took them to the biggest bedroom—Lizzy's grandfather's room. She led them to the wardrobe and opened the doors. She then proceeded to push aside the clothes and pushed against the back wall. It moved and opened.

Speechless, they all moved through the opening and followed the light from Hannah's lantern. They went down a corridor and came to a stop in a large room with several beds, end tables, a small kitchen table, and chairs.

"Hannah," Lizzy said, barely above a whisper, "How did you know this was here?"

"Since slaves ain't allowed to learn to read or write," Hannah began explaining, "we become very good storytellers. My great-grandmammy was yo' great-grandmammy's chambermaid. She helped yo' great-grand-parents wi' de hidin' of the sojers. Then she passed the story on down to her children. No one's seen this room till now, but we all knowed it was here."

"Thank you for showing us," Lizzy breathed. "This is incredible. Is this the only room, or are there more?"

"I believe dey's one mo' room," Sarah said. "Let me see if I can fin' it."

They left the room and moved to the guest wing of the house. Looking first in the biggest guest room, they found another wardrobe. This one was empty. Hannah pushed on the back wall. They were ecstatic to find that it too pushed open and led to an identical corridor with an identical room. The room held the same furnishings.

They admired the space a little longer, then Maggie spoke up. "We should probably take some inventory of what's here and usable, and then make a list of what extra provisions we'll need."

The others agreed, found some paper and a pencil, and began taking inventory of the rooms. Each room held eight bunk beds, eight end tables, one kitchen table, ten straight-backed chairs, six lanterns, thick blankets on each bed, and eight short trunks that fit under the beds. They took the lanterns outside to test them, making sure they were out in the open for safety. Four of them worked. They made their list of provisions needed: extra material for blankets and pillows, more lanterns and kerosene, and the extra food they would need. They decided on two different stores across town they would go to for the groceries, so as not to draw too much attention to themselves. They would buy the material from Mr. Parker. They made plans to begin the shopping the next day.

After their plans were made, the four women gathered cleaning materials and scrubbed the secret rooms from top to bottom three times over to get the hundred-year-old grime off. The room sparkled and the women were exhausted.

Hannah and Sarah insisted on making sure dinner was underway, in spite of protests from the other two. Lizzy and Maggie relaxed with tea in the parlor.

"I've been thinking," Maggie started, "this is going to be a huge undertaking. I might draw some undue attention coming over here every day. Plus, I don't know if my leg can handle that much traveling. I don't think it would raise too many eyebrows if I come to stay here for an unspecified amount of time, possibly under the guise of helping out with the running of things. What do you think?"

Lizzy's face lit up. "I would love that," she exclaimed. "I was wondering how we would do this. That's perfect."

The plan was set. They finished their tea, ate dinner, and retired for the evening, planning on shopping in town the next day and packing and moving Maggie the day after.

Maggie's parents compassionately agreed to let her move in with Lizzy, feeling sorry for Lizzy being alone as she was. No mention was made of the real reason for the move. They helped the girls pack and move.

A few days later, with Maggie settled in the room next to Lizzy, their purchases made, and blankets and pillows in the process, the girls felt ready to begin their part in the Underground Railroad.

CHAPTER 6

Tyler lay on his bunk after a long day of drilling. During their first evening off in a week of being at the fort, he found his first opportunity to write Lizzy. Some of the other soldiers had opted to go into town to a local pub for their evening off. Charley decided to try and catch up on long, overdue sleep, while Tyler composed his letter.

> Dearest Lizzy,
>
> It's been a week and a half since I saw you last, and this is the first time I've had to write. I wish I could say it's been an exciting week and a half, but in all actuality, it's been fairly routine. After receiving our assignments and reporting to the fort, we were fitted with our uniforms and received other provisions.
>
> Each day is the same. Breakfast early, marching all morning, lunch, marching all afternoon, dinner, more marching before bed. Right before bed, we're required to shine our boots and buttons and make sure all of our gear is in order.
>
> None of us are very sure why we're marching so much. It seems almost ridiculous. One foot in front of the other. No one wants to ask our commanding officer, but my guess is it has something to do with teamwork. All in all, it's not too bad.
>
> On a different note, Charley and I are definitely in the minority here. There are only two other Southerners in our

camp, both from South Carolina. On the outside, in our uniforms, we all look the same, but as soon as one of the four of us speaks and they hear our accents, the others become aloof and don't seem to want to get near us. No one has said as much, but I'm afraid they might think we're spies. I don't know what it will take to get them to trust us, but hopefully we'll find out sooner rather than later.

I wish I had the energy to write more, but I'm falling asleep. Know that I miss you and think about you often. Be safe; be smart. I look forward to hearing from you.

Love always,

Tyler

He folded the letter into an envelope and addressed it to be sent out with the next day's mail. Then he settled back to try to sleep.

"How long do you think it will be?" Charley's voice came out of the dark from the bunk below.

It was the standard question the two had been asking each other since they signed up. They'd heard rumors about Georgia seceding soon. Neither had misconceptions as to how the other soldiers would react to them when the inevitable happened. It wasn't a question of if anymore, but when.

"Soon …soon," Tyler answered.

The morning of January 20, 1861, dawned bright and clear. Lizzy woke from a peaceful sleep and began to get ready for the day. Her thoughts fell on the events of the previous week. "Events" was too exciting a word for the goings on of the week before. With the secret room finished and furnished, the household had eagerly awaited the arrival of their first fugitive guests. Lizzy and Maggie expected guests immediately. Hannah had to assure them that it took time.

After what seemed like weeks, but actually only three days, Jonathan, one of the barn caretakers, came to the kitchen door in the middle of the night with a family of four runaway slaves: a mother, father, two-year-old son, and three-month-old daughter. Hannah showed them to the room without waking Lizzy or Maggie.

When Hannah told them, they had been so excited and wanted to meet them. Instead, Hannah requested they be allowed to sleep and be awakened only at night. She explained that they would need to get used to this pattern, since they would be traveling at night. Since the girls were not used to this pattern, they only saw their guests briefly each night before turning in.

This brief time was not long enough to get to know the family. This was disappointing for the girls. However, they were greatly cheered by the intense gratitude the family shared with their hosts.

So far, it wasn't the exciting adventure the girls had hoped for, but it was definitely rewarding. Tomorrow was a new moon and would be the time when their guests would travel to the next station. Maggie and Lizzy hoped they would get to assist in the escape, but nothing had been decided yet.

The girls had a small breakfast in the front parlor by the fire. In spite of the uncertainty of the situation, both were very content.

As they were nearing the end of their meal, a knock sounded on the door. Hannah answered it and returned to the girls with two calling cards.

Lizzy took them. "Jackson Hill and Phillip Markley," she read. "Please, send them in, Hannah. Thank you." Hannah showed them in. After greetings were made, the gentlemen jumped right in to their reason for visiting.

"Have you heard the news?" Phillip asked.

"We haven't been to town to get the post yet," Lizzy answered, noting the newspaper in Jackson's hand.

"We assumed as much," Jackson answered, "and so we have brought the news to you." He handed the girls the paper with an excited glint in his eyes.

"Oh my," Maggie gasped, as they read the headline—two words in big, bold, capital letters on the front page:

"GEORGIA SECEDES!"

"It happened just yesterday," Phillip said.

"You know what this means, don't you?" Jackson asked, knowing Lizzy's father and Edward left to join the Georgia Army.

"War is inevitable," Lizzy breathed.

"Yes," Phillip answered excitedly. "The states that are seceding will form a new country. The Yanks won't like that, there'll be war, and we'll help the South win!" he finished triumphantly.

"Who do you mean 'we'?" Maggie asked.

Jackson answered more subdued than Phillip, all the time his gaze on Lizzy, "Phillip and I mean to join the Georgia Army two days from now."

Phillip left no time for response. "And we wanted to extend an invitation to the two of you to join us at the symphony for our last evening as civilians—as old family friends, of course."

"Tomorrow night?" Lizzy asked. Tomorrow night was when their "houseguests" were escaping. She wanted to be part of it. She glanced through the doorway into the hall where Hannah was standing, listening to the conversation. Hannah gave a nod saying the girls should accept the invitation.

"Yes, tomorrow night," Phillip answered.

Lizzy knew this was not a time to question Hannah, so, with a glance at each other, the girls accepted.

"Wonderful!" the men exclaimed. Then Phillip excitedly began to tell of the adventures they hoped to have.

Jackson moved closer to Lizzy. "May I have a word with you, in private?" he asked.

Confused, Lizzy answered, "Of course. Is the front porch sufficient?"

Jackson nodded, and the two left the room with a quick nod and gesture at the others. Phillip didn't even take a breath as he continued talking with Maggie.

It was comfortable outside for a January day. The two friends stood by the front door for their conversation.

Jackson began, "Before your parents' party, I had a much different reason for this visit in mind."

"What happened at the party?" Lizzy asked, searching her mind to see how she might have offended him.

"I saw you with Tyler Parker," Jackson answered simply.

"Oh?"

"I had intended to come here and ask permission to come calling," Jackson continued. "After the party, I have suspicions that your affections are already placed elsewhere. Are my suspicions correct?"

"Yes," Lizzy answered cautiously.

Jackson sighed then asked, "Have you declared your intentions already?"

"Yes."

"Well, for the two of you, I wish all imaginable happiness," Jackson said. "I have always considered you four to be good friends of mine. For you, I couldn't imagine a better suitor—unless, of course, it was myself. For Tyler, I believe he is the luckiest man. For myself, I only wish I had been sooner."

"Thank you for your kind words," Lizzy said genuinely. "We have always appreciated your friendship."

Jackson smiled and nodded, then asked, "Have you declared your intentions publicly yet?"

"Not yet," Lizzy replied. "We were waiting until he returned."

"That's a good plan," Jackson said. "May I suggest that you wait as long as possible until you declare publicly?"

"Why?" Lizzy asked.

"With the secession," Jackson began hesitantly, "There will soon be questions of loyalty raised. Your family is above scrutiny. However, I cannot say the same for the Parkers. I would suggest you lay low while he is away—for your own safety and freedom."

"Thank you," Lizzy said. She knew this was costing Jackson to reveal this information. He worked as an aide to one of the government officials, so she knew he would have correct information. "I will heed your warning and not declare anything publicly until absolutely necessary. Thank you."

Jackson nodded. "Well, that's all I had to say. Oh, do you think Tyler would mind my escorting you to the symphony tomorrow night?"

Lizzy smiled appreciatively at Jackson's concern for propriety. "I don't think he would mind. I think he would appreciate your concern, and he's always enjoyed your friendship. Thank you for asking. I look forward to tomorrow evening."

"As do I," Jackson replied. Then he looked in the window at Phillip and Maggie, "I'd better get him out of here before he scares Margaret away."

They shared a smile and went inside. After a few parting words, Jackson and Philip left. Lizzy and Maggie went looking for Hannah.

"Hannah," Lizzy started, after finding her in the kitchen, "I don't want to question your wisdom at having us go to the symphony tomorrow night. However, I cannot pretend not to be disappointed at not being able to help in the escape."

"I completely understand, honey," Hannah replied sympathetically. "There will be more adventures to go on, fo' sure. I think that, in order to remain above 'spicion, you should accept social invitations. We'll handle this one. There'll be 'nother one fo' you all to help wit."

The girls reluctantly agreed, though they were a little excited to go to the symphony. This was one social event they enjoyed attending.

An hour later, another knock came on the door. Hannah brought Lizzy the calling card. It was Aaron Thomas. Lizzy cringed and agreed to see him in the entryway. She did not want him getting comfortable in her house, so she would not offer him a seat unless it was extremely necessary. She asked Hannah to have Bartholomew near, in case he was needed for a hasty removal of an unwanted guest.

"Mr. Thomas, what can I do for you?" Lizzy asked coolly, but cordially.

"Miss Wyley," Aaron said, bowing formally, "I wanted to make sure you were appraised of the current news."

"If you're meaning Georgia's secession, we are appraised of the situation, thank you," she answered.

A look of disappointment at not being the first to share the news flashed across Aaron's face, but he quickly recovered. "I have come to also issue an invitation to dinner tomorrow night, as I am planning on enlisting in the army the day after."

"How very brave of you," Lizzy replied without feeling, "however, I am previously engaged tomorrow evening."

"Oh," Aaron said, obviously disappointed. "Might I be able to change your mind?" he asked confidently.

"I'm sorry, no," Lizzy said, feeling quite smug and trying not to show it, "I have important plans with another close family friend." How glad she was that Jackson had come to the door first!

"That's too bad," Aaron said. "Well, I will plan to see you when I return. I have signed for a three-year stint with the army. I'm sure whatever conflict that might arise between the North and the South will not last that long. In which case, I hope to be stationed in Atlanta, then we will be able to marry earlier," he added with a smile.

"I'm sorry," Lizzy said, obviously caught off guard, "what did you say?"

"Marry," he answered confidently. "Did you not know? I plan to enter into negotiations with your father. You are to be my wife."

"Excuse me," Lizzy said hotly and loudly, knowing this would bring Bartholomew into view, "I am not a piece of merchandize to be negotiated for. I will marry whom I please." Oh how she wanted to tell him of her intentions with Tyler, but she heeded Jackson's advice, knowing that Aaron Thomas would be one to use this information against her or Tyler for his own means.

"I'm not sure I like your tone," Aaron said condescendingly. "Your tendency to be headstrong will be something we'll work on once we're married. Make no mistake, we will be married. Your family and mine will make a wonderful alliance. You will satisfy me in many ways. I'll see to that. Don't forget your place as a woman, Elizabeth, leave the decisions to the men."

"Get out," Lizzy seethed. "Do not address me in such an informal manner—it is Miss Wyley to you. I will marry whom I please, and it will not be you. If you do not leave now, I will have Bartholomew escort you off my property." Lizzy backed him to the door, and Bartholomew followed her.

Aaron glanced at Bartholomew, a nervous look flashed on his face. He turned to leave. "I will return," he leered at her, leaving no question as to the lust he felt for her and her property. He turned and left through the door. Lizzy slammed it behind him.

Bartholomew watched through the front window to make sure Aaron had left, while Maggie and Hannah came to Lizzy's side. She was visibly shaken from the encounter.

"I know it wasn't much, and I won't marry him," she told them, "but the look in his eyes was pure lust, and it left nothing to the imagination as to what he really wanted to do with me."

"I know, honey," Hannah said in such a manner that made Lizzy wonder exactly how much Hannah knew about such looks from men and what men had looked at her that way. She shuddered. The three women went to the kitchen again for some tea to calm their nerves.

A few hours later, as they were preparing a small lunch, another knock came to the front door. Lizzy was scared that Aaron Thomas had returned for more and almost suggested they not answer it. She was relieved she had not when Bartholomew came with the calling card. It was Andrew Parker.

"Mr. Parker," Lizzy exclaimed when she saw him. "It's good to see you. How are you?"

"I'm fine, Elizabeth, and you?" he asked, smiling.

"Alright," she answered. "We've had a busy morning. You're our third call today."

"Really?" he asked. "So am I correct in assuming you've heard the news?"

"Georgia's secession? Yes, we've heard," she answered soberly.

"You know what this means then." It was more a statement than a question.

"Yes. We are not diluted in our thinking that this will not lead to war. We do hope that it won't last long."

"We can all hope that, but I fear that it will last longer than even the most realistic person can guess."

Lizzy nodded her agreement.

"This is what brings me here," Mr. Parker continued. "My brother has been looking to expand his shop in Washington City. I mean to pack up and move there. I am taking my workers with me. I think it will be safer there. I do not pretend to think that I will not be under intense scrutiny with my past behavior toward slaves, should I remain here. I'd like to extend the invitation to you as well, Elizabeth. I fear for your safety without your father and brothers here."

Lizzy was silent for a few moments. "I appreciate your offer so much, Mr. Parker," she said. "However, I can't leave my home. I have too much to do here."

"I thought you'd say as much," he answered. "I wish your response was different, but I believe you when you say you have much to do here. Tyler didn't tell me anything, but he hinted that your life will change a little during this time. He also hinted at a possible understanding between the two of you," he added hopefully.

Lizzy smiled. "Yes, sir. We have declared our intentions for each other."

Andrew Parker's face erupted into a huge grin. "I cannot tell you how happy that makes me. I immensely look forward to having you as a daughter."

"Thank you, sir." Lizzy smiled.

They paused for a moment, then Lizzy said, "Sir, have you, by chance, already purchased the ticket you intended for me?"

"Yes, I have," he answered. "Why?"

"I wonder if you might consider taking someone else in my stead," Lizzy said.

"Sarah, my mother's maid, has had a very rough time since mother's passing. She has mentioned wanting to go away. And surely you must know of her relationship with Joseph as well. I'm assuming you are planning on taking Joseph to Washington City." Joseph was one of Mr. Parker's former slaves. He currently worked in Mr. Parker's tailor shop.

"Yes," he said, "I am aware of their relationship. In fact, Joseph was unsure about coming with me because of it. In the end, he consented in the hopes of finding a place for them to live and coming back for her. He would be thrilled with this arrangement."

"Then you agree?" Lizzy asked hopefully.

Mr. Parker paused for a moment, then said, "Yes, I agree. I think it would be a wonderful plan. They would then be permitted to marry, provided Sarah was a free woman."

Lizzy's face fell. "Oh right," she said. She had no authority to set Sarah free. "How would we work that out, sir? According to the law, she is my father's property, not mine. I cannot set her free."

"What about selling her to me, and I would set her free?" he asked.

"Would that really work?" Lizzy asked. "I don't know the first thing about setting someone free. Though, I don't like the idea of selling her. She's a person, not property."

"No one agrees with you more than I do on that point, Elizabeth," Mr. Parker said. "However, she would need to be set free or sold to me in order to travel with me."

"I don't want a profit from her," Lizzy said adamantly. "What if the sale were just the price of the train ticket?"

"That would work," Mr. Parker said. "We'll just write up the bill of sale with that price on it, and then I'll immediately sign her manumission papers and set her free."

"Wonderful!" Lizzy exclaimed.

They went to Major Wyley's study and drew up the bill of sale, and then Mr. Parker signed Sarah's manumission papers. Lizzy was so excited.

"Thank you so much," Lizzy said gratefully. "I'll tell Sarah and have her ready to leave first thing tomorrow morning."

"Great," Mr. Parker said, "and I'll go tell Joseph the good news." Then he turned to leave the house. Lizzy stopped him.

"One more thing, Mr. Parker, if you don't mind."

"What is it?" he asked.

"Please, if you could, please teach her how to read and write so she can write me and tell me how she is," Lizzy asked.

"It would be my pleasure," he said. Then he turned and left.

Lizzy started toward Sarah's room. Maggie and Hannah met her in the foyer.

"What was that all about?" Maggie asked.

Lizzy told them. They were very excited.

"Hannah, I'm sorry it I couldn't have been you or any others for that matter," Lizzy said sincerely.

"Honey," Hannah exclaimed, "This is de mos perfect way! I couldn't have gone wit out Bartholomew. Sarah was the bes choice. I know you'd do it fo any one o' us, if you had de chance. I ain't upset a'tall."

Lizzy smiled her gratitude. "Now, let's go tell Sarah."

CHAPTER 7

After hearing the news, Sarah was stunned silent. "Free?" was all she could say.

"Yes, honey, you's free," Hannah assured happily.

"But why me?" Sarah asked. "There are so many."

"Don' even think about it," Hannah said. "We all get our chance soon enough. This yo' chance now. Take it, and don' question God's goodness."

Sarah smiled her appreciation. "Well then, I guess I best get ready to go." They began to help her pack her few belongings. Then they heard a knock on the door. It was Bartholomew.

"Sarah, honey, you have a visitor," he said with a smile.

Sarah looked confused. She had never had a visitor come to the big house before. She didn't know what to think of it.

A looked passed between Hannah and Bartholomew, and Hannah silently guessed who the visitor was. "Honey," she said to Sarah, "go on down and see who it is."

Sarah went downstairs. The others followed down the hall but stayed on the stairs where they could see but would be out of the way.

It was Joseph. Sarah's face broke into a big grin at the sight of him.

"Mr. Parker just told me the news," Joseph said quickly. "Is it true?"

"Yes," she said hesitantly. "I'm free." She smiled even bigger then.

"Are you truly coming to Washington City with us tomorrow then?" Joseph asked hopefully.

"Yes," Sarah answered.

"Then we can be married!" Joseph said excitedly.

"Yes!" Sarah exclaimed. They embraced.

"Wait…"

Sarah's face fell. She was afraid he would say he didn't want to marry her after all. "What is it?" She asked.

"I don't want to wait to get married," he answered. "I want to go to Washington City with you as my wife. Let's get married tonight."

Sarah paused for only a moment. Then her face erupted into the biggest grin yet. "Yes!" she shouted and wrapped her arms around his neck. He hugged her back, picked her up, and spun her around.

Hannah ran down the stairs. "Wonderful!" she exclaimed. "We gonna have a broom jumpin' tonight!"

"Is that what you'd like?" Joseph asked Sarah.

She nodded.

Hannah continued, "I'll go down and get Adam. Sarah, you get yo best dress on. We gonna have a celebration tonight!"

Sarah kissed Joseph on the cheek and turned to go upstairs to get changed. He held her back. "Wait," he said again. When she stopped, he said, "Wait right here." Then he turned and went out the front door. The others stood and waited, confused. When he returned, he had two boxes in his hand. One he gave to Sarah. "Open it."

She opened the box and pulled out a beautiful, but simple, white cotton dress. She looked at him. "Is this what I think it is?"

"Honey, it's your wedding dress," he said smiling. "I've been working on it in my spare time. I also made me a wedding suit. It's in this box." He pulled out the contents of the other box. It was a very simple white button down shirt and a pair of black slacks. "I didn't think we needed something too fancy. I wanted something nice but something we could wear again, if we needed to."

Tears were flowing down the faces of every woman in the room by now. They were all so happy for Sarah. Sarah smiled through her tears and flung her arms around Joseph's neck again and hugged him tight.

"Thank you, thank you," was all she could say.

After she was finished, Hannah took over. She sent Bartholomew to help Joseph get ready. She sent Sarah to her room to get ready with the promise that she would be there soon to help. Then she turned to run down and tell the others on slave row.

Lizzy and Maggie stopped her before she ran out of the house. "Wait," Maggie said. "What can we do?"

"I have an idea," Lizzy said. "I'd like to give them the night in the guest house. This way, they can start their lives as husband and wife alone, not in the small apartment above the tailor shop next to the other workers. Would that be all right?"

Hannah smiled. "I think that would be wonderful, honey."

Lizzy smiled back. "Great. So we just need to get word to Mr. Parker that Joseph won't be coming back and get his stuff ready to leave tomorrow. We also need to make sure the guest house is clean and ready. Maggie, will you help me?"

Maggie agreed. "We'll get it done, Hannah," she said. "When should we be ready?"

"Let's say an hour and a half," Hannah replied. "That should be plenty of time to get you two ready too. I'll lay out yo dresses."

The girls were grateful for that since they weren't sure what to wear to such an event. They didn't want to overdo it. Everyone set out to do their jobs. Maggie sent Eli to give the news to Mr. Parker and invite him as well. Then the two girls set out to fix up the guest house for the new couple. They had the kitchen staff make a few provisions for the evening and breakfast and extra food to take on the trip. Once they were sure the guest house was clean and how they wanted it, Lizzy and Maggie went back to change and get ready themselves.

The girls were dressed in simple, plain dresses that Hannah was sure would not make them seem as though they were putting on airs, but also would not make the others uncomfortable as though they were trying to come down to the slaves' level. Lizzy was worried about this since she had never even met some of the slaves. Her father was very strict about keeping the family away from the field slaves and away from slave row itself. Lizzy was never quite sure why he felt that way, but after this evening, she was determined to change that.

Sarah was radiant in the dress Joseph had made her. She looked so happy. Lizzy was very excited for her friend.

The ceremony was held halfway between the big house and slave row. Lizzy and Maggie didn't understand why Bartholomew continued Major Wyley's desire to keep them from slave row but decided not to argue this night.

Adam, one of the field slaves, performed the ceremony, and Lizzy and Maggie quickly understood why they called it "jumping the broom" when a broom was produced, and the couple actually jumped over it as part of the short ceremony.

The party afterward was lively and fun. A simple snack was prepared for the entire household. There was singing and dancing all around until late. Everyone enjoyed themselves.

Around eleven o'clock, people started wishing the couple well and saying good-byes. Soon it was only the couple left with Lizzy, Maggie, Hannah, and Bartholomew. Lizzy decided to give the couple her gift. They were overcome with joy.

"I can't believe you'd do that for us," Joseph said. He'd not encountered very many white people who were kindly toward blacks.

"It's the least I can do for all Sarah has done for my family, and you as well. Thank you both so much for everything. I wish you the greatest happiness in your life together. And Sarah, I want you to write me of all your adventures in Washington City," Lizzy said sincerely.

"Miss 'Lizabeth, I can't write," Sarah said.

"Perhaps not right now, but Mr. Parker will teach you," Lizzy said smiling.

Then they all wished the couple good night and everyone headed for bed.

The next morning dawned bright and clear. Those in the big house were up and ready to send the couple off as soon as Mr. Parker came to get them. They all hugged and waved good-bye through tears as they watched the couple drive off.

"I hope that's not the only happiness we'll see in the time to come, however long it might be," Maggie said.

"I hope so too," Lizzy agreed. "Well, we do have the concert tonight to look forward to."

"True," Maggie said hesitantly.

"What's wrong?" Lizzy asked.

"Oh, I guess I'm just worried about playing the part right."

"Playing the part?"

"I just don't want to give anything away, you know? With everything else going on tonight. I know I'm going to be worried that they'll all get where they're going safely. I just don't want to be too preoccupied."

"I understand," Lizzy said. "I guess we'll just pray for help and help each other. We do need to do this though. Hannah's right. If we don't, it will seem more like something is going on. We can't let there be any cause for questioning. We'll get our chance to help the runaways escape—just not tonight." Maggie gave a reticent smile in agreement.

"Oh," Maggie suddenly said.

"What is it?" Lizzy asked.

"Phillip and Jackson will expect an invitation for coffee after the symphony," Maggie said. "Should we oblige? Or should we decline, considering the events of this house tonight?"

"Let's ask Hannah," Lizzy said. "I don't know what to expect, so I can't say what we should do."

They set out to find Hannah and presented their dilemma to her.

Hannah thought for a moment and then replied. "When ya come home, if everythin's gone well, I'll say that coffee is ready to be served. If not, I'll say I have t' make it. Then ya'll know if ya need to be short or not. If ya need to be short, ya can preten' to be tired or somethin.'"

"That's perfect, Hannah," the girls agreed.

Dear Tyler,

What an exciting turn of events we've enjoyed the past few days. We have learned of the events of Georgia's secession. Though we are saddened by this news, it has brought joy to us with Sarah and Joseph. Sarah has been set free! She is now married to Joseph, and they are on their way to Washington City with your father. Their wedding was so beautiful. All of the slaves on the plantation turned out to celebrate their union.

I've never attended a wedding like it. Plus, I've never met some of the slaves that live right in my own backyard. It was quite an amazing night. All that was missing was you.

This evening, Maggie and I are headed to they symphony with Phillip and Jackson. I hope that's all right with you. They are joining the Georgia Army tomorrow. This is their celebration. Hannah suggested it was a good idea for us to accept their invitation.

I pray that all is well with you. I miss you.

Love always,

Lizzy

CHAPTER 8

That evening, the girls were dressed in their finest evening gowns. Their hair was done up in the latest fashion. Their jewelry sparkled. Everything was perfect for playing the part. The girls actually felt excited about the evening out. It wasn't often that they had been asked for outings. Lizzy, especially since her mother had been sick, had declined so many offers that the offers soon stopped coming. Most men, other than close friends, chose not to ask Maggie out, seeing only her disability.

Jackson and Phillip arrived at six o'clock to pick the girls up for dinner and then the symphony. The girls said good-bye to Hannah and took the offered arms into the carriage. It was splendid. The dinner was at a quiet restaurant near the concert hall. After dinner and pleasant conversation, mainly consisting of Phillip excitedly talking about adventures he hoped to have in the army, the four walked to the concert hall to hear the symphony.

The orchestra was incredible that night. Excitement was in the air with upcoming events surrounding the secession. Lizzy and Maggie couldn't help but be caught up in the excitement, even though they did not agree with the political side. The concert attendees were all in good spirits, even more after the concert was finished. It was a splendid night.

On the ride home, the girls even allowed themselves to get caught up in Phillip's excitement about the army. They almost forgot about the events of their house that night—almost. When they neared Lizzy's plantation, they tried to continue the conversation, but were a little distracted. Phillip didn't seem to notice, but Jackson eyed them curiously. Lizzy looked away and tried to be interested in Phillip's chatter.

When they pulled up to the driveway, the front door opened, and Hannah and Bartholomew stood in the doorway. They waited until the four were out of the carriage and up the stairs to address their mistress.

"Miss 'Lizabeth," Hannah began, "I hope your evenin' out was enjoyable. I have coffee made, if ya'd like it."

Lizzy and Maggie caught sighs of relief before they escaped.

Lizzy answered, "Yes, Hannah, we would enjoy that. Thank you. Please bring it into the front parlor." Then she turned to the men, "Won't you join us?"

The men graciously agreed, and the four settled themselves in the parlor. Soon, conversation drifted into pairs. Maggie continued to listen to Phillip's chatter. She couldn't understand how he had so much to talk about but actually was interested to see how long he would talk. It was somewhat interesting conversation.

Jackson turned his and Lizzy's conversation to more serious topics. "You seemed a little distracted tonight, Elizabeth. Is everything all right?"

"Oh yes," Lizzy said. "Everything is just fine. It was a wonderful evening out, Jackson. Thank you very much. We needed some fun after the events of the past few weeks and the impending events looming before us."

"I'm glad we could provide some entertainment for you," Jackson said.

A few moments of comfortable silence followed. The fire crackled in the fireplace. Jackson seemed to be gathering the nerve to say something. Finally, he spoke, "Elizabeth, I think there is something you're not telling me. I don't want you to tell me. I just want you to be careful. Whatever you do while we're all gone, please be careful."

"I will, Jackson. Thank you," Lizzy said.

"I know I have no right to feel so protective of you," Jackson said.

"I appreciate your concern," Lizzy assured him.

"Elizabeth," Jackson said, then paused. "As I said before, I'm extremely happy for you and Tyler. I wish it could have been me, but you two will be perfect for each other."

"Thank you."

"I hope I'm not out of line. I feel I must add something though."

"Please continue," Lizzy said curiously.

"If something should happen and things don't work out for you two," Jackson rushed on, "would you consider me as an alternative?"

"I appreciate your feelings, Jackson," Lizzy said, not wanting to hurt him. "You have been wonderful to us through the years. You have been a very good friend. I don't want to get your hopes up. My feelings for Tyler are very strong as are his for me. I don't foresee any change. However, in the very small chance that something should happen, I will consider thinking of you. Other than that, I want to remain friends with you. I don't want anything to change that."

"I appreciate your honesty, and I would be honored to remain good friends with you," Jackson replied.

"Thank you," Lizzy said.

"While I'm gone, would you allow me to write you, as a friend of course?"

"I would be honored. I would be very interested to know how you are doing and know that my friend is safe," Lizzy said.

Jackson smiled his response. Then the conversation became silent, and they listened in as Phillip seemed to be winding his monologue down.

Soon, Jackson decided the girls had probably had enough of Phillip's chatter and sensed they were ready for their guests to leave. The two men said good-bye and left the house. Lizzy and Maggie went in search of Hannah and Bartholomew.

They didn't have to search far. The couple was waiting in the foyer after they heard their mistress's guests leave, knowing the girls would want an account of the evening's events.

"Please," Lizzy asked, "if it's possible, tell us everything. We want to know what happened."

"Well," Hannah started, "everythin' went well, as I'm sho' you knew when you got home. Bartholomew and I took them in the boat 'cross the river and then through the woods to Mistuh Brown's cabin. They's all safe now."

"Mister Brown's cabin?" Maggie asked. "That's only five miles up the river. That's not very far. Why didn't you take them farther?"

"That's far as we go, Miss Maggie," Bartholomew answered.

"I don't understand," Lizzy said, agreeing with her friend. "I thought you'd take them farther. Surely each station along the Underground isn't that close to each other."

"Yo' right, Miss Lizzy," Bartholomew said. "Usually they's 'lot farther 'way from each other, so's to keep 'spicion low and so's to get them on they way."

"Then why did you only take them five miles away?" Lizzy asked.

"Befo' you offered this house, Mistuh Brown was already a station," Bartholomew began. "He's connected wit' everyone needed. They needed this house 'cause 'o da river. Riverridge is the closest plantation to the river of anyone offered on the Railroad. Really, the closest one to the river dat's near the city. Befo' you came 'long, da runaways had to go fifteen miles up river and den back down to Mistuh Brown's, or they had to travel twenty-five miles between stations and stay in da woods at night. Now, they jus' have to come here and cross. You's now a very important station, even though you's so close to Mistuh Brown."

"Oh," the girls said together. Now they realized that they really were an important part of the Underground.

"When is the next group coming?" Lizzy asked.

Hannah and Bartholomew smiled. They knew their mistress was excited to help. "We don' know when they's comin,' Miss Lizzy," Hannah said. "We usually only know a day or so befo,' if dat much. We let you know though, if we know when they's comin.'"

"All right," Lizzy said. "Thanks so much for taking them and for letting us know how it all went. I was surprised that you were back so soon, but now I understand why. That river can be heavily trafficked at times though. It will get fairly dangerous, won't it?"

"That's why we have to wait fo' the moon," Bartholomew explained. "Can't go on da river wit' a full moon."

"I see now," the girls said.

"All right, you two," Hannah said in a motherly tone. "You've had enough excitement for one night. There be plenty more in the day's to come. Off with you now. Go to bed. We see ya in da mornin.'"

The girls smiled and said good night as they headed up to bed, realizing how exhausted they really were. They were looking forward to a good night's sleep and, hopefully, an uneventful day tomorrow.

CHAPTER 9

"You must really like her."

"Why do you say that?" Tyler asked, smiling at his friend.

"Because you're smiling like a child eating candy as you read that letter." He gestured to the letter in Tyler's hand. "Who is she?"

"My best friend," Tyler answered. "Charley's sister."

"Really?"

"Yeah," Charley answered from across the tent.

"Is she pretty?"

"Very," Tyler answered, laughing. "Much prettier than anyone you could ever get, Jacob."

Jacob threw a pillow at Tyler, laughing.

Jacob was one of the first friends Tyler and Charley had made since coming to the military. He helped convince the other men that the two were not southern spies.

"What does she say in her letter?"

"That's none of your business."

"Aw, come on," Jacob pressed. "I can't ever keep a girl. I need to live vicariously through you." Jacob was known for attracting women at every pub he entered. Unfortunately, he was not known for having meaningful relationships with any of the women.

"It's personal," Tyler said. Then he turned to Charley. "She did mention that Jackson asked her to the symphony. Wanted to know my opinion on her going. Of course she already went, but it's the thought that counts."

Charley smiled a knowing smile.

"She must like you back," Jacob said.

"I hope so," Tyler answered meaningfully as he began writing her back.

Dearest Lizzy,

I am so glad things are going so well home. Your letter telling of Sarah and Joseph's wedding made me long for everyone. I wish I had been able to stay. Joseph has been a longtime friend of my family, and I know how much Sarah means to you.

As for your outing with Jackson, of course I don't mind. I appreciate you asking my opinion. He has been such a wonderful support to us and our families. I have no qualms about him taking you to dinner and the symphony, if I cannot be there to take you myself. Now if Aaron Thomas requests to take you, that is a different matter entirely.

As for me, we are still marching and shining shoes and buttons. I believe we shall soon begin rifle training. The thought of carrying a gun with the intent of using it against another man frightens me. I went hunting a few times with Charley on your land, so I know how to use a gun, but that was never intended for another human. This is entirely different than anything I ever imagined myself doing.

I know we told Maggie it was naïve of her to wish war would not come, but I share her sentiments. The closer I am to this, the farther away I want to be. I believe in the cause wholeheartedly, but the means to reach the end seems so far from godly that I am frightened. I pray that God will smile upon my intentions and not punish me for enlisting.

I miss you and pray for you every day. My heart is still yours, if you still desire it. Pray for me in this time.

Love,
Tyler

The next few weeks went by uneventfully. The girls were actually getting anxious and bored. They'd hoped that being part of the Underground Railroad would be exciting and adventurous, but not much happened. They had to wait for the runaways to come before they could do anything, and they wouldn't know if anyone was coming until a day or so before they came, if that.

Finally, toward the end of February, two women showed up at the back door in early morning escorted by Stella, one of the field hands. Lizzy and Maggie were excited to meet the newcomers, but Hannah and Bartholomew became nervous.

"The timin' ain't right, Miss Lizzy," Hannah said. "They's supposed to be here while it's dark. Someone may have followed them."

Lizzy then became nervous and agreed that a scout should be sent out to make sure no one followed them. Meanwhile, Maggie set out to fix breakfast for the women.

"We's sorry, ma'am," said one of the women. "We didn't want to bring harm yo' way. It's jes' that our massa was fixin' to bed Jessie here down with a mean ol' cuss of a man. He already done sol' her husband away. We didn't know what else to do, so's we jes' took off in the middle of the night. That was about five days ago. We jes' been walkin' in da woods at night and hidin' during the day. We kep near the river and walked in da water lots so's da dogs couldn't track us. Then we came by yo' people, an' they said to come up to da big house. Can ya hep us?"

"We'll try," Lizzy answered.

The women then ate in silence as they waited for Eli to come back from scouting and report on his findings. A half hour later, he returned and reported that he'd seen nothing.

After the women had eaten a good breakfast, Hannah showed them to the hidden room where they promptly fell asleep. When she came down, she found Lizzy and Maggie in the kitchen cleaning up from breakfast. "New moon's tonight," she said. "We's got to take 'em to Mr. Brown tonight. Who wants to come wit me?"

Maggie and Lizzy had already talked about who might get to go first and had decided Lizzy would go. Maggie was happy to help in any way she could, but she preferred helping at the house to the adventure part. The rest of the morning was spent with Hannah preparing Lizzy to help take the women. The afternoon was set aside for resting up for the mission.

After dinner, Lizzy was anxious to go, but Hannah continued to restrain her until late in the night. "We need to make sho' no one's on da river 'fore we cross," she reminded Lizzy.

Finally, the hour came. The four women, dressed in dark clothes, went down to the river and found the hidden flat-bottom boat. It was hidden under some brush in a heavily wooded area along the shore. As quietly as possible, which proved harder for Lizzy than the others who had having grown accustomed to traveling clandestinely, they got in and pushed off into the river.

The night was still, as was the river, making an eerie feeling fall over Lizzy. For the first time, she wondered if the risks were worth it. They were out in the open on the river which, at times, was heavily trafficked with fishing boats and riverboats. At any time, a night fisherman could come upon them and cause great danger. Lizzy kept her thoughts to herself, not wanting to worry the others. At last, they came to the other side, which was equally as wooded. They got out of the boat and pulled it ashore. Hannah showed them where to hide it, and then they were on their way on foot through the woods.

It was completely dark, which proved to be their ally as well as their foe. They knew it would be difficult for anyone to see them, for it was difficult for them to see each other. They could barely see two feet in front of them. Thankfully, Hannah knew her way well. Lizzy struggled some and tripped several times over the undergrowth, only to be slapped in the face by tree branches when she stood up. Other than the occasional twig snapping, there was no sound.

At last, they reached Mr. Brown's cabin. Hannah told them to wait hidden in the woods a few feet away from the door. Mr. Brown's cabin was pretty well-hidden in the woods. He preferred solitude to company. This proved well for the Underground Railroad, since most people forgot his existence.

Hannah knocked on the door in a prearranged pattern of knocks. Soon, the door opened. They exchanged words the others couldn't hear. Then Hannah ushered them in. Hannah made quick introductions but said she and Lizzy couldn't stay since they needed to return home. They said good-bye and left through the woods the way they had come. It was a bit quicker this time, Lizzy's eyes having become more accustomed to the dark and having only two travelers. They continued in silence and reached the boat.

Hannah stopped a ways away from the boat to see if anyone was coming on the river. About a mile up, they made out the outline of a small fishing boat on its way down. Lizzy was scared. Hannah remained calm and just motioned for them to hide in the brush until the boat passed. It seemed agonizingly long to Lizzy. Finally, the boat passed. After about twenty more minutes to be sure the boat was gone, Hannah motioned for them to go. They uncovered the boat and continued across the river. After making sure the boat was well-hidden again, they made it home.

Maggie was pacing in the parlor when they arrived. "I was so worried," she said. "I don't know if it's better to wait here or be in the danger there." She smiled and brought them both some tea.

Lizzy told her all about the trip. "It wasn't such a hard trip, and I'm sure it will be easier next time, but the fear of being caught sure is taxing," she said.

"Perhaps I'll go on the next one," Maggie offered.

"You's welcome to do whatever," Hannah replied.

Soon they all retired and slept in a little later the next morning.

CHAPTER 10

Dear Tyler,

Several weeks have passed by since my first trip. We have had a few more visitors since. Maggie and I have both participated in the journey. The fear never ceases. However, the knowledge of doing what is right pushes us forward.

The coolness of winter has passed by, and spring is blooming all over the land. I look forward to mild enough weather that I can return to my willow tree by the river.

Thank you, and thank Charley as well, for your letters. I'm sorry life is not more exciting, but I am glad you are safe. I have heard from Jackson as well. He sounds just as bored as you do!

I do read in each of your letters about the tensions between the North and the South. Being secluded as we are, we don't feel what you do. I guess it makes it easier on us. I believe you when you say war is coming, though we don't know when. With the formation of the new Confederate States of America in the South, I wonder if the North won't storm in and try to crush the rebellion. Why has it not happened yet?

I guess President Lincoln has his heart set upon preserving the Union, but does he want it enough to start a war? Only time will tell, I guess. We sure are tense waiting for it.

I pray for you every day and night. Please be safe.

Love,

Lizzy

Lizzy hoped her letter would be safe and reach Tyler. She worried over the contents and what they might give away should someone read them. She prayed the envelope would remain unopened until Tyler received it.

On the morning of April 15, 1861, Lizzy thought she'd go stir crazy if she had to stay in the house a minute longer. She decided to go into town to pick up some much needed supplies and newspaper to see if she could get any news on the situation. She went to the mercantile and placed her order. While her wagon was being loaded, she decided to take a walk with her newspaper. The whole town seemed abuzz with excitement. Lizzy opened the paper to read the shocking news. "Ft. Sumter, South Carolina, Returned to Proper Ownership," the headline read. Lizzy stopped in the middle of the boardwalk to read the news.

A strategic Union fort off the coast of South Carolina had been under siege for forty hours with continuous shelling by the South. Since the fort was on Confederate soil, the Confederates wanted control, so they attacked. Fortunately, the southern general gave the Union soldiers safe leave out of the fort when they surrendered.

"It has begun," Lizzy whispered, fear beginning to creep up her spine.

Then the full realization of what this meant hit her. She crushed the paper in her hands and ran to her wagon, throwing propriety aside. She pushed her way through the crowds of excited people. Thankfully, her wagon was loaded and she was able to take off toward home.

Once she reached the house, Bartholomew ran to meet her. The fear in his eyes matched the fear in her heart.

"What's de matter, Miss Lizzy?" he asked.

"We need to talk, now!" she said as she jumped out of the wagon and ran inside.

Bartholomew took the horses to the barn for Eli to care for and unload the wagon, as he went into the house to see what had so frightened the mistress. Lizzy was pacing the kitchen with Hannah and Maggie sitting on the edge of their stools waiting to hear the news.

"It's started," Lizzy said when Bartholomew came in. "War has started and the Confederates began it." She then read the news article out loud so they would all know the details she knew. They had earlier agreed that all four should share any and all information they heard with each other. They were all in this together.

"Since the South started this," Lizzy continued, "if I understand Tyler and Charley's letters correctly, the North will probably do something to cut off supplies from the South. The Confederates are too dependent on others, yet too stubborn to give up, they'll have to starve us into in to surrendering if they don't win the fight," she predicted.

The next few days passed in more excitement and tension as the girls took turns riding into town to get news. Sure enough, on April 20, the girls read that the day before, President Lincoln had declared a blockade on the South. Thankfully, they had had the presence of mind to buy what provisions they could without rousing suspicion. The plantation was fairly self-sufficient, but there were a few things they needed to buy.

During these days, they also realized the increase in the risk of their involvement, or anyone's for that matter, in the Underground Railroad. People were going to be more vigilant in watching for runaways. Hannah had spread the news to the others involved through the intricate network. Everyone was on higher alert. For a while, this slowed down many of the runaways. They were all afraid the punishments would be more severe now. A few runaways came and went safely through Riverridge Plantation, though not without intense fear. However, there was no sign that anyone had caught on to their involvement.

"Letter for you, Lizzy," Maggie said as she brought the envelope to her friend.

Lizzy's heart leapt. She had been hoping for a letter from Tyler, praying for one to lift her spirits. Her hopes were let down as she read the signature on the page. Nonetheless, she was pleased to hear from her friend.

Dear Elizabeth,

By now, I am sure you have heard of the beginning of the war. Ft. Sumter in South Carolina has been attacked. We are now in full swing of war. Our training has stepped up greatly. We are marching to our first destination of battle, though I don't know where that is. I probably wouldn't be able to tell you anyway.

I think of our time together at the symphony. I greatly enjoyed your company. I wonder how Margaret was able to put up with Phillip's chatter. He has calmed down a little. So far, war has not turned out to be as glorious as he thought—what with all the training and little actual fighting we are doing.

The men in our unit are congenial enough. We know several of them from school. I hope I am able to make you proud in my accomplishments with the army. I still hope there is a chance for a future with you, however small. I suppose I must be content with friendship, though I will cling to the smallest hope of more.

I continue to pray for your safety, especially now that war has begun. Please pray for me as well.

Jackson

The weeks passed, and everyone fell back into routines. The news didn't bring much information, as not much was to be had. It almost seemed as if the North might be content to let the new Confederate nation stand, though President Lincoln had called for army volunteers after the incident at Ft. Sumter. Along with the slowdown of news from the newspapers, Lizzy was frustrated to experience a cease in correspondence from Tyler and Charley. She still received letters from Jackson, but it seemed the North was determined to block correspondence as well as supplies.

Even though war was looming, business needed to be conducted as usual on the plantation. Crops needed to be planted. Livestock needed to be taken care of. Lizzy had run the household for over a year since her mother fell ill, so she knew what needed to be done. The fields were a new matter. Her father's white overseer had left when her father did. She put Bartholomew in charge of finding a proper overseer from among their current workers—she did not like thinking of them as slaves. He would then report to her daily about the progress in the fields. This arrangement worked well. Lizzy felt she could trust Bartholomew and the rest of the workers. She was determined to find some way to pay or compensate the workers. She hated that they worked for so little.

One day in June, Lizzy and Maggie decided to take water down to the field hands. The heat was sweltering, and they knew the people could use refreshments. They also wanted to sneak a look at slave row. Bartholomew still hadn't let them see it with him. They gathered a water pitcher and a basket with some food and headed out into the muggy day.

They were in high spirits as they walked, enjoying the sun and being out of the house. As they walked, they came upon a few rundown buildings that could only be described as shacks. The buildings were poorly constructed with holes in the walls and roofs. A dirt path ran down the middle of the two rows. Each row held five shacks each.

"Do you think this is it?" Maggie asked.

"Surely not," Lizzy replied. "Perhaps these are the old buildings and the new ones are down the lane a bit."

But smoke was coming out of one of the chimneys, and two little boys scampered out of one of the buildings. The boys stopped when they saw Maggie and Lizzy and stared at them. The girls stared back. Surely no one was forced to live here, the girls hoped.

Then one of the boys spoke, "Mammy, some lady folks here."

A heavyset black woman who looked to be in her sixties came out of the shack and stared back at the girls. "Can I hep ya, ma'am?' she asked, in shock that the mistress of the house would be at slave row.

The girls didn't know what to say. Finally, Lizzy asked, "Do you live here?"

"No'm, I live der," she said, pointing across the path.

"But you actually live in these buildings?" Lizzy asked. "This is what my father had for you?"

"Yes, 'm."

"Could we see inside?" Maggie asked.

The woman hesitated, then, seeing that her guests were truly waiting for permission, she nodded and led them inside. The girls were shocked at what they saw. The building was a one-room shack. It was about the size of one of the bedrooms in the big house. The floor was dirt. The two windows had no glass. The furniture consisted of one bed, the mattress made out of cornhusks; a table with one broken leg leaning against the wall; and two chairs. The curtains and blankets were old and worn, each having at least one hole in it.

Six children looked up at them from the game they were playing on the dirt floor. Lizzy figured her face matched the shock on the children's faces—she could see Maggie's expression did.

"What's your name?" Maggie asked the woman.

"Ida, miss," she answered. The girls introduced themselves.

"Are these your children, Ida?" Maggie wondered.

"No 'm. I watch the chillun's while der folks work in da field. I's too old to work in da fields no mo'."

"How many people live in this house, Ida?" Lizzy asked.

"Dose three chilluns dere," Ida pointed at two girls and one of the boys, who all looked to be younger than ten, "an dere mama an daddy."

"Five people?" Lizzy asked incredulously, looking at the single bed.

The girls stayed for a while longer talking with Ida and looking around slave row. After a while, they left and walked back home, completely forgetting their original errand.

"They need a better place to live," Lizzy said.

"Yes, but how can we make that happen?" Maggie asked doubtfully.

"I don't know for sure," Lizzy said, "but I need to do something. I have access to some money, perhaps I could buy some wood and we could build new houses. I think Father hired out one of the men to learn carpentry. I'll talk with Bartholomew and find out."

Later in the afternoon, Bartholomew found Lizzy and Maggie in the front parlor. His face wore a stern look of disappointment. "Ida say you come down today," he said unhappily. "I thought I tol' you not to go down dere."

Lizzy knew she was being scolded. "I know you didn't want me down there, but I had a right to know how my workers were living."

"Now you know?" Bartholomew wanted to know her reaction.

"Something needs to be done," Lizzy said strongly. "I won't allow them to be forced to live that way any more."

"Miss Lizzy," Bartholomew said. "I know ya want good things fo' dem, but ya gots ta think 'bout yosef in dis. If ya do anything, word will git 'round and people gonna come talkin' to ya. Den we might not git to do da Unde'groun' Rai'road. Ya might git in trouble."

"I understand that, Bartholomew," Lizzy said, "but how can I work to get people to safe places and better homes but not be willing to have better homes for my own workers? I'm not asking for a whole lot. Maggie and I have already been coming up with plans for new housing. And didn't Father have someone trained in carpentry? So we won't have to ask for outside help."

"Yes, 'm, Eli is trained in de carpentry," Bartholomew replied.

"I'm sure we have a lot of extra material and clothes for blankets, curtains, and clothes we can give too." Lizzy said excitely, "So there should be little we would need to buy besides wood and stoves."

"I see ya planned a lot o' dis," Bartholomew said uneasily. "But I don' think ya get da danger."

"Bartholomew, I know the danger. I know the danger of the whole operation. But how can I live in all this finery when my workers are living in dirt and rags?" She paused, then added quietly, "More pointedly, how can you as well?" Bartholomew and Hannah lived in the big house with Lizzy. Their room wasn't as big as hers, but they had access to everything in the house.

Bartholomew's face registered shock. He didn't know what to say. He stood silent for a few minutes. Neither of the girls said anything. Lizzy feared she had said too much. Finally, he spoke.

"Yo' right, Miss Lizzy," he said sadly. "I didn't think o' dat. I was too busy thinkin' o' yo safety and the Unde'groun's. An' mine too. Yo right. Dey needs better houses. I'll hep in any way I can."

"Thank you, Bartholomew," Lizzy said quietly.

"Ya won' even haf to buy wood," Bartholomew said.

"What do you mean?" Lizzy asked, confused.

"Las' fall, yo daddy ordered wood fo' a new, bigger barn. It's all in da ol' barn under canvas. Dere's enough dere, should build a few houses. I check wit' Eli."

The next day, Lizzy, Maggie, Bartholomew, Hannah, and Eli met together to talk about the new houses. Eli needed a little convincing for the same reasons, but, seeing the mistress was more than serious and determined, he became excited about the project.

They planned to build five buildings. Three of the buildings would be for the three families. Each building would have one great room for the kitchen and living areas, as well as one room for the parents and another for the children. The other two buildings would be the same layout, but one would house the five single female workers, and the other would be slightly larger with two extra rooms and house the ten single men. This one would also have another stove.

They went out to the barn to look at the wood. Eli thought there should be enough for the new buildings. Lizzy felt confident that they could get more without rousing suspicion, should they need it.

As they were walking back to the house to take a look at material for clothes and blankets, Maggie spotted a small stone building to the side of the barn. "What's that building?" she asked. "It looks out of place with the wooden barn."

Bartholomew and Eli exchanged looks. Eli looked fearful.

"Bartholomew," Lizzy said, "what is it?"

He looked at Lizzy for a few moments trying to determine if he should tell her. He finally resolved not to keep anything from her anymore. He simply turned toward the building and motioned for the others to follow. He opened the door slowly. The girls did not know what to expect, but absolutely nothing could have prepared them for the horror of what they saw.

Chains, whips, clubs, and other torture devices hung on the walls. The room was just big enough for two men to stand in. There were no windows. The room stank of human waste and blood. No questions needed to be asked about the purpose of the building.

Maggie was speechless and immediately sorry she had asked about the building. Lizzy was furious. How could these people have been treated this way? How could her father have done this? What could any of the slaves possibly have done to deserve this treatment?

Bartholomew began the explanation. "It was put up almos' two years ago. Massa Edward thought some o' de men needed dis'plin. Thought dey wasn't workin' hard enough an' needed to be taught to mind. After da beatin's, dey was left in here fo' a day or two. He used it 'bout once a month or so to git da men to work more."

"So it wasn't my father?" Lizzy asked, relieved, yet angry all over again at her brother.

"No, 'm," Bartholomew answered.

"Did he agree with this punishment?" Lizzy asked.

"No, 'm," Eli answered. "He treated de slaves mostly fair, 'ceptin' fo the houses," he said with a wry grin. "When yo mama took sick, Massa Wyley turned a lot over to Massa Edward. It was bad times with Massa Edward."

"But my father didn't stop it."

"No, 'm," Eli answered sadly. "He was busy wit' yo mama an' let Massa Edward take over."

There were a few minutes of silence. Finally Lizzy spoke. "I know exactly what to do with these stones."

"What?" the others asked, interested to see what this cunning look on her face meant.

"I think each house deserves a porch or at least a patio. These stones would be perfect for walking on!"

They all laughed and agreed. This building would be knocked down and the stones used as patios or stairs in front of each house. The chains and whips would be melted and made into something else more useful.

Material was found in the house to make at least one blanket for each person. Old clothes were found for children, as well as adults. Everything was gathered and ready to begin construction. The workers were told, and everyone agreed to begin construction on the houses after the harvest. Blankets, curtains, and clothes would begin immediately, as well as beds and other furniture. The torture building was demolished immediately by all the men.

The workers were a little skeptical at first, especially since most of them didn't know of their mistress's involvement in the Underground Railroad—and still weren't told for safety reasons. However, her genuineness was well-received, as well as her and Maggie's willingness to help sew and learn to build.

Everyone was tired after the day's work in the field, but excited about the project. Work began, and a fast pace toward completion was set. The goal of having everything completed by Christmas was well on its way to completion.

After a long day of marching, Tyler sat near the campfire rubbing his feet.

"You don't think about all this marching when you sign up for the army," Charley said, as he sat down next to Tyler and handed him a tin mug of bitter coffee.

Tyler sipped the coffee and coughed. "Did Jacob make this batch?"

Charley laughed. Jacob usually made strong, bitter coffee. The others tried to get to the grounds before he did, but tonight they were unsuccessful.

Charley noticed the pen and paper next to Tyler. "Are you going to write Lizzy?"

"Yeah," Tyler answered. "I know the Union has cut off communication lines, but writing helps me wind down and process what's going on. I hope to one day give her the letters I write. I have a feeling that we're going to see and experience things that will be difficult to put into words later on. I know she's going to want to know as much as I can tell her of my experiences. This way, I'll have them fresh from the time they happen."

"You know my sister well." Charley smiled. "She will pester you for every bit of information you can give her. She'll want to live vicariously through your experiences, knowing she'll never get to share them."

Tyler smiled, then sobered. "I'm nervous, Charley," he said. "What if I'm not up to the challenge of battle? What if something happens?"

"I understand what you're saying," Charley said. "But we can't think that way. If we live in a world of 'what if,' we're going to die in that world. We just need to live one day at a time and get through them with God's help."

Tyler gazed into the flickering flames of the campfire, watching the smoke rise through the trees. "Pray for me that I can do that," he said as he picked up his pen and paper.

Dear Lizzy,

I have determined to continue writing you, though I know communication lines between the North and South are severed. I hope I will be able to deliver these letters to you in person someday soon.

I'm sure you have heard about the beginning of the war. We are all put on high alert now. We've moved out of camp and are headed south. I don't know where we're going, but our commanders seem confident that we will strike hard and fast, and the war will be over quickly. I pray they are right.

We have made some friends in the company. They have seen our hard work, and I don't believe they consider us spies anymore. Unfortunately, that is not the case for all Southerners in our company. There are a few others. Their work ethic is lacking somewhat. The other men in the company are frustrated with them and, in some cases, have targeted them for abuse. I fear for them when battle comes. We have friends that we know will stick by us and help us out, should we get in danger. The other Southerners don't have that. I'm afraid they might even be placed in certain danger by some of the men.

We've had to prove ourselves in many ways to gain the trust of the other men. It's been hard work, but I believe it has been worth it. The commanders have given us more duties and more difficult duties than some of the Northerners to try to get us to prove ourselves. I believe we have gained their respect in all we've done. Time and battles will tell.

I pray that you know I love you with all my heart. I pray for your safety and the safety of all you are helping.

Love always,

Tyler

On July 22, Lizzy read of the first major battle of the war. It happened at a place called Bull Run Creek at Manassas Junction near Washington City. This news was met with fear and concern by the entire household, but none had much time to dwell on it with all the work needed to be done.

Little else was heard in regard to the war for the next few months. Lizzy heard from Jackson a few times about the deplorable conditions in which he, Phillip, and the other soldiers lived. The house received runaways at least once a month. All were promptly and safely moved along the Underground with seemingly no detection from the outside world.

One night in November, a knock came on the front door. Hannah answered it and went to get Lizzy. She looked scared.

"Who is it, Hannah?"

"Some men wit guns, Miss 'Lizabeth," she answered.

"Tell Bartholomew and Eli to come," Lizzy said as she grabbed her father's pistol and hid it in the folds of her dress. She went to the door, and Maggie followed, staying just out of sight with another pistol in hand.

"Can I help you, gentlemen?" Lizzy asked as sweetly as her shaking voice would allow. She recognized one of the men as Oliver Patterson, the owner of the Highland Plantation ten miles southward. His son, Seth, was with him. Oliver was a friend of her father, and Seth was one of Edward's friends. She did not like either of the men nor the look of anger and determination in their eyes.

"Sorry to bother you, Miss Wyley." Seth did not sound sorry at all. "We're looking for a couple of runaway darkies. You seen any?"

"No, sir," Lizzy answered truthfully. None had come by the house tonight. They'd taken a family across the river last week, but she was sure they were from a different plantation.

"Mind if we have a look around here to be sure?" It wasn't really a question.

Lizzy was about to object when Oliver broke in. He was a little nicer than his son.

"We would just like to have a look around, Miss Wyley, to make sure no one has come and hid here without you knowing."

Lizzy thought for a moment. She knew she needed to allow them to, in order to remain above suspicion. "That would be all right, Mr. Patterson, but I would like Eli and Bartholomew to go with you to make sure everything is in place." The men hesitated and seemed about to argue, but the Southern gentlemen in them agreed.

A tense half hour later, the men returned. "Everything seems in order," Oliver said. "However, I would like to inquire as to the purpose of the building project you have going on."

"We're building housing for the slaves," Lizzy answered.

"Why?" Seth asked, as if that were the stupidest thing he'd heard.

"Because, Mr. Patterson," Lizzy answered defiantly, "their former housing was uninhabitable. And I believe that I will get more production if my workers are well taken care of."

The men laughed. "They're slaves, Miss Wyley," Oliver replied. Then his face took on a hard look. "You'd do well, Miss Wyley, to be careful of how you treat your slaves. We don't want them getting too uppity. Neither do we want word getting to other slaves on other plantations. Might start a riot."

"You'd do well to heed the example of your brother, Edward, in dealing with the slaves," Seth said. "He was a good learner under my teaching, and I believe he got great production out of his slaves."

"Thank you for the suggestion," Lizzy said. "Is there anything else, gentlemen?"

"No, ma'am," Oliver said. "Only that you might want to keep an eye out for runaways now with the hostilities heating up with the North. If you do see anything suspicious, please let us know."

Lizzy smiled her good-bye and shut the door. She watched until the men had all ridden out of sight.

CHAPTER 11

"Silent night, Holy night. All is calm, all is bright…"

The sound of the men singing Christmas hymns was more haunting than comforting. Tyler sat in his tent alone as he listened to the men around the campfire. They were excited for the upcoming holiday. Tyler missed Lizzy more and more. He felt alone. Christmas was supposed to be a happy time. A time for family. Instead, he was alone in a tent surrounded by other men from other states. How he wished life were different.

> Dear Lizzy,
>
> The prospect of spending Christmas without you does not please me. I know it was my choice to join the army and be away from you, but especially when I look ahead toward Christmas, my heart misses you most. We are spending the winter months in tents in the snow. Needless to say, it is not pleasant. I comfort myself with thoughts that you are cozy at home by the fire.
>
> My teeth are chattering and my hand is shivering, so I will say good-bye for now.
>
> Love,
> Tyler

Dear Elizabeth,
    Merry Christmas!
    I hope this letter finds you well and warm by the fire. I envision you wrapped in a quilt, sipping hot cider.
    As for me, I am in a tent sipping cold coffee. We are supposed to be getting some much needed sleep, but the wind is whipping our tent flaps so harshly that it is difficult to relax.
    We are marching somewhere to fight someone. We never know what we're doing until we get there.
    Stay warm and have a merry Christmas!
    Jackson

Lizzy smiled as she read the letter. She was glad for Jackson's missives, though it made her long for Tyler all the more. She worried that she was unable to hear any news of him and Charley. She prayed they were still alive and well. She did not allow herself to think otherwise.

During December, no runaways came. Hannah reported that word was spreading that Oliver and Seth Patterson were on the lookout for runaways, and those who wanted to try to escape now were too scared to make the attempt. Hannah assured them that the fear would subside, and they would be able to help more in a few weeks.

    Christmas rolled around with mixed feelings on the Riverridge Plantation. It had been a year now since the last time they had seen Tyler or Charley. It had been a year since they had seen or heard from Major or Edward Wyley, both choosing not to write home. This saddened Lizzy, but she was not surprised, having never been close to either of them. It had also been a year since the death of Lizzy's mother. Lizzy took some time to think of each one, doing her best to think positively. She was able to remember several wonderful memories, though so many were clouded by bad ones. Maggie's parents also moved to Kentucky to help

Maggie's aging grandmother, so both girls had reason for sadness during this holiday time.

On the positive side, the new workers' village was completed. Everyone had moved in with new furnishings, mattresses, drapes, and clothes. Lizzy was overwhelmed with excitement for the occupants. The workers all expressed extreme gratitude to their strange new mistress. Most of them were still unsure of Lizzy and Maggie and the kindness the ladies showed, but they didn't want to question the generosity, lest it be taken away.

After a quiet Christmas morning with small gifts and a light breakfast, Hannah told the girls that the workers had invited them all to a Christmas party in the workers' village. The girls had excitedly told Hannah that they would love to go.

"Is this something new?" Lizzy asked, thinking she had never heard of the slaves holding a Christmas party or any party for that matter.

"No," Hannah answered. "Dere's a party down dere every year. Y'all jes' don' know 'bout it since yo mamma always had parties."

That night, everyone from the big house traveled down to the workers' village with much excitement. They found all the workers outside engaged in various activities. Lizzy had shared money from the cotton harvest with the workers by getting lists of what they wanted and needed and buying supplies. They had asked for a pig, which she bought. That pig was now being roasted over a fire. Several men were tending to the pig. The women were putting out breads and desserts they had made and vegetables from their gardens. Children were playing with new handmade dolls and other toys. Lizzy felt great satisfaction in the happiness of her workers.

They all milled around talking for a while and watching the children play. Soon, the food was ready and they all sat down to eat. The newly made tables and chairs had been brought out from the houses so everyone would have a place to sit.

After dinner was eaten, and everyone was full, a few of the men brought out some homemade instruments that Lizzy couldn't identify and began to play songs. Although the songs were foreign to Lizzy and Maggie, they enjoyed them. The songs were upbeat, and many of the workers got up to dance. The rest of the night was filled with laughter, music, and dancing.

By the time the evening was over and Lizzy and Maggie had danced with several of the men, most of the discomfort and suspicion held by the workers had eased. They had a new respect for and comfort with their young mistress.

Lizzy and Maggie went home well after midnight, exhausted and in high spirits. They both agreed they had never had so much fun. All the glitter and glamour of Mrs. Wyley's Christmas parties didn't hold a candle to the fun and ease of the workers' party.

The girls looked forward to enjoying the new relationships cultivated with the workers due to the Christmas party. They hoped to now be welcomed without suspicion in the workers' homes. They knew the workers would still not be comfortable to come to the big house, but Lizzy and Maggie felt that a big chasm had been bridged.

The day after Christmas, Lizzy woke to the sound of ice pelting her windows. She rose from her bed, wrapped a robe around her, and went to take a look. They sky was dark gray. Ice was already freezing to the bare branches on the trees lining the driveway. Ice crystals stuck to the window making it increasingly difficult to see out.

Lizzy turned away from the window and quickly dressed. She met Maggie in the hallway, and they descended the stairs to breakfast.

"Quite a storm out der," Hannah said as she served the food.

"I'm glad it waited until after Christmas," Maggie said.

"It would have put quite a damper on the party," Lizzy agreed.

Bartholomew entered the kitchen, arms laden with wood for the fires. "Pretty fierce one out der," he said, as he shed his coat and went to add wood to the stove. "We'll have to stay in here. Can't go down to de village for a while."

The girls were disappointed. They wanted to see their new friends. They tried to salvage the day by bringing out some of the games they enjoyed playing.

The storm continued through the day. The pitter-patter of ice on the windows was deceiving as to the severity of the storm, which continued into the night.

As the girls were reading in the parlor, snuggled in blankets close to the fire, Hannah came in followed by a young man and woman. They were clothed in very little and stood shivering behind the housekeeper.

Lizzy and Maggie jumped up and immediately, without needing to say anything, wrapped the couple in their blankets and led them to the fire.

"Stay here and try to warm up," Lizzy said. Then she and Maggie left to get warmer clothes for the runaways.

Bartholomew met them in the hallway. "Dese folks got to go out tonight," he said worriedly.

"What?" Maggie asked.

"They just got here," Lizzy said. "They're freezing. They can't go out in this again. It can't be safe."

"Dis storm's not lettin' up, Miss Lizzy," Bartholomew said. "It gonna get worse. Tomorrow night's the new moon. Dey gots to go."

Lizzy had long ago learned to trust Bartholomew's weather sense. Reluctantly, she agreed, and the two continued on their mission to find warmer clothes.

Hannah fed the couple and gave them hot coffee. After a few hours, they seemed warm enough and rested enough they could travel.

Lizzy insisted on accompanying them since Maggie's foot would not allow for ease of travel, even under normal circumstances.

Lizzy and Bartholomew wrapped in warm clothes and led the couple out of the house down the path to the river. Ice pelted them the entire way. They each slipped at least once down the path.

They finally reached the boat and had to break it away from the shore since the ice had formed all around it making it freeze to the ground.

The river was rough with rapids and ice. Lizzy was afraid, but she trusted Bartholomew with her life. She prayed that God would protect them, hoping that no one else would be foolish enough to be out in this weather.

They struggled to row across the tide, Lizzy and Bartholomew using every ounce of strength to push through the freezing water. Finally, they reached the opposite shore. The woman slipped as they pulled the boat up the bank. She stopped just before the water. Her husband pulled her up after them.

Their travels were precarious through the woods. The sound of their feet crunching on frozen branches and leaves seemed louder than normal to Lizzy. She became extremely paranoid.

Bartholomew suddenly stopped them and motioned for them to hide behind a bush and be quiet. They crouched down, pulling their dark coats over their heads and around their faces.

Lizzy held her breath as she heard other footsteps come near them. She peered through the barren branches of the bush and saw the breath of a man frozen in the air. The man stopped a few trees downstream from their hiding place and glanced all around him. All four held their breaths, lest the man see the frozen vapor.

He finally moved on, seeming satisfied with his scouting.

The four in hiding waited for what seemed like hours before Bartholomew motioned them onward. He kept them close to the thick bushes as they continued on their way.

They were all freezing and shivering by the time they reached Mr. Brown's cabin. He welcomed them in and offered them hot coffee. Lizzy and Bartholomew accepted but left quickly.

True to Bartholomew's prediction, the storm was continuing to worsen. They went as quickly as they could back along the path to their hiding boat. The faster pace proved more difficult for Lizzy, who slipped several times. The warmth from the coffee quickly wore off as they traveled.

Finally, they reached the boat. Lizzy helped untie it and, as they were getting it into the water, she slipped and fell in. Bartholomew grabbed her and pulled her into the boat. Knowing nothing could be done for her drenched state, they pushed on. The rest of their trip was thankfully uneventful.

When they reached the house, Lizzy could no longer feel her fingers or toes. Hannah and Maggie had blankets ready and a raging fire.

Maggie helped Lizzy out of her wet clothing into warm, dry ones. She wrapped her in blankets and sat her as close to the fire as safely possible.

"We saw a man in the woods," Lizzy said through chattering teeth.

Maggie stared at her friend in fear. "Did you recognize him?"

"No," Lizzy answered.

"Did he see you?" Maggie inquired.

"I don't think so," Lizzy answered. "We hid behind some bushes and covered our heads and faces with our coats. I would have never thought to cover my face, but I'm glad for Bartholomew's sharp thinking. We could hear the man, but what truly gave him away was the vapor from his breath in the air. He would have caught us had we not covered our faces."

Maggie simply exhaled in thankfulness for the safety for her friends.

Lizzy stayed inside for the next few days, nursing a cold from her dip in the frozen river. She continuously thanked God that she did not suffer more.

Finally, the storm abated. Lizzy felt better, but Hannah would not let her out of the house for over a week. Bartholomew and Maggie walked the grounds to the workers' village to help where needed. When Hannah finally let Lizzy out, she was overjoyed to spend time with her new friends.

In her elated state, she forgot the fear of the trip in the ice storm and concentrated on the joy of the workers. The next few weeks were exciting, as they found new relationships and new roles on the plantation.

> Dear Tyler,
>
> What an amazing start to this year we've had. The workers (I refuse to call them slaves) invited us down to the new workers' village we've built for a Christmas party. They have so much fun. We danced throughout the night with the workers. I believe they are more comfortable with us now. At least I hope so. We've worked hard to make it possible.
>
> We make regular trips to the village now with food and clothes and conversation. I believe it has helped a lot with their comfort level. We've started taking books to read to them. We read the Bible every day. We try to teach them and have a church service on Sundays. Bartholomew and Eli lead the service. Hannah and Mimi lead the music, while some of

the other men play some instruments. They've told us that they'll teach us how to play sometime.

We've even stepped out more and have started teaching the workers how to read and write. Actually, Maggie has taken this up. She's very good. The women have really taken to her. Some of the men have started attending classes, but they are a little more nervous. I help, but Maggie is really a great teacher. They really look to her as their teacher and see me more of an employer. Hopefully, they'll start to look to us as friends as well.

Hannah and Ida have taught us the most amazing job! They are the midwives of the plantation. They have allowed us to learn along with them. Mimi and Eli had a baby girl, which I was able to help deliver. Ella and Marcus had a baby boy, which Maggie helped deliver. What an amazing experience. We were both so scared, but it was wonderful. No more babies are foreseen anytime soon, but perhaps someday we'll get to help again.

It is horrible not being able to correspond directly with you. I pray you are all right and that the communication lines will be opened soon.

Love,

Lizzy

February 1862 brought more fighting between the states. The Union army captured forts along the Mississippi River, with Union General Ulysses S. Grant stating, "No terms, except unconditional and immediate surrender, can be accepted." They captured thousands of Confederate prisoners and effectively cut off the Confederate supply line from the territories in the West.

With the fighting picking up and supplies being cut off, naturally tensions began to run higher among Southerners. Lizzy and Maggie tried to counteract this fear and tension by spending more time with the workers. This helped them to keep their minds off of the lack of information from their loved ones.

"Miss Lizzy, Miss Lizzy."

Lizzy was awakened by the urgent knocking on her bedroom door. She wrapped her robe around her and answered the knock.

"Hannah," she said surprised. "What is it?"

"We have a visitor," Hannah said. "She in trouble."

Lizzy followed Hannah to Maggie's room. They woke her up, and all three went down to the kitchen.

Maggie and Lizzy were shocked at what they saw. Mimi was carefully washing a young woman's back. The woman was a runaway. She had been badly beaten. Mimi was carefully pulling strips of clothing away from open and gaping wounds on her back and arms. When Lizzy looked closer at the horrific sight, she gasped. The woman was pregnant.

CHAPTER 12

"Oh my goodness!" the girls exclaimed together as they ran to their new visitor.

They thought she was unconscious until she gave out a great cry of pain.

"It de contractions," Mimi said.

"She's having contractions now?" Lizzy asked.

"Yes'm" Mimi answered. "She a bit early, but de beatin's brought 'em on."

"Who did this to her?" Maggie asked angrily.

Mimi and Hannah looked at each other.

"Seth Patterson," Hannah answered sadly.

"He beat her, even though she's pregnant?" Maggie asked incredulously.

Mimi and Hannah looked at the girls with meaning in their eyes.

"He's the father of the baby," Lizzy said, understanding.

"What?" Maggie asked. "He did all of this?" She gestured toward the woman.

"It not uncommon, Miss Maggie," Mimi answered. "De massa's find a pretty girl. He bed her down. Make more slaves fo' de fields."

"They would father children and make them slaves?" Maggie asked sadly. Maggie's family didn't own field slaves. Her father was a banker. The only slaves they had were a few house slaves. They had no need of more.

Lizzy was too stunned to speak. She prayed her father and Edward never did this, but she was too scared of the answer to ask.

The woman screamed again when a contraction ripped through her.

"We's got t' get her lying down," Mimi said as she finished cleaning the wounds. "She gonna have dis baby tonight."

They carefully wrapped her limp form in blankets and carried her to one of the guest rooms upstairs. It was slow going since she had contractions every few minutes, and they tried not to jostle her and make the wounds hurt worse. A half hour later, the woman was settled in a bed with cloths and basins of water. The other four women were ready to assist any way possible.

The contractions came quickly and intensely. Mimi headed the team of midwives, giving orders to the other three for cloths, water, and massages.

An hour later the baby still hadn't come.

Hannah pulled Lizzy and Maggie aside. "De contractions are too close. She losing a lot of blood. Dis beyond what we know."

"Are you saying we need to call for a doctor?" Lizzy asked.

Hannah nodded.

Lizzy looked toward Mimi, who glanced a pleading look in their direction. Mimi was covered with blood as was every cloth they had brought. The woman, whose name was Rita, looked as pale as her dark skin would let her.

"I know de risks, Miss Lizzy," Hannah continued. "But Rita in de biggest risk of all. She gonna die if we don' get a doctor here."

Lizzy looked to Maggie who agreed with her eyes.

"All right," Lizzy said. "Maggie, go get Bartholomew to take you to Dr. Ryan's house."

"Dr. Ryan and not Dr. Harrison?" Maggie asked. Dr. Ryan was a new doctor. He was born and raised in Atlanta but went to medical school in New York. He had just returned home to practice medicine a few months before the war started.

"Yes, Dr. Ryan," Lizzy said. "I know he's young, but he's been in the North for a while. Perhaps his views on slavery are different. Besides, he's married to a New Yorker. I can only hope."

"All right, I'll go," Maggie said as she flew out the door and down the stairs to get Bartholomew.

As they waited for Maggie to return with the doctor, the three women did what they could to make Rita comfortable. It was terrifying. One minute she would be screaming in agonizing pain. The next minute she would be limp on the bed breathing so shallow that they couldn't tell if she was still alive.

The clock ticked the minutes by.

The fire cast a frightful, eerie glow across the room. The shadows dancing like demons coming to claim the woman's life.

What seemed like hours passed.

None too soon, they heard the front door fly open and feet crashing across the floor and up the stairs. Lizzy had the bedroom door opened for the doctor. He ran in to the bedside. Taking one glance at Rita's limp body and the blood surrounding her, he began barking orders. Sending Lizzy and Maggie outside, he instructed Hannah, Mimi, and his wife, who had accompanied him, in the final stages of the birth. Lizzy and Maggie paced the darkened hallway listening to the frantic orders.

Twenty minutes later, Rita gave an excruciating cry that ripped through the house. Lizzy and Maggie stopped dead in their tracks at the end of the hallway. When her scream ceased, the girls ran to the room, stopping at the doorway. They were greeted with the sound of slapping and then a boisterous cry from a newborn.

Tears of fear mingled with tears of joy streaming down every woman's face.

Peeking in the room, Lizzy saw Rita lying back, nearly unconscious. Dr. Ryan cleaned the baby and then placed it with the mother. He instructed Mimi and Hannah to gather clean blankets and take the soiled ones to the wash. They also finished cleaning Rita and helped her hold the sleeping baby.

Dr. Ryan glanced up to the doorway after he had given his last orders. Rinsing his hands in the last of the fresh water, he strode to the doorway.

Lizzy expected him to allow them into the room to see the new mother and her baby. Instead, she was greeted with a cold glare. "We need to talk, now," Dr. Ryan seethed through clenched teeth as he continued through the doorway.

He stood in the hallway waiting for Lizzy to lead him to a private room. She and Maggie took him to the study.

"What is going on here, and why do you have another man's slave in your house?" Dr. Ryan asked.

Lizzy and Maggie remained silent. They knew he already knew enough to cause them harm, should he so choose, but they didn't want to make the situation worse.

"Elizabeth," Dr. Ryan continued angrily. "I have known your family for years. I went to school with Edward. I know your father would be furious at you harboring another man's slave. Why is she here?"

More silence.

His eyes flashed furiously. "As a law-abiding citizen, I am required to report what I saw here tonight. I will ask you one more time. What is going on here?"

Lizzy took a deep breath. "She came here for help."

"What kind of help?"

"You saw the condition she was in," Lizzy snapped. "What kind of help do you think?"

"She belongs to Seth Thomas."

"He's the one who did this to her," Lizzy countered.

He looked at her curiously. "Did what do her?"

"Everything." Lizzy replied hotly.

"Everything?" he questioned.

"You saw that baby. That is not a black man's baby."

"How do you know? The mother was light-skinned."

"You're not stupid, Franklin," Lizzy said. "That baby's father is Seth Thomas. The man who beat the baby's mother is Seth Thomas. I cannot send her back there. As a God-fearing woman, I am required to help her."

Dr. Ryan glared at her. He had been brought up in the South. His family had slaves. He had always been taught that the black men and women were inferior and belonged to the white men and women. His time in New York had opened his eyes to another way of thinking, but the Southerner in him had not gone away.

"You took a huge risk in calling for me," he finally said. "I will be back tomorrow, and we'll discuss it further. He turned to leave the room.

"She'll be gone tomorrow," Lizzy said defiantly.

He whirled around to face her. The doctor in him replacing the Southerner. "She'd better not be. She lost much blood during the delivery. She has been torn badly. She cannot be moved for several days." He raised an eyebrow as the Southerner took over. "I'll see you tomorrow."

He stormed out of the room, throwing open the study doors.

His wife blocked his tracks out of the room.

"I am ashamed of you, Franklin," she said heatedly. "I have never heard you talk like this before. Did you mean anything you said in my father's parlor?"

His shoulders slumped slightly. Then he glanced back at Lizzy and Maggie. His eyes turned cold again as he turned back to his wife. "Go to the carriage. We're leaving now." He pushed past her and out the front door.

Anna Ryan looked defeatedly at Lizzy and Maggie. With tears in her eyes, she slowly turned to join her husband.

Lizzy and Maggie quietly returned to the bedroom. Rita was sleeping soundly with the baby next to her. Mimi and Hannah had taken the soiled clothes to the workers' village to be cleaned as they returned to help Rita.

"She can't be going nowheres anytime soon," Hannah said.

"That's what Dr. Ryan said," Lizzy replied wearily. She sank down into the rocking chair and watched the reflection of the flames flicker on the wall. The sight which, a few minutes ago, had been so frightening, now seemed comforting. The shadows were still and everything seemed peaceful.

"Dr. Ryan gonna say somefin to Massa Seth?" Mimi asked shakily.

"We don't know," Maggie answered. "He said he would be back tomorrow, and we'd discuss it more." She turned to Lizzy. "I know he said not to move her, but I'm afraid Seth will come looking for her and want to search the house again."

"I agree," Lizzy said. "We need to move her to the secret room, but how?"

"You leave dat to us," Hannah said.

"But Dr. Ryan said not to move her," Maggie protested, worried about their patient.

"We's got plenty o' practice movin' people carefully, Miss Maggie," Mimi said. "She won' feel a thing."

"Mimi right," Hannah said. "Now, you'uns go on t' bed. We take care o' dis."

Feeling too tired to protest, Lizzy and Maggie returned to their rooms for a few hours of fitful sleep.

Morning breakfast was interrupted by a knock on the door. Lizzy answered the door herself, as Hannah was working on the food.

Thinking it would be Dr. Ryan, her heart skipped a beat when she was met by Seth Patterson.

"Mornin,' Miss Wyley," he said almost nicely.

"Good morning, Mr. Patterson," Lizzy said, not inviting him in.

"I'm sorry to bother you this pleasant morning, but might you have seen a runaway slave girl in the night?"

Lizzy cringed at the drippy sweetness of his voice. "No," she lied.

He seemed to take her at her word. Then he sniffed the air. "My goodness, something smells delicious. Am I in time for breakfast?" he started to step through the doorway.

"We were just finishing," she lied again, blocking his entrance into her house. For once, she was thankful for the hoops her skirt required.

He made a pouty face as he stepped back. "Too bad. Perhaps another time." He reached out and stroked her arm.

She jerked her arm back. "I'll thank you never to do that again. Good day, sir." She slammed the door in his face.

First Aaron Thomas, now Seth Patterson? Good heavens, what was next? She didn't even want to think about it. Oh, how she wished Tyler and Charley were here.

That afternoon, another knock came to the door. Lizzy sent Bartholomew to answer it. He returned with Dr. Ryan's calling card. They met him and his wife in the front parlor.

"Good afternoon," Lizzy said coldly to him, then smiled at his wife.

"Good afternoon," they answered.

Dr. Ryan's shoulders were slumped, though he looked her in the eye. "I want you to know that I have not gone to the authorities yet," he said.

Lizzy let out a breath.

He continued slowly. "What you have asked of me is an extremely dangerous proposition, Elizabeth."

She shook her head. "I have not asked anything of you beyond your help last night," she corrected.

"On the contrary," he said, holding up his hand for her to allow him to continue. "I believe that Rita was not the first, nor will she be the last to come through your doors for help. I now have a choice to make. On one hand, I could do the southern thing and go to the authorities to turn you in. You would then be arrested, and I could wash my hands of the whole affair."

Lizzy and Maggie avoided each others eyes, knowing the fear they would see in each.

"Or," Dr. Ryan continued, "I could help." He took a deep breath. "After talking at length with my wife, together we have come to a decision."

He paused. Their hearts beat loudly in their ears. This could be the end of their involvement in the Underground Railroad. This could be the end of their freedom—the freedom of each of the workers.

"We have decided to help," said Anna Ryan, ending their anxiety.

They remained silent; the relief too shocking for words.

"While studying in New York," Dr. Ryan said, "I had the privilege of meeting several people of several viewpoints. My wife and her family were among them. I worked alongside of several people of color. My view of them changed as I saw their hard work and dedication to their jobs. I heard about the Underground Railroad and even met some people who had arrived to the city via that route. I never became thoroughly involved, believing I would never need to. Then you called me last night, and I was forced to make a decision. I am a Southerner, but, first and foremost, I am a Christian. I cannot, in good faith, turn you in for doing what God has called you to do."

"Thank you, Dr. Ryan," Lizzy said.

"However," he continued, "I cannot be fully involved in anything. I will offer my medical services as needed. And we can discuss any other necessities I might be of service with. I can make regular house calls in such a manner that I believe will be above suspicion."

"How can you do that?" Lizzy asked curiously.

He turned to Maggie. "Miss Swanson," he said, "I noticed last night that your limp was more pronounced than I'd seen it before. Are you having troubles?"

"Actually, yes," she said. "We have been working a lot at the workers' village. The walking takes a great toll on my leg."

"Might I suggest a treatment to help?" he offered.

"What kind of treatment?"

"While in medical school, we learned about braces and splints," he explained. "I believe I could fashion a brace for your foot to help with your limp. It might be painful at the beginning, but eventually it should feel better. The idea is to slowly and gradually turn the foot out to its proper place."

He continued talking and showed her an example of the brace. After several minutes of explanation, he began to fit her foot for a brace.

"You see," he said, "I will need to return to the house for weekly visits to check up on your progress."

They all smiled.

"Therefore, giving an excuse to make house calls," Maggie finished.

"Exactly," Anna Ryan said.

A month later, Rita was on her way with her new baby along the Underground Railroad. They were all sad to see her go. Having so much time with her gave them the opportunity to actually get to know one of their visitors. They were happy she was on her way to safety.

Dr. Ryan gave the baby, whom Rita named Franklin, something to keep him quiet on the way.

Seth Patterson had been by one other time to see if anyone had seen Rita. Lizzy made herself conveniently busy and had Bartholomew show him to the door.

CHAPTER 13

"Are you sure you don't want to come out and play cards?" Charley asked hopefully, poking his head into the tent.

"No," Tyler snapped.

Charley hung his head in dejection. "You haven't wanted to play cards in weeks. You sit by yourself in the tent. Are you sure you don't want to be with us?"

"I said no!" Tyler retorted. He rolled over on the ground, covering his head with his blanket.

"I know it's been hard since Jacob died," Charley said sympathetically, "but we all have to bear his death. You're not alone in this. We're all hurting."

Jacob had died three weeks earlier. He wasn't the first friend Tyler had lost, but he was the closest.

"He was my first friend here," Tyler said quietly, "the closest to me besides you."

"I know," Charley said. "He was my friend too."

Tyler threw the blanket off him and turned to face Charley. "It could have been me!" Tyler snapped. "It should have been me."

"Why do you say that?" Charley asked, aghast that his friend would feel that way.

"The bullet barely missed me," Tyler said. "His body slammed into me. His blood was all over my uniform. Some stains still won't come out." He fingered the hem of his tunic where the red blood from his friend's fallen body still stained the blue material.

"It was close to me too," Charley said. "His equipment hit me. It could have been me."

Tyler shuddered at the thought but refused to allow it to form. "But it should have been me," he whispered.

Charley rushed to his friend's side, fearful. "Why do you say that?"

Tyler looked him in the eye. "Because you both are so good. You don't suffer from the dark thoughts I do. You don't imagine inflicting pain on the enemy. You don't feel almost gleeful during battle when you see a fallen rebel, knowing you are the one who ended his life…" His voice trailed off.

Charley was speechless. He hadn't known his friend felt this way. He backed away.

Tyler dropped his head into his hands and whispered again, "It should have been me."

Shuddering at the darkness he felt from his friend, Charley turned, closed the tent flap, and went to the other men.

Tyler groaned. Charley was right. What was the matter with him? He'd become somewhat of a recluse. He was still cordial with the other men and they with him, but he didn't seek out their company. He preferred to be alone with his dark thoughts. And dark his thoughts had become of late.

Shoving the blanket aside, he reached for his pen and paper.

My Dear Lizzy,

How I hate being away from you while our country is in turmoil. As the fighting continues on the northern and southern soils, no end seems in sight. We foolishly hoped this war would be over quickly. How naïve we all were.

The fighting is intense. I never imagined what war would be like. Seeing comrades killed in front of me and beside me is an experience I would not wish on my worst enemy. What was I thinking when I enlisted?

I thought war would be grand. I thought I could become a hero. Instead, I am sickened to see the horror of war—bodies strewn across the battle field, bloated and bleeding in the sun, no relief in sight for those still breathing.

I confess I find myself feeling pleasure in killing the enemy. I believe it is their fault we are in this mess. Who in their right mind could believe that owning another person is not wrong? At times, I actually look forward to battle. I find a gray uniform, put it in sight of my gun, and fire. Not taking my eyes off of my target, I lower my gun and watch the man fall.

I am glad you cannot receive this letter. What would you think of me? I am not the man you said good-bye to in your foyer so many months ago. I am a hardened veteran of war. I will never be the same again.

Tyler

He could not even bring himself to sign the letter to his beloved with the word "love."

Fighting continued throughout the coming months. In mid-April 1862, Lizzy received news she had dreaded since the initial announcement to go to war. On April 6, the Confederates launched a surprise attack on Union soldiers at Shiloh, Tennessee. Even though the Confederates had the initial momentum, more Union troops arrived to the rescue of the surprised troops. The ensuing battle ended in a victory for the North.

Along with the announcement that all men between the ages of eighteen and thirty-five must serve in the Confederate Army, Lizzy received the dreadful news. She had lost both her father and her brother Edward. She was in sorrowful shock for the next few days. She'd never been close to either of them, but they had always been the head of the household. Now, not only was she the acting mistress in charge of the plantation, she was actually in charge. She had no idea how her father's will was written; she assumed everything would now go to Charley. She would worry about that later and talk with her father's lawyer after the funeral.

The funeral was joint for both Major and Edward Wyley. It was largely attended, as her father was a prominent man in the community. The preacher was comforting in his words. Her father and brother were buried next to her mother in the family plot on the back acres of the plantation on the opposite side from the workers' village. Lizzy was glad for this, knowing she would not need to field questions. Edward's fiancée carried on pathetically, looking forlornly at the property she would never be mistress of. After everyone had left the reception, Lizzy collapsed on the sofa and slept until the next morning, releasing much of her grief.

Two days after the funeral, Lizzy paid a visit to her father's lawyer. She had a small idea of what he would say regarding her father's will. She really wasn't sure what to expect, but she was not prepared for what she discovered.

"Miss Wyley," his lawyer began, "your father came to me the day before he left for the army and changed his will. Originally everything was to be left to Edward. He changed his will to leave everything in equal shares to you and Charles. With Charles at school, he also gave special access to several bank accounts to you. Your father had several accounts and investments he kept secret from your mother, simply to make sure you and your brothers would be well taken care of."

Lizzy knew her father was wealthy but looking at the ledgers his lawyer showed her was staggering. How much she could do for her people with this! Her father had also had the foresight to change all of his currency to gold, not knowing what might happen to it should war ensue. With all of the legalities taken care of and paperwork signed, Lizzy gathered her things and prepared to leave.

"Thank you, sir," Lizzy said as she took the papers. She thanked the man again and left for home. When she arrived, she gave the horses to Eli to care for. She then went down to the river to her favorite tree to grieve her father's passing and wonder at the turn of events brought by his will.

Dear Elizabeth,

I am terribly sorry about your father and brother. The fighting at Shiloh was awful. We lost so many men. Your father and brother fought hard and bravely. I am proud to have fought with them.

I am also writing with the news of Phillip Markley's death. I don't know if you have heard already. He was killed during the same battle as your father and brother.

I feel so lonely now that he is gone. We had been friends for most of our lives. We enlisted together. We bunked together. We had mess duty together. We fought together. He was hit right next to me. It was terrible. I couldn't even go help him. We were pressing toward the enemy, and I couldn't go back.

It's at times like these that I wish I had never enlisted. I know I would have been conscripted in the end, but at least it would not have been my choice. I pray I am doing the right thing.

I apologize for the morbidity of this letter.

I pray for your safety and for a safe return home to you.

Love,

Jackson

Dear Jackson,

Thank you for your kind words about my father and brother. I am terribly sorry for the loss of Phillip. I had not heard. We were so busy with the funeral arrangements for Father and Edward, I did not hear about Phillip. I am so sorry. This must be terribly hard for you. I know how close you two were.

I pray for your safety every day. As for whether or not you are doing the right thing, that I cannot tell you. I pray you find peace with yourself and God through this nightmare.

Thank you for your prayers and letters.

Elizabeth

Days passed by, and Lizzy was able to use some of the money from her father's accounts to replenish some much needed supplies for the workers' village and the big house.

What they could learn of the war was confusing. Each side was winning battles. No one seemed to be gaining ground. After a series of Union victories during the spring in New Orleans; Yorktown; Corinth, Mississippi; and Memphis, Tennessee, the Confederates pushed other Union soldiers back to Washington in June in what became known as the Seven Days' Battle, costing thousands of casualties on both sides.

Another battle was fought at Bull Run in August, ending in a victory for the South. The Union Army had been trying to reach Richmond, the capital of the Confederacy, and was again pushed back to Washington. In September, another bloody battle ensued in Sharpsburg, Maryland, ending in yet another victory for the Confederates.

The North would win a series of battles, and Lizzy would become hopeful, then the South would turn the tide and gain major victories. The spring and summer of 1862 was a succession of emotional ups and downs for the entire country.

Adding to the emotions, every day the newspapers would post what names they had of dead and wounded soldiers. Lizzy knew she would not hear news about Tyler and Charley from the newspapers, but she feared reading other names she knew, such as Jackson. Many of her brothers' other friends were in the army, now that it was mandatory for men ages eighteen to thirty-five to join. Somehow, some of the most prominent men were exempt. Lizzy was sure it had to do with putting the right amount of money in the right person's hands.

Unfortunately, Seth Patterson was one such person excused from the army. Lizzy deeply resented this fact. One day in May, he paid the plantation a visit. He said he had come to visit Lizzy, but she suspected it was more to check up on her relations with the workers, since he had seemed so suspicious of her activities while building the village. He'd come on what seemed to be a social call.

He must have been unaware of the fact that Maggie was living at the plantation as well, because he seemed genuinely surprised to see her there. This turned out for Lizzy's advantage. She had difficulties being pleasant to people she despised. Maggie was much more adept at social niceties and was actually quite congenial during his visit.

He asked permission to come calling on Lizzy again. Maggie motioned for Lizzy to agree to see him. Grudgingly, she agreed but made it perfectly clear she was only interested in friendship.

"How can you stand that man?" Lizzy asked Maggie after Seth had left.

"Only by the grace of God," Maggie answered dryly.

"Then why have me agree to see him again?"

"We have to keep up appearances," Maggie answered. "We can't hide out here. People already think us strange for building the workers' village. We can't ward off prosperous men as well. You've only agreed to chat with him from time to time. You can make it clear that you want nothing more and will have nothing more."

Lizzy was skeptical but said nothing else. She knew her friend was right about appearances. However, she didn't have to like it.

Seth came by several more times throughout the next few weeks.

Lizzy became nervous. They had a number of runaways come through during this time. Everyone acted as typical as possible and seemed to pull it off. Seth didn't show signs of suspecting anything any more.

Though he said he was visiting both women, Seth would often try to figure ways to be alone with Lizzy. The girls never allowed for that. One day this was not possible, and his advances became too strong.

On this particular day, Maggie was out in the garden when Seth arrived at the door. Lizzy answered, and he let himself in before she could ask him to wait.

Once again, as he had several times before, Seth told Lizzy he would like to court her. "No, thank you, Seth," she replied. "I fear I cannot accept any advances with my brother away. Besides, I'm simply not interested in you as more than a friend." She gave him what she hoped was a smile, though she was shaking inside. Seth had a reputation for getting what he wanted. Lizzy was also quite frightened of him knowing how he treated his slaves.

Seth's eyes became hard. "Miss Wyley," he said, "Elizabeth, there is no earthly reason why we should not court. I believe you would make a fine mistress for my home. Now, let's forget this foolishness and be done with it. You know I always get what I want." He stepped closer to her, almost touching her.

She tried to step back, though her step took her up against the wall. She tried to steady her voice, "Mr. Patterson, I am firm in my decision. Now I must ask you to leave."

He grabbed her arm with one hand and put his other arm around her waist. Pulling her close, he pressed his lips against hers in a rough, menacing kiss. She tried to push him away but couldn't free her arms. At that time, Maggie and Bartholomew came up to the house.

"Lizzy!" Maggie shouted. She ran to her friend and pushed Seth away. Bartholomew was right with her, ready to fight the man off, if need be. "What is going on here?"

"Leave us alone," Seth barked. "This is none of your business."

"This is my friend," Maggie growled back. "It is all of my business. Now, I suggest you leave."

Seth glared at her and then at Bartholomew. They stared at each other for what seemed an eternity. Bartholomew did not back down. Seth finally turned to Lizzy and said, "You're not worth my time. I'm disgusted I even tried. And you," he turned to Maggie, "you're nothing but a cripple. It's all I can do not to wretch when I look at you." Then he pushed past Bartholomew and stormed out the door.

Horrified at the words, Lizzy turned to Maggie who was actually laughing. "I can actually say I'm thankful for this thing," Maggie said pointing to her foot.

Lizzy tried to giggle at her friend's feeble joke.

"I'm fine, Lizzy," Maggie assured her. "Today, I can actually thank God for my infirmity. I would not have wanted to go through what you just went through. Are you all right?"

"Could be better," she answered. "It's over, and hopefully he won't be coming around again."

"We'll pray for that."

"This is a nasty bruise on your arm, Elizabeth," Dr. Ryan said the next day, as he came for one of his weekly visits. "What happened?"

She was unsure of how much to tell him. She hesitated.

"Elizabeth," Anna Ryan said. "You can tell us. Is everything all right?"

She looked down, embarrassed at having been so vulnerable. "I had an altercation with Seth Patterson."

Dr. Ryan's eyes narrowed. "What did he do?"

Lizzy was afraid of the look in her friend's eyes.

"It's all right, Elizabeth," Anna said. "Please tell us."

Lizzy took a deep breath and recounted the terrible experience.

"That man thinks he can have whatever he wants and has no respect for anyone or anything," Anna said.

"I'm so sorry, Elizabeth," Dr. Ryan said meaningfully. "I worry about the two of you out here alone."

"We're not alone though," Lizzy said. "We have Hannah and Bartholomew, Mimi and Eli, and all of the rest of the workers."

"I know," Dr. Ryan said. "But you know how people like Seth Patterson view your workers. They would hurt them more than you and wouldn't see them as much of a threat."

Lizzy nodded in agreement.

"I'm not saying you need to leave or even need to find someone to stay here to protect you," he said. "All I'm saying is I worry for you and hope you're doing everything to stay safe."

"Thank you, Franklin," Lizzy said. "We appreciate your concern and all you do when you come here. We're doing everything we can."

"Good." He wrapped her wrist in a bandage to keep it stable to help it heal. "Well, I think my work is finished here. Everyone looks healthy. Be careful with Samson as you take him across uneven ground. His ankle is pretty sprained from the fall. Margaret, your leg is stretching nicely. Keep working on the exercises I showed you. Elizabeth, keep your wrist wrapped. The bruise and sprain should heal with little movement."

He and his wife stood to leave when he finished packing his bag.

"Thank you both for all you do," Lizzy said.

"We appreciate it more than you know," Maggie added.

As Lizzy was going through her father's affects a few days later, an envelope dropped to the floor. She knelt to pick it up. Reading her name on the outside, she opened the envelope. Her pulse quickened in anticipation as she began to read:

My dear daughter,

How strange that must be for you to read from my pen. I have never been one for showing emotion, but being faced with possible death makes one reevaluate his life.

Before I go on, I want to be sure to write that I have always thought of you as my dear daughter. I have always been proud of you and know you to be a true gentlewoman in every sense of the word. You have grown into everything a father could want of his daughter. I have been very impressed with how you have handled the affairs of the house with your mother's illness and know you will handle it extremely well in my absence.

Next, I want to address the contents of my will. You may well be confused at many items. I will try to address each.

First, the adjustment of my will from Edward to you and Charles: Edward has received more responsibilities on the plantation due to his position in the birth order. I have not agreed with his tactics with the slaves. He has become more and more tyrannical and, frankly, I am disgusted. If he does not go to the army as I plan to do (I have no doubt he will at least consider this, as he tends to follow where I go), I will leave him a handsome sum to sustain him and his new wife, as well as a letter of explanation as to my decision. Rest assured, dear daughter (it feels good to write that), the decision will be irrevocable. You and Charles will inherit the plantation and everything with it.

Second, the extra money: yes, I hid money from your mother. It was basically so it would not tempt her to use it. I wanted all of you to be well taken care of after I was gone and not want for anything.

Finally, I want to address an issue that may well shock you with my knowledge. This is the issue of slavery. I know you and Charles do not agree with the institution. I do not know to what extent you do not agree (I sincerely hope you are careful and discreet with your disagreement). I have been wavering with my own feelings toward the issue. I do not approve of the tyrannical, barbaric way of treating slaves that Edward has adopted. However, I do see the need for the workers. Perhaps I can either mull this over after the conflict is finished, if I survive, or the decision will be made for me, either with my death or the victory of the northern states. If this letter reaches you, the slaves belong to you and Charles now. I specifically left them to both of you so nothing could be done in haste. I am under no illusions that Charles hasn't at least entertained the idea of joining the northern army. I'm sure he is either fighting (I hope not to answer this question face-to-face with him on a battlefield), or he is working in some business up north. Either way, a decision on the freedom of slaves must come from both of you. I did this for your protection, Elizabeth. If the slaves were to be set free (as I would assume you would do), you would come under intense scrutiny by other Southerners. Life would be miserable for you. I know you'll do the right thing when the opportunity arises.

Now, as I've become long-winded, I must end my missive. Please know, dear Elizabeth (it feels so good to call you that), I am proud of you and, yes, I love you. You have brought great joy to your mother and me. You are a lovely young lady, and I have no doubts you will make some young man a wonderful wife. I did see the looks you gave young Tyler. Please know you would have every blessing from me should you desire to marry him. He is an amiable, pleasant, fine, upstanding young man. I would be proud to call him my son-in-law.

With those final words, I will say good-bye. I look forward to seeing you in heaven and saying these words face to face. I love you.

Your father

Lizzy took a deep breath and wiped the streaming tears from her face. Her father was proud of her and actually loved her. How she had longed to hear those words from him. Now she had them on paper in his own writing. How wonderful. He also knew her feelings about slavery and was supportive. Lizzy had not felt this good in a long time. She decided not to dwell on the awful thought that her father might have met her brother on opposite sides of the battlefield before his death. She prayed that they never met, and Charley and Tyler were still all right. She went to the kitchen to share the good news.

Maggie, Hannah, and Bartholomew shared in Lizzy's joy. Somehow, they all felt more at ease knowing the true views of the late master of the house. The next mission with runaways to Mr. Brown's house a few weeks later seemed easier than the ones before, and Lizzy and Hannah were less frightened on the trip.

The next few weeks were filled with a peace and joy that had not been felt in the big house for a long time. The women hummed with their chores. More laughter could be heard wherever anyone went on the plantation. Lizzy truly felt she had the blessing of her heavenly Father, as well as her earthly one. Life seemed good. They all wished this peace would last forever.

One day at the end of September, Lizzy and Maggie rode into town together. Neither had wanted to be alone in town or at the plantation during the weeks following the altercation with Seth Patterson. As they shopped for their supplies, they overheard some men talking.

"That man can't tell us what to do," one man said. "He ain't our president."

"Who does he think he is?" another man retorted. "No one's gonna free our slaves. That Lincoln's tryin' to steal our property."

"What does he think we're gonna do without them?" the first man asked. "He's trying to run us all out of business."

The girls gave each other questioning looks and moved out of ear-shot of the men so as not to be caught eavesdropping. Neither said a word to each other as they continued shopping. When they reached the counter, Lizzy casually asked Martha, the storeowner's wife, about the conversation.

"Oh, deary, have you not heard?" Martha asked. "That Lincoln's issued a proclamation saying all the slaves in the South are free. I don't know who he thinks he is though. Does he just expect us to say, 'All right, whatever you say, sir,' and let them go? He's not our president. He can't tell us what to do." She lowered her voice and leaned closer to the girls, "Be careful what you say though, deary, if any of the slaves hear about this, we're bound to have an uprising. Keep a tight hold of your slaves, deary, is all I can say."

She finished ringing up the purchases and had one of her slaves take the parcels out to Lizzy's wagon. The girls were excited about the news as they discussed it on the way home. Through their excitement, they were realistic and also discussed the possible challenges to come along with this. They both knew that fear among slave owners would run high and most would place a stronger hold on their slaves, which also meant harsher punishments for runaways.

Lizzy and Maggie wanted to tell their workers of this freedom, though they realized it was freedom in name only. The South would never recognize any orders President Lincoln gave. If Lizzy freed her slaves, they would more than likely be captured by another Southerner, enslaved again, and treated very badly. As much as she hated to be a slave owner, she decided it would be safer for her workers if they contin-ued as they were. She still treated them as if they were free, though still living on her land. It was a strange situation, but she believed it was best for their safety. She would soon receive confirmation for her thoughts.

CHAPTER 14

A few nights later, Lizzy was awakened by crashing thunder and bright flashes of lightning. Rain beat on her window. She had always enjoyed storms. Something about the powerfulness of God was revealed to her during these times. She knew God was big and mighty, but listening to the driving rain and the deafening claps of thunder, as well as watching the blinding flashes of lightning, had always been awe-inspiring. She lay in bed, curled under her quilts, and listened to the thunderstorm.

In between claps of thunder, she heard a sound out of place in the squall. She cocked her head and listened. There it was again. It sounded like shouting. "Surely not," she mused. "Who would be out in this?" Again came the shouts.

She crept to her window, not lighting the lamp, to see what was happening. The sights she saw would haunt her dreams for the months to come.

A flash of lightning revealed a group of white men chasing a pack of dogs. As she strained to see what the dogs were chasing, lightning flashed again revealing three runaway slave men, fleeing for their lives.

Lizzy watched through flashes of lightning as the runaways ran along the shore, trying to find a safe place to jump into the river.

A lull in the lightning frustrated her as she strained to see what was happening.

Then she heard the most terrifying sound she'd ever heard. Screams echoed through the night, accompanied by snarling, growling, and barking. Shouts of menacing encouragement mixed with the awful sounds.

A flash of lightning revealed faces. A few yards down the river on her land, she could see Seth Patterson and his men with rifles. Running down stream toward her house, they were chasing five huge, frightening, attack dogs. The dogs were in the water tearing at something. She could hear one of the men calling the dogs off their prey. Reluctantly, but obediently, the dogs returned to their masters. Moments later, Lizzy saw the most horrifying sight she had ever seen in her life.

Lightning split the sky in several places, illuminating the horrific scene. Floating within plain sight of her bedroom window were three black bodies, chillingly mangled. Their clothes were ripped to shreds. Their arms floated cockeyed from their bodies. Their eyes stared sightlessly into the sky. Their throats were grotesquely missing from their necks.

Lizzy was too shocked at first to utter a sound. Then, out of nowhere, she gave a bloodcurdling scream. Almost as soon as she screamed, a hand clamped over her mouth, cutting off the sound. She tried to fight the intruder but was quickly held down.

"Hush, Miss Lizzy," Bartholomew hissed. "They's gonna hear you. You want them poundin' on our door?"

Lizzy stopped, but not before the men outside heard her scream. A loud banging on the front door snapped her out of her current fright into a new one. Would these men do to her what they had just done to the runaways?

"You got to go get dat door, Miss Lizzy," Hannah urged from her husband's side. "Dey's gonna spect somethin' if you don."

They helped her into a robe and down the stairs. The storm raged on.

Maggie joined them. Hannah handed Lizzy a lantern as she attempted to light a few lanterns in the foyer. Bartholomew handed both girls a pistol, while he held the rifle just out of sight. The pounding continued. Finally, Lizzy attempted courage she could not muster and opened the door. Facing her was Seth Patterson and five large men with torches, their faces lit in the demonic red flicker of the flames.

"What's going on?" Lizzy asked, not attempting cordiality.

"We're just taking care of some runaways, Miss Wyley," Seth sneered.

"Seems to me you could take care of them a little more humanely and off my property," Lizzy snapped.

The men were dripping wet. Puddles were forming around them on her porch and attempting to run small rivers into her foyer. Lightning flashed, immediately followed by thunder.

"Looks like they were running this direction for a purpose," Seth shouted above the din. "You have any idea what that purpose might be?" he asked, seeming to hope to catch her in something.

She did not know what he knew or thought he knew, but she wasn't going to divulge any information. Her fear was quickly turning to anger. "No, Mr. Patterson, I don't," she answered.

"They seemed mighty purposeful in coming this direction," he said, attempting to wipe the rain from his eyes. "My dogs caught them trying to get into one of your little boats. Any idea how they might have known where your boats were?"

"We live on the river, Mr. Patterson," Lizzy answered testily. "Everyone who lives on a river has a boat. They probably figured they were lucky when they found one and tried to get away from those mongrels."

Seth bristled at the insult of his dogs; he'd paid a high price for his purebreds and trained them well to be attack dogs.

"Still seems mighty coincidental to me," Seth said.

"Think what you want," Lizzy retorted. "I have no idea who they were or where they were going." She answered truthfully, thankful now that they never got to know the runaways well. It was definitely good protection for all involved. She truly had no idea if these people were trying to find safety in her house or accidentally found one of her father's boats and tried to escape.

The brightest flash of lightning yet, accompanied by instantaneous thunder, made everyone jump.

"You're seeming mighty upset and defensive, Miss Wyley," Seth said, as they gathered their composure.

"Of course I'm upset," Lizzy shouted. "You would be too if you'd been awakened in such a manner, along with the powerful storm. No one should live in fear of being chased down to that terrifying a death.

And no one should be woken up in the middle of the night to hellish screams and horrific visions outside their window. Now, I have nothing further to say to you gentlemen. I suggest you get off my property."

"Are you threatening us, Miss Wyley?" Seth almost laughed at the idea. "We'll leave when we're good and ready."

"I think you're ready now," Lizzy said ominously, as she drew up her pistol.

Seth did laugh now. "She probably doesn't even know how to use that," he said to his men.

A shot rang out, then a yelp. One of Seth's prize dogs lay dead on the ground. Seth whirled to look at his dog. Then he jerked back to find himself looking down the barrel of Lizzy's smoking pistol.

"I think you're ready now," Lizzy repeated.

Seth paused for a brief moment. The still smoking gun seemed to make his decision for him. He ordered one of his men to pick up the dog and turned to go. He turned back to Lizzy. "You'd better watch yourself, Miss Wyley," he threatened.

She stopped him before he could threaten any more. "Unless you want to have to carry another of your prize dogs home, you'd better go right now," she said.

He clamped his mouth shut, turned on his heels, and strutted away from the house into the driving rain.

Lizzy shut the door when she could no longer see the men. She was shaking all over. Bartholomew took the gun from her hand, while Hannah helped her to the sofa. Lizzy finally broke down and cried. Their peace was shattered by the nightmare they were all fighting so hard against.

The back door crashed open. "Help! Come quick!" Eli ran through the house trying to find them.

Bartholomew met him in the foyer. "What's happenin'?" he asked, afraid to hear the answer.

"Lightnin' hit a tree," Eli panted. "It done fell on one o' de houses. Dey's a big fire!"

Everyone jumped up and ran out of the house toward the workers' village. As soon as they left the house, they could see the flames reaching to the sky. They ran through the torrential rain, ignoring the lightning and thunder all around them.

At the workers' village, everyone carried buckets and ran to form a human chain to the river.

"Why is the rain not putting the fire out?" Maggie shouted.

"Don' know, Miss Maggie," Mimi shouted back. "Jes grab a bucket and go!"

At that moment, Lizzy saw a sight that immediately made her wretch in the bushes. Josiah, one of the young, unmarried field hands, ran out of the burning house carrying a young boy Lizzy couldn't identify. Both were on fire.

Bartholomew grabbed a blanket out of one of the workers' hands and ran to Josiah and the boy. He flung the blanket on the two and tackled them to the ground rolling them in the blanket.

Soon the two were no longer on fire, but both were screaming in pain.

"Go get Dr. Ryan!" Bartholomew shouted.

Maggie ran as fast as she could to the barn and jumped bareback on one of the horses. She flew out the door and down the path in search of the doctor.

Lizzy stood rooted to the ground in a horrified stupor.

Mimi and Ida grabbed her out of her daze and pushed her along the path to the river. She was strategically stationed at the river so she could not see anything going on at the village. The two women had the foresight to see their mistress needed to be as far away from the carnage as possible.

For the next forty-five minutes, everyone worked together to haul water and put out the fire. The wind blew harder and harder, making their task more difficult. Finally, they got a break in the storm. The wind died down minutely, and the lightning ceased momentarily. The bucket brigade drenched the devastated house and put out the fire.

Too exhausted to move, everyone collapsed in the open area of the village, panting in the rain.

The fire was out. Dr. Ryan was working on the patients along with Maggie and Ida's help.

Soon, Dr. Ryan made his way over to Lizzy. "Praise God the burns are not worse," he said.

Unable to speak, she simply stared at him through the veil of rain.

"They had enough clothes on, and Bartholomew reached them in time that most of their burns are not too extensive," he continued with his diagnosis. "The boy, Michael, should heal with minimal damage. He was hiding in a corner, afraid of the storm when the tree hit, his mother told me. Everyone in the family made it out of the house and realized he was not with them. Josiah ran in to get him. He found him hidden under some blankets in the corner of his room. Josiah grabbed him and ran out of the house. By that time, the fire had consumed the door. Since Josiah had wrapped his arms around the boy, his arms were the first through the fire. He sustained most of the trauma on his arms and hands."

Dr. Ryan proceeded to tell Lizzy about the treatment he would prescribe, but she barely heard him. She surveyed the damage to the village she was so proud of. Some of the workers had risen from their exhaustion and were attempting to sift through the carnage to find anything salvageable.

Mimi and Eli took the family into in to their house. Lizzy overheard them say they could stay until another house was built.

Lizzy felt her heart hardening against her will. They had lost so much during the past few months. What they had gained now seemed so little. Seth Patterson and a lightning strike proved that tonight. She felt as if she were hanging by a thread. She tried not to give in to the hard feelings, but, looking at the devastation around her, it was difficult. She felt the weight of everyone leaning on her.

Lizzy wasn't sure how much more she could take.

December 1862
En route to Fredricksburg, VA

It seemed all they did was march—from one town to another, from one battle to another, marching all the way. Through mud, dirt, dust, frozen ground—depending on the season—marching and more marching. Each stint of marching was punctuated with intermittent periods of excitement and horror due to confrontation with the Confederate troops. These confrontations were either in the form of large scale battles or small skirmishes along the way. This excitement resulted in taut nerves and short tempers for all in the army; Tyler and Charley were no exception.

They were miserable. What made it more miserable was that there was nothing to do while marching but think; think about what they had lost, wonder what might be still at home for them to gain, think about fallen comrades, wonder if they would be next. Not only did the marching tire them out physically, but mentally, they were exhausted from all the thinking. Lately there had been little positive to think of while marching.

The only positive Tyler could think of that they had gained during their months in the army was that their fellow soldiers had finally come to accept them. It had taken a long time. When they first arrived, their southern accents had made the others suspicious of them. Charley and Tyler had felt the need to prove themselves more than the other soldiers. They had drilled with a fervor their superiors had picked up on. They had gained the respect of those around them as true soldiers for the North; their accents did not matter any more. Some of their comrades were not so lucky. They had a few other Southerners in their unit. Some worked hard as well and gained the respect of the others, but some did not. Those who did not were immediately ostracized and had remained so throughout the ordeal.

Now, those who chose not to work for the respect and approval of their comrades were dead. By their choices, they had also lost on the necessary training and valuable companionship needed to survive the war. They had no one to look out for them and help them during the battles. As it was, Tyler and Charley stuck together like glue, always looking out for each other. Most of the rest of the unit did the same. Tyler thought the bad apples had been weeded out of the bunch. Now, the unit was a tight, cohesive entity. Each soldier looked out for the other and each loss was felt greatly.

Again, Tyler's thoughts turned to the comrades they had lost. He realized he had lost more than just friends. The people were so important to him that he felt each loss immensely. However, the mental toll this conflict had taken on him seemed almost heavy enough to crush him at times. Cynicism had replaced his naïveté. War had stolen his innocence. He had seen the viciousness of humanity and witnessed the senseless destruction that blind devotion created. He felt himself being pulled into a pit of despair daily.

The only reprieve from this misery was thoughts of Lizzy. Tyler clung to Lizzy's memory as the only hope to rise from his anguish. She was his light in this darkness. However, even her light was marred with a cloud of uncertainty. Would she know him when he returned? Would he be lucky enough to return to her? Would he be able to climb out of this pit and have the heart for her he once had? He was so different than when he had left her.

This misery and anguish did not leave him after his thoughts slowed when the marching was over. As bad as it was during the marches, it was worse after a battle. Tyler found himself drawn to the battlefield after a fight. It seemed as if he was bent on torturing himself. He would walk through the scattered bodies of dead and dying men as the medics attempted to reach them. There was nothing he could do for them. He simply walked among the men, morbidly assessing their pain—dwelling on the pain he had inflicted on some of them. Then his thoughts would turn to a desire for revenge as he thought of the pain the others had inflicted on his comrades.

What scared him the most, though, was the thought that he was losing his relationship with God. He knew God was still with him and would never abandon him, but he felt himself pulling away. He had seen too much destruction, too much death. How could God allow this? Couldn't God see the pain His creation had inflicted upon itself? Didn't He care? Could he continue to serve a God who allowed this to happen?

After his mind had run through these thoughts, inevitably, the same questions would return: Why was he here? Why were any of them here? What was this fighting all about anyway? It seemed harder and harder to remember as the grief and tension mounted.

Finally, they reached their destination, giving Tyler a brief break from his musings. The unit set up camp and prepared to remain until given their next orders.

The Union army had a new general replacing General McClellan, who had proven himself incompetent over the past few months. Their hope was that General Ambrose Burnside would lead them to victory. His plan at their new position near Fredricksburg was to try to overtake Confederate General Robert E. Lee and his defensive position north of Fredricksburg.

Nothing in the battle seemed to go right for the Union soldiers. In the end, it was a massive slaughter by the Confederates. There were so many wounded and dying men on the battlefield that the medical staff was unable to reach many of them in time. The air was filled with the screams of the suffering and the curses of the tormented. It was a sound that would haunt the dreams of many of the survivors for a long time to come.

At one point during the battle, Tyler, Charley, and a few of their fellow soldiers were pinned down behind a small ridge. The Confederates were shelling them mercilessly. Between them and their enemies lay a vast chasm of wounded men. Tyler, Charley, and the others remained hiding for some time, barely able to raise their heads to look for safety. After a while, a soft snow began to fall, dusting each soldier, not discriminating between live or dead.

After a time of silence, a soldier from Massachusetts, whom his friends called "Preacher," spoke up. Preacher had wanted to become a pastor before the war started. He was unofficially the chaplain of their little group within the unit. What he said confused the men.

"This is an actual, visual representation of God's Word in Isaiah 1:18," he said.

Preacher had exhibited much wisdom throughout the months. No one questioned his authenticity when he spoke of these things.

"How so, Preacher?" Charley asked.

"In Isaiah 1:18," Preacher began, "the writer says, "Come now, let us reason together," says the Lord. "Though your sins are like scarlet, they shall be as white as snow; though they are red as crimson, they shall be like wool." I believe God has sent us this snow to remind us why we are here."

"I don't understand," one of the soldiers commented, curious to see what Preacher would say.

"I believe," Preacher began, "we are here, fighting this awful war, to cover the sins of our fathers. God's word also says that the sins of the fathers will be passed down to the sons through the generations. I believe we're here trying to make amends for the sins our fathers committed by owning slaves."

"I can see how that applies to me and Charley," Tyler said, "but how does it apply to the rest of you. You're Northerners."

"It doesn't matter where you're from," Preacher said. "My father owned slaves, as did his father before him, and on back as many generations as have been in this country." This was a new admission on his part. He had never mentioned this before. "The slaves were passed down to the eldest son. My father inherited his slaves from his father. He tried it for a while but eventually set them free. I remember having slaves in my house until I was ten years old."

A few of the other men in the group grudgingly admitted that their ancestors had owned slaves. Along with this admission, they also apologized to Tyler and Charley for keeping this information.

The men then fell silent as they contemplated Preacher's words. Tyler had a renewed sense of purpose. Watching the snow cover the blood of the dying soldiers was indeed a visual reminder of why he was here. The scarlet blood of the fallen was being covered, now looking white as the fresh fallen snow. He was here to atone for the sins of every man who had ever owned a slave. He knew slavery was wrong. He knew the institution of slavery needed to be abolished forevermore by any means necessary.

Though the battle of Fredricksburg was an undeniable slaughter of the Union forces, Tyler had won a great victory over his despair. He continued to battle his thoughts questioning humanity, struggling with cynicism. However, he less frequently questioned God and never again questioned his purpose in this war.

CHAPTER 15

June 1863
Pennsylvania

They had been marching far too long. They were all exhausted. They had lost so many men during the Fredricksburg campaign. It was an utter failure. They were just now feeling like they were getting back some strength in the company. Now they were marching again. Confederate General Robert E. Lee had invaded Pennsylvania this month, and now Charley and Tyler and their company were on the way to help fight the Confederates off.

A few days later, they had camp set up and were preparing for their fight. Charley, Tyler, and their friends gathered around the campfire to pray for the upcoming battle. The prayer was much the same as others had been. They sought God's guidance during the ensuing fight. They prayed for safety for each other. They also prayed to be spared from fighting against someone they knew. When they were finished praying, they fell into a comfortable silence as they rested. The silence was punctuated with a few talks of former battles, what they missed from home, and anything else they could think of. When they ran out of things to talk about, they remained silent for a while. One by one, they left the group and went to bed.

The morning of July 1, 1863, dawned, and the company was awakened. They had breakfast and gathered their things. Marching again, they came to a field just outside the town of Gettysburg. Across the field stood a sea of Confederate soldiers. Charley and Tyler's company was one of many facing the Confederates. They had taken the Confederates by surprise, therefore were more prepared than their enemies.

Each side lined up preparing for battle. Each soldier stood at the ready, waiting for orders. It was an intense wait. All too soon, the order was given, and the battle began. The front line shot their volleys, then dropped down to reload as the lines behind them fired. This continued until the order was given for hand-to-hand combat. This was always the scariest for the men.

For Tyler, it was especially harrowing. He had trouble not looking at the faces of the men he was fighting. The first battle was the worst. He still remembered the faces. They had haunted his dreams for weeks after the fight. Since then, he had fought in several battles. There were too many faces to remember afterward. However, he was still haunted during the fights. The eyes of the men rolled back in pain or lifelessness was what disturbed him the most. Nevertheless, he needed to fight. He ran ahead with his comrades to do his duty. Charley was never far from his side.

The battle continued; one of the fiercest they had ever fought. It seemed God was again answering their prayers for safety and guidance during this fight. Each face Tyler looked at was unfamiliar as well. Their prayers were all being answered, until…

The men fighting around them parted for an instant. In that brief period of time, Tyler looked up. Charging toward him were two Confederate soldiers, one was none other than his old friend Jackson Hill. Each man registered recognition and surprise. In the next moment, something happened that would change Tyler's life forever. Jackson turned to the Confederate soldier charging with him and shot the man.

A split second after, Charley, Tyler, and Jackson all fell to the ground in shock. They were near the edge of the field at this time, and they all crawled for the cover of the nearby trees; Charley and Tyler seeking refuge from the battle behind one tree and Jackson another. After they caught their breath, Tyler was the first to find his voice.

"Why did you do that?" he asked, yelling over the battle sounds.

After a few deep breaths, Jackson answered, "She deserves to have you come home."

Charley and Tyler glanced questioningly at each other, unsure of what that meant.

"You need to go home to Elizabeth," Jackson panted. "She needs you to come home." Then he reached into his coat and pulled out an envelope. "Give this to her when you get there," he said. "You can read it, if you want to."

He reached across the space between the trees to hand the letter to Tyler.

The movement must have caught the attention of someone on the other side of the battle. Seconds later, the unmistakable sound of a shell was screaming toward them. Before they knew it, Jackson had hurled himself toward Tyler and Charley. Then, the explosion hit. Dirt and tree limbs flew everywhere. Jackson's limp body slammed into them, and everything went black.

Riverridge Plantation
Atlanta, GA

Lizzy locked the door and flung herself on the bed, crying. Why did life have to be so tough? They had just taken another set of runaways to Mr. Brown's cabin. She wanted to help these people, but when would it end? When would the cruelty of their situation and the necessity of their flight cease?

How long would she live in the darkness of unknowing? How long would she fear the worst of her brother and the man she wanted to marry? How long would she live in fear of detection?

It all seemed too much for a person to handle.

The positives seemed too few and far between. She tried to focus on them, such as healing for Josiah and Michael. Dr. Ryan said their wounds were healing well. Michael had begun playing with the other children who seemed to accept him, in spite of his wounds. Josiah was slower in healing but was on the mend. His hands seemed to bear the brunt of the burns. Dr. Ryan was helping him learn how to use his hands with as much ease as possible.

She slowly moved to her writing desk. Grasping her pen and paper always ready on the table, she began to write.

> Dear Tyler,
>
> I am so tired of writing letters not knowing if I will ever be able to give them to you. The stress of this stage of life is really weighing heavily on me. The clandestine activities, keeping our lives secret, treating our people humanely, yet not being able to be open about it because someone might arrest us …The list goes on and on.
>
> Father has left us a generous living in his will. I have entertained thoughts of leaving and starting over in the North where I would be accepted for my thoughts and ideals and not shunned if I am open.
>
> The only thing keeping me back is knowing that I cannot free the people without Charley. I will wait here until he returns or I hear otherwise.
>
> As much as I hate to think about it, each day that passes without word from either of you, I lean more toward believing the worst. I think there is no way you could survive this hell.
>
> As awful as I feel here, reading about the events of the war, I cannot imagine what you are going through, actually being part of it. Have you lost friends? Have you been hurt? Are you still alive?…

Field Hospital
Gettysburg, PA

Everything was blurry. Pain shot through his body. He couldn't move his left arm. He felt around himself with his right arm. He was in a bed or something like it. Overhead, the sky looked green.

He shook his head to try to clear the blur in his eyes. That resulted in a massive headache. When his vision cleared after a few minutes, he realized he was in a makeshift hospital bed under a tent. His whole body ached, and he still couldn't move his left arm. He had no idea what happened or how long he'd been there. He didn't know what happened to Charley either. That thought scared him more than anything. He tried to move his legs to get out of the bed. This resulted in knocking over a tray at the foot of his bed. The clatter wasn't loud on the grass below, but the noise did get the attention of a nearby nurse.

"I see you're finally awake now, laddie," came the Irish accented reply. "I'm Nurse Katherine Johnson. Nice to finally meet you."

Tyler stared at her dumbly, then, finding his raspy voice, asked her, "What happened?"

"You've had a nasty blow to the head which knocked ya out for the past three days," she answered.

"Why can't I move my arm?" Tyler asked.

"The same shell what knocked you out also tore a lot of things in your arm," she began. "The doctors were able to save yer arm, but you'll need to wear it in a sling for the rest of yer life; ya won't be able to use it." She was matter-of-fact in her explanation. She didn't try to sugarcoat anything. Tyler was grateful. He wanted the facts. This gave him hope for his next question.

"Do you know what happened to my friend, Charles Wyley?" he asked, hopeful. "He was fighting next to me."

Nurse Johnson smiled. "He's finally asleep, the next bed over." She pointed to Tyler's left. He hadn't been able to roll on that side due to the bandages. "He wouldn't let anyone separate the two o' ya. He's been so worried about ya. Said you needed to get home to marry his sister. He wanted me to wake him as soon as ya were awake, but if ya don't mind, he needs the sleep."

"Of course," Tyler said. "But if I fall asleep before he wakes up, would you wake me when he does? I don't think I'm in need of much more sleep."

She smiled. "I'll do that."

"Can you tell me what happened to him?" Tyler asked, concern etched on his face.

"He told me 'twould be fine to tell ya," she said. "The same shell that hit you busted his right foot so badly the doctors needed to amputate."

Tyler groaned in sympathy for his friend.

"The war is over for the two o' ya," Nurse Johnson said. "But you two were lucky." Tyler looked at her questioningly and waited for her to continue. "When the medics found ya, you were buried under what was left of a Johnny Reb. I don't know if that reb was tryin' t' attack ya or protect ya, but he saved yer lives."

Tyler didn't know how to respond. Was that Jackson Hill she was talking about? He was confused over what he remembered of the battle.

Nurse Johnson could tell Tyler was unnerved about something. She didn't want to pry, so she simply said, "I'll go let the doctor know yer awake and see if he can be seein' ya soon." Then she walked away.

Tyler lay in his bed trying to remember all he could about the battle. He remembered seeing Jackson. He remembered Jackson killing the rebel soldier charging with him. Why would he do that? Why would he kill someone fighting on his own side to protect his enemy? What had Jackson said? He had talked about Lizzy, said, "She needs you to come home." What did that mean?

He was feeling agitated. That only worsened his throbbing headache. A fly landed on his nose. He tried to swat at it with his left hand, forgetting it was immovable. Frustration swept over him, aggravating the aches.

The doctor came and confirmed everything Nurse Johnson had said. He gave Tyler a few instructions and some medicine for the pain. "As soon as we can," the doctor said, "we'll move you two to a real hospital in Washington City for your recovery."

After the doctor left, Tyler tried to relax awhile and waited for Charley to wake up.

"Tyler. Tyler, you awake yet?" Charley's hopeful voice penetrated Tyler's restlessness.

Tyler rolled as much as possible so he could see his friend's face. "Yeah, I'm awake," he said sleepily.

Charley's face relaxed in unmasked relief. "I was so worried," he said. "You'd been out for three days. Did they tell you what happened?"

"Yeah," Tyler sighed. "The war's over for us both."

They relaxed, both thankful to be finished fighting; both thankful to have not lost the other.

"Charley, Jackson saved our lives, didn't he?" Tyler asked.

"Yes, he did," Charley answered.

"Why?"

"I don't know."

They fell silent for a few moments. Then Charley spoke up almost excitedly, "Do you still have that letter Jackson gave you before the shell hit?"

The letter! Of course. Tyler had forgotten the letter. He reached awkwardly into the pocket of his torn uniform jacket. He fleetingly thought it would be nice when they reached Washington City to get other clothes.

He found the envelope in his pocket. After opening it, he pulled out two letters—one addressed to Lizzy and the other addressed to him. He was genuinely surprised to see the one addressed to him. He read Lizzy's letter aloud first.

The letter evoked mixed emotions. It spoke of Jackson's feelings for Lizzy, which apparently she knew about. However, Jackson went on to say that it was good that Lizzy didn't return his feelings and that he was unworthy of any feelings she might ever have for him. He concluded the letter saying:

> You deserve someone who is strong in his convictions to match the strength you have in yours. I am realizing more and more that I don't know who's right in this war. I'm leaning more toward agreeing with you. But if you are right, then I'm fighting for the wrong side. I'm having a hard time living with the choice I made.
>
> Tyler has the convictions you need. He fights for those convictions. You two belong together. As much as I want to be with you, I know he is better for you. If I get a chance, I will do what I can to ensure he returns to you.

When he finished, they sat quietly for a minute, not knowing what to say. Charley spoke first.

"He saved our lives so you could go back to Lizzy, even though he was in love with her," Charley mused.

Tyler didn't know how to respond. He opened the letter addressed to him. The letter explained that Jackson had feelings for Lizzy and recounted his conversation with her before he joined the army. It reiterated his desire for her to be with someone with deeper convictions who believed in what was right, stating Tyler had the qualities she needed.

"That soldier was coming straight for you," Charley said. "God used Jackson to give you a second chance and get you home to Lizzy."

Still unable to say anything, Tyler rested his head on his pillow and thanked God for this second chance.

Tyler found himself with conflicting feelings for the next few days. On one hand, he was excited to go home to Lizzy. He was excited about the prospect of getting married. On the other hand, he was worried that she might not want him. It had been three years since they had even shared a letter. Had she given up on him? Would she want this battle hardened cynic? Would she want a man with only one working arm? Did she actually want him in the first place? She had not made a commitment before he left. He kept his concerns to himself, not wanting to bother Charley.

"Good mornin,' laddies," Nurse Johnson's cheerful voice broke through Tyler's melancholy. "How does a change o' clothes, clean sheets, and walls sound to ya?"

"Like heaven," Charley answered. They were tired of being in the hospital tent still wearing their tattered uniforms. "Where do we get it?"

"Washington City," Nurse Johnson said. "We're loadin' up tomorrow and takin' the soldiers to real hospitals. You two are comin' t' my hospital, so you're not rid o' me yet," she smiled.

Tyler was looking forward to the change of scenery. He was also glad they would still be with Nurse Johnson. She had been kind to them and kept them together. He also noticed Charley seemed to especially enjoy her company. He wondered her story. Surely she must be a widow.

Unmarried nurses weren't allowed. He liked her and thought she might be good for Charley.

The next day they were loaded onto wagons for the ride to Washington City. Nurse Johnson was in their wagon.

"How did you become a nurse?" Tyler asked her.

"My husband was a lieutenant in the army before th' war started," she began. "He was injured at th' battle of Shiloh. When he was sent to th' hospital, I went t' help nurse him. I was put t' work nursing others as well. He died from his wounds. My parents had died on th' trip here from Ireland four years ago, so I had no family t' go to. I decided to remain at th' hospital. I enjoyed nursin' and the doctors said I had a knack for it. I stayed on learning as much as I could."

"I'm sorry you lost your husband," Charley said. "How long were you married?"

"Only two years," she answered. "His father was th' pastor o' th' church I attended when I arrived from Ireland. I knew no one. His family took me in and took care o' me. The other nurses helped me get through his death."

Tyler listened as Charley and Katherine talked. Throughout the next few weeks at the hospital, their relationship grew into more than nurse and patient. Tyler was happy for them, but it made him long for Lizzy even more.

When the doctor released them from the hospital, Tyler and Charley spent a few weeks recovering more at Tyler's father's house. They enjoyed conversing with the people who had worked for his father for many years, as well as talking with Andrew Parker.

"It's great being here with you, Dad," Tyler said one afternoon, as he was sitting alone with his father.

"It's wonderful to have you here," Andrew said. "How are you feeling?"

"I'm doing all right," Tyler answered. "The pain is pretty constant, but it is getting less severe. More dull now than sharp."

"I'm glad you're feeling better. How long do you think you will stay?"

"I don't know. I think we might return within the next few days or so. Our wounds are healing pretty well. I know Charley wants to get home."

"And you?"

"What about me?" Tyler squirmed under his father's scrutiny.

"Do you want to get home?" his father pressed.

"I think so," Tyler said hesitantly.

"Not certain, huh?"

"Not really," Tyler said sadly.

"What about Elizabeth?"

Tyler hesitated.

Andrew cocked an eyebrow. "Are you having second thoughts about Elizabeth?"

"No, sir," Tyler said. He took a deep breath. As he spoke, he did not look his father in the eye. "I guess I'm wondering if she has second thoughts about me."

"Why would she?"

Tyler looked up at his father. "I've changed so much, Dad. War haunts me in a way I never thought possible. I definitely am not the same man I was when I left her three years ago."

"War changes everyone, son."

"I guess so," Tyler said defeatedly. "I'm just afraid to face her, I guess. I've been through so much heartache in the past two years. I don't know if I can handle more."

"I understand about heartache, son," Andrew said sadly. "I lost your mother long before I thought I would be ready to. But, son, I would not have given up the joy I had with her for anything. Had I known our life together would be cut short, I would have married her anyway."

Tyler looked at his father and saw a single tear roll down his aging cheek.

Soon their wounds had healed enough, and they began to talk about returning home to Georgia. Tyler was still excited and anxious. He still had his doubts. The closer the time came for their trip home, the more anxious and nervous Tyler became.

One day, as Tyler sat in his father's study staring out the window, Charley came in and sat in a chair facing him. "What's going on, Tyler?" Charley asked, coming right to the point.

"What do you mean?" Tyler asked, stalling.

"You know what I mean," Charley answered a bit testily. "You've become more and more withdrawn the closer we get to going home. You've been moody and simply not yourself. Are you having second thoughts about going home? About Lizzy?" he asked with the protectiveness of an older brother.

"I still want to marry your sister," Tyler replied defensively.

"Then what is it?"

"I guess I just don't know if she'll want to marry me," Tyler said.

"Why would you think that?" Charley asked, concerned.

Tyler didn't answer for a moment. "I've changed so much since I last saw her," he said. "I've become more cynical and less content. My relationship with God is rocky, at best. I've found more in life to be angry with than happy." He paused, not sure how to say what he wanted to next. "And I just can't imagine her wanting a man with only one arm."

Charley looked at him with a mix of sympathy and understanding. He knew his friend very well. Though Tyler had kept his concerns from Charley the past few weeks, Charley now fully understood his friend's apprehension. They sat in silence for a few minutes.

"I understand what you mean," Charley said.

"How could you possibly know what I mean," Tyler snapped.

Charley was taken aback by his friend's tone and comment. In reply, he lifted his right leg with the amputated foot and laid it on Tyler's lap. "That's how I can possibly know what you mean."

Tyler simply stared at his friend's leg, embarrassed at his outburst. Of course Charley knew what he was talking about. He was a farmer without a foot, just as Tyler was a clothes maker without an arm.

"Will she still want me?" Tyler asked fearfully.

"Of course she will," Charley answered. "She's loved you forever. She might not have known it, but Maggie and I did. You two are meant for each other."

"Those are all nice words," Tyler said, unbelieving. "I know Kate and you have worked through it and she loves you anyway, but how do I know for sure about Lizzy? I haven't had any contact with her for three years, Charley, three years! How do I know she hasn't changed as much as I have and wants nothing to do with me?"

Charley had no answers. Katherine had been a dream come true for him. She accepted him and loved him even without his foot. She had helped him begin to work through the anger and other issues that fighting in a war brought about. They had plans to marry before the trip home. Tyler was supportive of this, but Charley suspected his support came with some grudging.

Thankfully, Katherine was passing by the study and heard part of the conversation. "Pardon me for eavesdroppin', boys," she said, standing in the doorway. She had fit in with the boys so easily that they did not feel her interruption an intrusion. "Tyler, there is no way for you to know her feelin's without askin' 'er. Ya'll never know unless ya see 'er face to face and ask 'er. Until then, ya'll just have questions—unanswered questions. Don't ya think she deserves th' courtesy of hearin' 'er side straight from 'er mouth?"

"But what if she doesn't want me?" Tyler asked painfully.

Katherine smiled sadly, "Then at least yer questions will be answered." She stood in the doorway for a few moments, letting her words sink in. "Good night, fellas," she finally said. "See ya in th' mornin.'" She turned and left.

Tyler and Charley sat in silence for a long time. Charley knew his friend needed this time to think over Katherine's words. What she said made perfect sense. Charley hoped his friend would take his fiancée's advice.

"She's right," Tyler said at last. "I will never know unless I ask her. I will always wonder what could have been. I need to go ask her myself and find the true answer."

Charley breathed an inaudible sigh of relief for his friend and his sister, praying God would see fit to keep them together. The last thing he wanted was either of their hearts broken.

"How soon can we leave after your wedding?" Tyler asked. Charley and Katherine were scheduled to get married in two days. They hadn't set a departure time yet.

"We can leave the next day, if you want to," Charley answered, thankful for Tyler's eagerness to get back to his sister.

Tyler smiled. "How about the day after that?"

Charley agreed. They would leave for home in four days.

CHAPTER 16

"He out der agin, Miss Lizzy," Bartholomew said, as he hauled in water to the kitchen one morning.

"When did you see him?" she asked irritably.

"Jes last night," he said.

"I've had it!" she practically shouted, flinging the vegetables she was chopping across the table. "We're reduced to prisoners in our own home! Why won't he leave us alone?"

"He suspects something, Lizzy," Maggie said. "And rightly so."

"What's that supposed to mean?" Lizzy spat.

Maggie gave her a patronizing look. "You know what that means. We're involved in several illegal activities."

"According to the Confederacy."

"Yes, Lizzy, according to the Confederacy. But, unless you forget, we live in the Confederate South. Therefore, what we are involved in is illegal according to the laws we live under."

"I don't accept those laws." Lizzy scowled. "They're stupid and idiotic and hateful."

"I couldn't agree with you more," Maggie said. "But they are the laws and we are breaking them."

Lizzy scowled more and chopped the vegetables harder. "Well, with him prowling around, scouting every move we make, we're not doing much to break the laws, now are we?"

The past few months had been extremely stressful on the plantation. After the confrontation with Seth Patterson and his attack dogs, several people on the plantation, Lizzy and Maggie included, had seen someone looking a lot like Seth prowling around the grounds with a low lit lantern late at night. These spottings were sporadic, but everyone gave the same descriptions of the person they'd seen. Lizzy knew he was trying to find something with which to trap her. They had halted their involvement in the Underground for a few months, hoping not to endanger anyone. Bartholomew set up night scouts to try to trap Seth, but no one had been successful yet. They'd seen him, but he had gotten away quickly. Everyone was frustrated and on edge, especially Lizzy.

Lizzy took it the hardest because she had made it her personal life mission to save the runaways. Without being able to help, she felt as if she was letting them down. She felt defeated by the world. Before this, she had felt she had a purpose; now that purpose was stolen away from her. She thought the halt in their participation would only last a few weeks or so, and they would catch Seth, perhaps putting him in jail for trespassing. The weeks turned into months and still no capture.

Lizzy's frustration had turned into depression. Everyone felt it. No one knew when she would be crying or angry. Everyone tiptoed around her, not wanting to upset her. For the house staff, it was reminiscent of when Lizzy's mother was still alive.

"I hate seeing her like this."

"I know, Miss Maggie," Hannah consoled.

"Everyone depends on her. I've tried to help and guide everyone, but I'm just not as good as she is. I'm their teacher, not their leader. She needs to lead them. I've tried almost everything I can think of to pull her out of this chasm. Nothing has worked yet."

Maggie put her head in her hands and cried.

Hannah knelt beside her friend and rubbed her back. "Somethin's gotta work, Miss Maggie. What else is der to try? We's got t' think o' somethin.'"

"I don't know," Maggie cried.

Lizzy lay in bed, unable to muster energy to get up for the day. "God, help me!" she cried. "I'm so tired. I feel so defeated. Help me get out of this! Why have you left me here alone? Where are Tyler and Charley? I'm going mad not knowing anything. Why can't I know something? I miss them so much. God, I wish they were here to advise me on what to do and protect us. I am so tired of being the protector." She punched her pillow and cried.

When the tears were spent, she sighed. "I know I haven't been on the best terms with you lately, God. I'm sorry for not praying and not reading my Bible. I just can't do it. It feels like you are so far away. It feels as if you've left us."

A soft knock on her door broke her tirade.

"Yes," she said testily.

Maggie opened the door and slipped in. "Good morning, sleepy-head," she said cheerfully, but cautiously. "Need help getting up?"

"I'm not getting up," Lizzy said.

Maggie pulled up a chair and sat down by the bed. She decided to come right to the point. "I know you're hurting," she said. Lizzy didn't answer. "I know this is very hard for you. You've put so much into being part of the Underground. You've done so much to help so many people. You've been amazing and now everything's been taken from you."

"Thanks for reminding me," Lizzy snapped. "Is there a point to your sermon?"

Maggie went on undaunted. "I know it's hard for you not to have Tyler and Charley here too."

"What's your point?" Lizzy snapped again, not wanting anyone to dive into her feelings.

"My point is," Maggie snapped back, "you're not the only one who's hurting. We all want to continue helping. It's hard for all of us to have this taken from us. It's hard for all of us to be so uncertain about Tyler and Charley. You need to get over your fears, get back to God, and lead us again."

Lizzy shot up in her bed. "First of all, I'm not afraid of anything. Fear is for the weak and vulnerable. Second, who are you to judge where I am with God? Finally, why do I have to be the leader? Maybe I don't want that responsibility. How about you step up for a change and lead something?" She slumped back in her bed and pulled the quilts over her head.

Maggie had been prepared for this outburst. She knew what she was doing when she confronted her friend. "Just something to think about," she said as she left the room.

Lizzy felt Maggie drop something on her bed, but she refused to come out from under the quilts until she heard the door shut as her friend left. How did Maggie know her thoughts and feelings so well? She felt sure that, had she given Maggie the opportunity, she could have pinpointed every thought and feeling Lizzy had.

She came out from under the quilts and found what Maggie had dropped. It was a Bible. It had a piece of paper sticking out of it. Lizzy pulled out the piece of paper. Maggie had written some verses on it. She wanted to fling the book across the room. She lifted it up several times to do just that, but her hand fell back to the bed each time.

She dropped the Bible out of her hand and stared at it for several minutes.

She pulled the quilts over her head again and tried to go back to sleep. When sleep wouldn't come, she peeked out from under the quilts and stared again at the Bible.

I am with you.

She looked around the room, certain someone was in there with her. Seeing no one, she shivered and cuddled further under the blankets.

I am with you.

She heard the voice again.

"All right, I'll look," she said, "but I'm not promising anything."

Grudgingly, Lizzy looked up the verses Maggie wrote down.

"After these things the word of the LORD came unto Abram in a vision, saying, 'Fear not, Abram: I am thy shield, and thy exceeding great reward.'"

Genesis 15:1

"Behold, the LORD thy God hath set the land before thee: go up and possess it, as the LORD God of thy fathers had said unto thee; 'fear not, neither be discouraged.'"

Deuteronomy 1:21

"Ye shall not fear them: for the LORD your God he shall fight for you."

Deuteronomy 3:22

"Be strong and of a good courage, fear not, nor be afraid of them: for the LORD thy God, he it is that doth go with thee; he will not fail thee, nor forsake thee."

Deuteronomy 31:6

Lizzy broke down and cried.

Maggie had sent exactly what she needed.

She spent the next few hours rereading the verses, praying and crying. She was broken and she knew it. She knew she needed to come out of this depression. She knew her friends were afraid of her, but she didn't know how to change. Finally, she realized that she needed to go down and confess her fears.

Lizzy felt a tear trickle down her face. "God, I am afraid," she cried. "I don't want to be afraid. I'm scared of so much. Please forgive me. Please help me to trust in you. Please help me to lead your people."

"I think we're ready to start reading the newspaper," Maggie said. "Perhaps we'll start that tomorrow."

"I think dat's a wonderful idea," Hannah replied. "We's all so thankful to ya for teachin' us to read. You's such a good teacher."

Maggie blushed and turned to the sewing she was doing. In her embarrassment, she missed a stitch on the baby dress she was making for the newest baby in the workers' village. She cut the thread with her teeth and began fixing it.

They heard a sound at the parlor door. Looking up they saw her.

The look in Lizzy's eyes begged her friends for forgiveness and help. Maggie dropped her stitching and went to embrace her friend.

"I'm so sorry," Lizzy said, through more tears. "I'm so sorry for everything: for my behavior over the past months, for snapping at you, and for not being honest. You're right. I am afraid. I'm afraid of so many things. I'm afraid of not being able to help with any more runaways. I'm afraid of getting caught, if we are able to help. I'm afraid I'm going to need to shoot someone other than a dog. I'm afraid I won't be a good leader to you all. I'm afraid Charley won't come back. I'm afraid Tyler won't come back. I'm afraid Tyler will come back and not want me anymore. I'm afraid of losing my relationship with God more than I have." Her sobs overwhelmed anymore speaking.

Maggie just held her friend and let her cry. Hannah and Bartholomew sat near and silently prayed for their friend. Finally, Lizzy stopped crying and they went to sit down. They led her to her favorite seat in the parlor—the window seat overlooking the front porch.

She gazed out at the oak trees. The leaves were blowing in the wind. The dogs were lying lazily on the driveway. Birds chased each other through the trees.

Lizzy was spent from her morning, so she sat quietly and let her friends comfort her.

"Honey," Hannah began, "we knows you's tired. We knows you's afraid. But you don' need to go it alone. We's here to hep ya."

"Chile," Bartholomew said, "you don' need to fear nothin.' God be with ya. He your strength. He fight for ya. He love ya more than we do, an' dat's a lot!"

"They're right," Maggie said. "We're here with you, but, more importantly, God is too. He's fighting for us. This is His war. He doesn't want His people suffering any more than you do. But everything's got to come out of His time. We can't push anything. He wants to use you to help accomplish His goals, but He doesn't want you to do it alone. That's what we're here for."

"But why do I have to be the leader?" Lizzy asked.

"Because you're good at it." Maggie answered. "God gave you the strength and the gifts to lead us. You see all you've done for the workers already. They have new housing because of you, better food, and they can read and write."

"You're the one who teaches them to read and write," Lizzy interrupted.

"God put me there to help you with that." Maggie smiled. "You've made all this possible for them. You've also made it possible for many runaways to pass through on their way to safety. I know it's not been easy, but you've done it."

"What about Charley and Tyler?" Lizzy asked timidly.

"I know you miss them," Maggie answered. "We all do. I know it's harder for you though. It's so hard for me, and they're only my friends. I can't imagine how hard it is for you, with it being your brother and your hope of a fiancé. But you need to give them to God. Put them in God's hands. He will see them through to whatever their end is, whether it ends in a battle or here with you decades in the future."

Everyone sat silently for a while. Lizzy didn't have any energy to say much more. Finally she spoke up, "I know you're right. It might take me a while to act like it, but I know you're right. Thanks for helping me through this. Thanks for loving me enough to confront me with it. I'll do the best I can." She took a deep breath. "Can we pray?"

They all prayed together for each other. They prayed for strength in all circumstances. When they had finished, Lizzy felt as if a tremendous weight had been lifted from her shoulders.

A few days later, Lizzy came practically running into the kitchen where Hannah and Maggie were making breakfast. "We've got to get him!" she almost shouted in her excitement, "And we've got to do it now. I'm not going to sit in one more minute of fear if there's anything I can do about it."

They knew she was talking about Seth and his prowling around the plantation. "How you think we gonna do it?" Hannah asked.

"I've been talking with Ida. She believes he'll be around soon." Ida had shown some gifts of prophecy, or at least very in-tuned intuition, in the past. Everyone on the plantation listened when Ida talked.

"We've got to all go out together. One person isn't enough to catch him. He's too quick. Two people aren't even enough. If we get as many from the village to go too, we can catch him. I say we start tonight and stay out as many nights as we need to until he's stopped. What do you think?" She was out of breath for talking so fast and excitedly.

They looked at each other and smiled. Their Lizzy was back. "Let's do it," they exclaimed.

That night, Lizzy, Maggie, Hannah, Bartholomew, and at least twelve others from the village were out scanning the property for their trespasser. They all wore dark clothes and were on the lookout for the low lit lamp. They didn't carry lamps for fear he might see them. This put them at a disadvantage, though they hoped their numbers would be their advantage. Lizzy prayed they would not have to do this for too many nights. Her prayer was answered.

Two nights later, she was scouting with Eli when he silently and quickly caught her arm. He turned her to face the direction he saw the light. They quickly moved toward it.

Seth didn't see or hear them coming. He moved his light up to look at something and, for the first time, Lizzy caught a clear glimpse of his face.

"Seth Patterson," she called out.

He froze at the sound of her voice. Then he turned to run away and ran right into Bartholomew. He struggled to get out of the grip, but Bartholomew held him fast. Lizzy and Eli moved in to challenge him, making sure he could see the rifle she carried.

"I thought I told you to stay off my property," she challenged. "What have you been doing all these nights?"

He looked shocked that she knew he'd been here before.

"That's right," she said. "I know you've been prowling around my land for months now. What are you hoping to find?"

"I know you're involved in something," he hissed. "I'm going to find out what it is."

"Have you found anything out yet?" she asked.

"I will," he replied.

"I don't think there is anything for you to find out," she said. "I think you're just trespassing. I aim to bring you up to the law for that."

He struggled again, but Bartholomew's grip tightened.

"I'd come along peacefully, if I were you," Lizzy said. "Unless you want to end up like your dog."

He stopped struggling. He shouted threats and curses as Bartholomew held him, and some of the other men tied his hands and feet together. They threw him in the back of a wagon, and Lizzy and Bartholomew drove him to the sheriff. They thanked God as they drove away from the sheriff's office.

A few days later, Seth was convicted of trespassing. As far as Lizzy knew, he didn't come around her property again. They weren't naïve enough to think he couldn't or wouldn't, so they took even more strict precautions as they began helping runaways again.

CHAPTER 17

Christmas 1863 rolled around. Lizzy invited everyone to the big house to celebrate. It was a quiet celebration but a rejuvenating one. Everyone enjoyed being together. They all felt more peace than they had in months. Seth Patterson hadn't been seen again. Several runaways had been helped. The fate of the Union was still unsure, but, for this night, everyone on Riverridge Plantation was joyful.

A few days after the New Year, a lone soldier in a Confederate uniform was spotted riding down the driveway. They had not had many visitors since the war started—never one in a Confederate uniform. Everyone felt the tension wondering what might be going on. Had they been found out? This was the question on everyone's mind.

Lizzy and Maggie patiently waited in the parlor for the visitor to be announced. They heard the knock on the door and Hannah answer it. Hannah came into the parlor to announce the visitor. She was visibly shaken. Her eyes showed fear Lizzy had never seen before.

"Who is it, Hannah?" Lizzy asked.

"It's Master Aaron Thomas, Miss 'Lizabeth," Hannah answered fearfully.

Lizzy shuddered. "Send him in," she said, trying to sound cheerful in case he was listening.

Before Hannah could turn around, Aaron Thomas strode to the doorway. Lizzy had to stop herself from audibly gasping. He looked frightening. Before the war, he had had some handsome features. Upon returning, his face had several scars, and he wore a patch over one eye. It was the eyepatch especially that made him look foreboding. There was no smile in his other eye. He looked angry.

Hannah slipped from the room to find Bartholomew, in case he was needed.

"Good afternoon, Mr. Thomas," Lizzy said, trying to sound bright.

"Good afternoon, Miss Wyley," Aaron said, then turned to Maggie. "Miss Swanson."

"Mr. Thomas." Maggie nodded.

He didn't waste time. "Miss Wyley," he began. "I told you when I left for the war that I would return for you and would have you as my wife. I've come to keep my promise."

Lizzy ignored his statement and wasted no time asking the question burning in her mind. "What happened to you?"

"I was wounded," he said.

"Obviously," she said sarcastically. "Where were you? What happened?"

"It was the battle at Gettysburg, Pennsylvania," he replied flatly. "I was hit by shrapnel from a bursting shell."

"I'm sorry to hear that," Lizzy said genuinely, not relishing anyone's pain, even Aaron Thomas. "Have you been recuperating all this time?" she asked, knowing the battle had taken place seven months prior.

"I have," he replied. "I have now been honorably discharged from my post in the Confederate army, where I served my newfound country proudly. I have returned to make you my wife," he repeated.

A log snapped in the fireplace. Lizzy jumped. Aaron's eye remained fixed on her. Maggie remained silent, observing the situation.

Lizzy was nervous, but she would not let him think there was any hint of a chance she would marry him. "I'm glad you're well and honorably discharged," she began. "However, your visit to my house was unnecessary. As I told you before you left, I will not marry you. I know you have not talked with my father about acquiring my hand, and I know he would not approve of the match and neither do I. Thank you for letting me know you're well, but I must now ask you to leave."

"You're a headstrong woman, Miss Wyley," he said, "but I am equally determined." He looked at her menacingly. "We can do this the easy way, or we can do this the hard way. Either way, I will get what I want."

"You're mistaken, sir," Lizzy challenged. "We will not be doing this any way. You'd better leave, or my men will escort you off my property."

Aaron turned around and saw Bartholomew, Eli, and two other field hands standing in the foyer, openly glaring at him. He glared back, sizing up his chances against them. Wisely, he turned to leave. Before he was out of sight of the parlor, he turned back to Lizzy. "I'm a man who gets what he wants, one way or another," he growled, then turned and left.

Maggie went to Lizzy's side. Lizzy was shaking. Hannah brought some hot tea. The three women sat together shaking. The men stood around protectively. They all knew Aaron Thomas could be dangerous. He seemed much more so now than he had in the past. He was a man who generally did get what he wanted. Everyone in the household was determined to see that didn't happen where Lizzy was concerned.

Bartholomew took it upon himself to make sure men were around the house at all times. He also set up scouts all night to make sure no one came while they were sleeping. They all knew Aaron Thomas and Seth Patterson were friends. They had no delusion that Aaron wouldn't be back and might not possibly be back with Seth to harm Lizzy in some way.

The next two days were tense and extremely fear-filled.

The third day from their initial visit from Aaron Thomas, the household was awakened by a severe ice storm. It had begun the night before and gained strength as they were sleeping. All around the plantation, branches snapped off trees under the heavy weight of the ice, littering the ground.

Everyone still felt tense about Aaron Thomas, but hope began to rise that perhaps they might not be visited again, especially with the severity of the storm. That hope was quickly shattered.

Mid-morning, Lizzy was in the parlor reading and watching the fresh ice fall out the side picture window, trying to calm her nerves—unsuccessfully, since she jumped every time a branch snapped off a tree.

Hannah and Maggie were in the kitchen baking for lunch. Bartholomew was on the porch looking out. Lizzy heard a noise from the front of the house that confused her. She began to put her book down to go take a look when the front door crashed open.

Aaron Thomas flew in the door. The sound she had heard was Aaron smacking Bartholomew in the head with the butt of his gun. Bartholomew lay slumped on the front porch, knocked out from the blow. Aaron was obviously drunk, which scared Lizzy to no end.

Why had Bartholomew not alerted her when he saw Aaron coming up the drive? Had Aaron come a different way? She shuddered. Having no idea where any of the other men were, she prayed they were close by.

Aaron stood in the doorway of the parlor sneering at Lizzy. "Your man is down," he said, gloating over Bartholomew's misfortune. "I don't see anyone else around to stop me from getting what I want now," he said with an evil grin that sent chills up Lizzy's spine.

"I told you, Aaron, I will not marry you. You might as well go back to town and find someone else who wants you instead of wasting your time on me." She tried to sound brave in spite of her quaking nerves. She remembered her fear when Seth tried to force himself on her. Compared to Aaron, Seth was gentle. She knew Aaron would be fierce.

He stepped toward her. "I want you, Elizabeth," he said. "And I will have you. Again, we can do this the easy way or the hard way." He leered at her. "Frankly, the hard way sounds a little more fun to me."

Lizzy knew exactly what he meant by the "hard way." She was determined to make sure that didn't happen. She glanced around trying to find a way to escape. He was blocking most of the door. She hoped he was drunk enough that his reflexes weren't good. She tried to slip around him to the foyer.

She was wrong. His reflexes didn't seem to be hindered from the alcohol at all. He grabbed her and pulled her close. She almost gagged from the smell of alcohol on his breath. She tried to scream. He clamped his mouth over hers. She bit him. He flinched back but didn't let go. Blood oozed out from his lip. His grasp on her arm pinched tighter. He pushed her up against the wall, grabbing at her dress. She squirmed and tried to get away. His hold on her was vice-like.

He pulled her from the wall and pushed her onto the sofa as he continued kissing her harshly and grabbing at her dress. He fell on her tearing at her collar. She screamed clawing at his face. He slapped her and tore her collar more, ripping the shoulder off her dress.

Pain hit her stomach. Something was digging into her. Coming to her senses, Lizzy remembered the secret pocket Hannah had sewn on the inside of her dress. She kept her pistol hidden in that pocket. It was the pistol that was pushing into her stomach. She reached inside and grabbed the gun. She pulled the trigger.

Aaron snapped back, screaming in pain. He fell to the floor in a pool of blood clutching his knee. She had blown his kneecap. He rolled back and forth cursing her and clutching his knee. Jumping off the sofa, she stood frozen in horror. He looked as if he still might come after her, though he was in tremendous pain. She looked around the room to find an escape route. He lay on the floor, trapping her between him and the sofa. Her skirts were too cumbersome to step over him or climb over the sofa. She tried to step around him.

Finally, rage overtook reason. He lunged at her, grabbing at the hem of her dress. Before he reached her, his head snapped forward and he fell at her feet, unconscious.

Lizzy looked up to see Maggie behind Aaron, holding a frying pan. She looked a mix of anger and fear. Finding her feet, Lizzy moved around Aaron to Maggie. The two fell into each other's arms crying.

Hannah came through the front door with Bartholomew leaning on her. Eli came running up behind them.

"What happened out there?" Lizzy asked Bartholomew.

He rubbed his head as Hannah steadied him into a chair. "De storm's bad out der. I couldn't hear nothing wit the storm goin' on. Somehow, he come up behin' me. Sorry, Miss Lizzy."

"Are you all right?" Lizzy asked him, concerned.

"I be fine."

Hannah spoke then. "We got to get him to de doctor."

Lizzy looked up incredulously at her. "After what he did to me, I need to take him to get healed?" she asked.

"Hannah's right," Bartholomew said groggily. "We got to make sho' he don' die from any o' dis. We also got to make sho' we tell someone what happened, so's none o' us gets in trouble."

Lizzy stared at them, speechless for a few minutes. She wanted to take him to the road and dump him off there and leave him to his own fate.

She grudgingly agreed realizing they were right. Eli hitched up the wagon. They put Aaron in the back of the wagon and wrapped him in blankets. Maggie rode in the wagon with Eli and Bartholomew. Lizzy rode a horse so she could go to the sheriff to tell him what happened. She found Aaron's horse down the road. Picking up his reins, she led the horse behind her and left him with the sheriff.

Eli, Bartholomew, and Maggie took Aaron to Dr. Ryan's. Lizzy met them there with the sheriff. There, they told him what happened. Dr. Ryan began to operate on Aaron. Sheriff Jones listened to everyone's story. Then he told them he would come out to see them in a few days after Aaron had a chance to recover enough to tell his side of the story. Before they left, Anna Ryan came out of the operating room to assure them that the doctor believed Aaron would live through this.

Weary, the four left and returned home, thankful the storm seemed to be letting up.

The next two days passed quietly. They were all nervous about Aaron's recovery and what he might do when he was recovered. They felt calm that he wouldn't be able to do anything for a while but not assured enough that he wouldn't try. They also had no idea what he would tell the sheriff.

Lizzy and Maggie jumped at every noise. They still had lookouts posted to see if anyone was coming. Learning that Aaron had snuck around the trees to the side of the house, this time, they posted two lookouts together so they wouldn't have a repeat of what happened to Bartholomew.

The storm stopped and the men went about cleaning up the fallen tree branches. Lizzy and Maggie wanted to help but were ordered to remain inside in case something happened.

Two days after the confrontation, Lizzy and Maggie were drinking apple cider in the parlor. One of the lookouts came running into the house. "Someone's comin.' Someone's comin.'" He shouted.

"Can you tell who it is?" Lizzy asked.

"No'm," he said. "It's three people though. Two's in uniform and one's a woman."

"What color uniform?" Maggie asked.

He sighed. "Gray, ma'am."

161

CHAPTER 18

Their nerves taught, Lizzy and Maggie thanked him and went to the porch with him. Eli was standing there holding a rifle. The three visitors came closer. The four on the porch stood still, waiting to see who was coming. A steady, light snow was falling. Through the flakes, they could tell that one of the soldiers walked with crutches, which was making their progress slow. The other soldier had one arm in a sling.

Lizzy squinted through the snow, trying to get a better look. She took a step closer. "Oh, God!" she cried, dropping the mug she still held in her hand. She took off running down the driveway. The mug shattered where her feet had been.

Maggie stepped closer to get a better look. "It's Tyler and Charley!" she cried as she took off running.

Lizzy was already to the trio. Tyler wrapped his good arm around her, hugging her close. Charley handed his crutches to Kate and hugged his sister and Maggie. Lizzy would not let go of Tyler, even as he hugged Maggie. Unashamedly, Lizzy let the three years of frustration and fear run down her face in a torrent of relieving tears. Tyler cried with her.

Kate stood back, observing the emotional reunion of her new family. She had heard much about the closeness of the four friends. She looked on patiently, anticipating her new role in the group.

After the initial excitement was over, everyone stepped back. Lizzy and Maggie took notice of Kate for the first time. They became slightly shy.

"Lizzy, Maggie," Charley began proudly, "this is my wife, Kate. Kate, this is my sister Lizzy and our best friend Maggie."

"Your wife?" Lizzy asked, smiling.

"Yes," Charley said matter-of-factly. "We met in the hospital. She was our nurse. We would have loved to have you two at the wedding, but we wanted to travel properly."

"Of course," Lizzy said. "We're sorry to have missed it. Congratulations and welcome to the family, Kate." Lizzy stepped forward and gave her new sister-in-law a hug. Maggie did the same.

"Naturally, we want to know what happened to you both," Lizzy said, gesturing toward their wounds, "but would you first please tell us why you're in Confederate uniforms?"

"You gave us quite a fright," Maggie said.

"Sorry about that," Tyler answered. "We needed disguises to get behind enemy lines. We were afraid of being captured and becoming prisoners of war."

"Even with your obvious wounds?" Maggie asked.

"Spies will fake wounds and have been caught before," Charley answered. "Even with our disguises, we were still questioned."

"Where did you get them?" Lizzy asked.

"My father made them," Tyler supplied. "When we were able to leave the field hospital, we were taken to a hospital in Washington City. After we were released, we spent some more time recuperating at my father's."

"I'm glad you were able to see him," Lizzy said. "I trust he's doing well?"

"Very well," Tyler answered, smiling down at her.

"Let's go back to the house," Maggie said. "It's freezing out here. We'll get warm, and you all can sit down and tell us what happened to you."

They walked back to the house, all of their spirits higher than had been in three years. Tyler and Charley hugged Hannah and Bartholomew and introduced Kate to them. Hannah went to get more cider, and they all relaxed in the parlor.

"Where were you wounded?" Maggie asked when they had all settled in.

"We were fighting at the battle in Gettysburg, Pennsylvania," Charley answered.

"Gettysburg?" the girls asked together. They glanced nervously at each other, thinking about Aaron Thomas.

"Did you see anyone you knew there?" Lizzy asked apprehensively.

Tyler and Charley looked at each other, wondering if the girls knew. "Yes," Tyler answered. "We saw Jackson Hill."

"Jackson Hill!" Lizzy exclaimed.

"He saved our lives," Charley said.

"What?" Lizzy asked in astonishment.

"Twice," Tyler said.

"What happened?" Maggie asked.

Charley and Tyler went on to tell them their experience. "When I woke up, I had forgotten the letter," Tyler said, "until Charley reminded me." He reached into his coat pocket. "Here it is." He gave Lizzy the letter.

She took it gingerly and laid it in her lap, staring at it. Jackson had told her he loved her. He could have let Tyler and Charley die and come back to claim her for his wife. Instead, he had laid down his life so Tyler and Charley could come back to her. She had become so used to fearing the possibility of people trying to hurt her over the past three years that she didn't understand this act of love.

"You've read it?" She asked.

"Yes, we both have," Tyler answered.

"He died so we could be together," she said. "I'm not sure how to accept this act. Do you mind if I read it later?"

Tyler squeezed her hand in assurance. They sat in silence for a few moments.

"Charley, Kate, tell us your story," Maggie asked softly, changing the subject.

They smiled, enjoying their new relationship and told their story. Lizzy relaxed as she took pleasure in her brother's happiness.

"I'm so sorry we missed it," she said. "Kate, we're so glad to have you as part of our family, and we really look forward to getting to know you."

Maggie agreed.

"Thank ya," Kate said. "Charley's told me so much about y' all, I look forward to being part o' th' family."

"Tell us what's been happening here," Tyler said.

The girls filled them in on their involvement in the Underground Railroad, the building of the workers' village, and Major and Edward Wyley's deaths. They left out the incidents with Aaron and Seth for the time being, not wanting to worry them during their first moments home.

"Charley," Lizzy turned to fully face her brother, "before Father left for the war, he changed his will. As I tell you what's next, keep in mind that Edward had not yet decided to join the army when this happened."

"All right," Charley said curiously.

"When father changed his will," she said slowly, "he left Edward enough money to take care of him." She paused. "The rest he left to us."

Charley stared at her.

"He left everything to you and me," Lizzy said.

"Everything?" Charley asked.

"Everything," Lizzy answered. "The land, the house, the money—of which there is a lot." She smiled. "And…" she paused again, not sure how he would take this last part, "and the people."

His face fell. "The people?" he whispered.

"Yes, Charley," Lizzy answered. "We're slave owners."

He didn't know what to say. Everything he had fought against, he now was. He'd lost his foot fighting to abolish the institution he was now unwillingly a part of.

"They're left to us in such a way that they need to be set free by both of us."

Charley brightened, "Let's sign the papers and set them free now!"

Lizzy braced herself for this conversation. "We could do that," she said, "I hate owning people as much as you do. I know we've both fought in our own ways to get rid of this awful institution. I've talked with Maggie and Hannah and Bartholomew at length about this." She paused, weighing what she was about to tell him. "They've all advised me not to set them free yet."

Charley gaped at her, then at Maggie, Hannah, and Bartholomew in turn. "Why would you, of all people," he questioned, looking at Bartholomew and Hannah, "not want to be set free?"

"It's not dat we wants to stay slaves, but it safer dis way," Bartholomew answered calmly.

Lizzy explained, "If we set them free, word would get around that there are free colored folks. Anyone could and would come and kidnap them and sell them back into slavery. If we don't set them free, we at least have the legal claim on keeping them here and away from slave traders. I know it sounds awful, but I think they're right. We can set them free whenever we want to—whenever it's safest."

"What about the Emancipation Proclamation?" Tyler asked hopefully. "President Lincoln set the slaves free."

Charley looked expectantly at Lizzy, hoping to get out of this situation.

"That's true," Lizzy said, "but the people of the South don't recognize Lincoln as their president. They're refusing to let the people go free."

"It's hard, Missuh Charley," Hannah said, "but it's de right thing ta do."

Charley looked to Kate, pleading for help.

"Honey, I think they're right," she said, laying a hand on him for assurance. "I'm in this with ya. I don't like it either, but what they're sayin' sounds like this might be the safest for the people."

He looked back to Lizzy. "You really think there's danger of someone trying to come get them?"

Lizzy and Maggie looked at each other. "You might as well tell them now," Maggie said.

Tyler tensed, sensing something was wrong, "Tell us what?" he said evenly.

Lizzy sighed. "We've had some trouble." Lizzy told them about Seth Patterson. "There's more," she continued, fearing what she was about to tell them about Aaron Thomas. "When I asked earlier if you had seen anyone you knew at the battle at Gettysburg, I didn't mean Jackson. I meant Aaron Thomas."

Tyler's eyes narrowed. Charley visibly tensed. They knew Aaron had desired Lizzy before the war. They were uneasy, wondering what Lizzy might tell them.

"He was wounded at Gettysburg too," she went on. "He's now back and quite incensed with life." She went on to tell him of Aaron's advances on her.

Charley clenched his fists. Tyler's face darkened with fury. Lizzy shivered. She had never seen either of them so upset. She was almost afraid of them. She pulled slightly away from Tyler. This movement seemed to snap him out of his wrath for a moment. He shook his head and looked at her with all the love and compassion he felt for her. He squeezed her hand reassuringly. She immediately calmed.

Charley jumped up. "I'm going to kill him!" Kate caught his arm to keep him from running Lizzy and Maggie both shouted for him to stay.

"Lizzy took care of him," Maggie said.

"What happened?" Tyler asked with amusement, wondering what his little Lizzy would have done to "take care of" big Aaron Thomas.

"Well," she shyly began, "I could barely move my arms, but I could reach inside my apron to the secret pocket Hannah made for me to keep my pistol in." She reached into her apron and pulled out her pistol to show them. "I didn't waste time trying to pull it out. I just pulled the trigger and blew off his knee. Then Maggie hit him over the head with a frying pan."

Tyler, Charley, and Kate looked at Lizzy and Maggie with a mix of amazement and amusement on their faces. They simply stared at them for a few moments until Tyler began to giggle. Kate and Charley followed. "I guess you don't need my protection," Tyler chuckled.

Lizzy smiled, knowing full well she would gladly let him protect her.

They all relaxed as Lizzy told them about taking Aaron to Dr. Ryan and waiting for the sheriff. "So, that's why we were so nervous when we saw you coming down the driveway wearing Confederate uniforms." Maggie said.

They sat in peaceful silence for a few moments. Then Tyler turned to Lizzy. "Can we take a walk?" he asked.

"In the snow? Sure." She smiled at him. They got up to leave.

"I'll go get started on supper," Hannah said.

"I'll help," Maggie offered.

"I'm pretty tired from the walk," Charley said. "I think I'll go rest for a while, if you don't mind."

"That's fine," Kate said. "Could I help with supper?"

"We'd love your help and company." Maggie smiled.

Everyone left to their own tasks, agreeing to come back together for supper.

Lizzy grabbed her wrap and bonnet, and she and Tyler headed out the door. "Where do you want to walk?" Lizzy asked.

"I'd love to see the village," Tyler said, taking her hand. They began a leisurely walk to the workers' village. When they got there, Tyler stood staring. "This is beautiful, Lizzy. I'm so proud of you."

She beamed at his praise. "Would you like to see inside one of the houses?" At his nod, she went to knock on one of the doors. Mimi answered. Lizzy introduced Tyler and asked for permission to show him the house.

"Sho," Mimi answered. "You knows you's always welcome to come to da house."

"Thank you," Lizzy said. "How's the baby?"

"Doin' fine." Mimi beamed.

Lizzy showed Tyler around. He was genuinely impressed.

"Miss Lizzy's been real good to us," Mimi said. "We preshiate all she done fo us."

"Nothing's going to change, Mimi," Lizzy said, sensing her friend's apprehension at the new masters' arrivals. "Charley and Tyler are good men. You have nothing to worry about."

Mimi smiled and visibly relaxed.

"Would you mind telling the others of their arrival?" Lizzy asked.

"Sho' nuff," Mimi said.

"Thanks," Lizzy replied. "Thanks for letting us see your house. You keep it very nice."

"Thank ya, ma'am." Mimi smiled at her employer and friend's approval.

"We'll see you later," Lizzy said.

"Good-bye," Tyler said. "Thank you."

Lizzy and Tyler left and wandered around the plantation for a while. Soon, they reached the river and Lizzy's favorite tree.

"Let's sit here a while," Tyler said.

Lizzy sensed he wanted to talk about something. She agreed, and they sat on the bench Eli had made, gazing at the freezing water. After a few moments, Tyler spoke.

"Lizzy," he began, "I'm not the same man who left you three years ago. This war did something to me. I've become more cynical and, at times, morbid. I've become less sure of myself at times. I'll be honest with you, I thought about not coming back home."

She looked at him, not sure how to take his words. Had she misinterpreted his affection since he'd been back? Was he going to tell her he didn't love her anymore? She stiffened and waited for him to continue.

He noticed her change of demeanor and hurriedly continued. "Please believe me, I never stopped loving you. When I entertained the thoughts of not returning, it was all because of my insecurities. I wasn't sure if you could love me how I'd changed. I wasn't sure you'd want me with this." He gestured toward his immobile arm. "I wasn't sure I could like myself the way I was."

Lizzy relaxed and smiled sympathetically at him. She waited for him to continue.

"I was still a little unsure until we started walking down your driveway." He smiled lovingly at her. "When I saw you standing on your porch though, I thought my heart would melt. Then when you ran down to us, I thought I would burst with love for you. Lizzy, I love you. I have always loved you. I have never stopped loving you. With God's help and thoughts of you, I made it through the war. Now I'm back."

He paused to see if she would say anything.

"I understand how the war would have changed you," she said. "I have changed as well. I cannot imagine what it was like for you. I have battled depression and anger here. God has brought me through. God has given me these wonderful people to help me through. Thinking of you has helped as well."

He took her hands in his. "Lizzy, I love you," he repeated. "I want to marry you. I want to protect you. I want to take you away from all this, perhaps back to Washington City with my father." He paused. "Will you marry me?"

She gazed up at him full of love. "I love you too, Tyler. As for your arm, don't worry about it. It's what brought you back to me. And yes, I will marry you. I will gladly turn over the role of protector to you. But I cannot move away from here. These people need me. I need them. I won't leave them."

He smiled. "Of course. We don't need to go anywhere."

"Thank you." She sighed and leaned into him. "So," she teased, "when shall we get married?"

He smiled mischievously, "I was thinking maybe tonight?"

She shot him a look to see if he was serious. "Tonight? Really?" she asked.

"I've been without you for three years. I don't want to be without you for another minute. I keep thinking that, had I not been so foolish in my own insecurities, I might have been here to protect you from Aaron in the first place. I want to be your official protector now. I don't want him coming back without you being mine."

She liked the way he made it sound. It didn't sound possessive and hungry like Aaron made it sound. "I would love to marry you tonight, Tyler," she said sweetly.

"I wrote you several letters while I was away," Tyler said. "I knew the communication lines had been severed, but it helped me to talk to you in this way."

"I did the same for you." Lizzy smiled.

"When would you like the letters?" Tyler asked.

"Let's exchange letters tomorrow, after our wedding."

"Sounds good. I do have one that you might like to read now though."

"Really? Why?"

He pulled an envelope out of his coat pocket and handed it to her.

She saw her name scrawled on the outside but didn't recognize the writing. She looked at Tyler for explanation. He simply smiled and kept silent. Opening the envelope, Lizzy felt tears fill her eyes as she read the letter.

Dear Miss Lizzy,

    I have so much to write. These three years have been so wonderful. The North is great. Mister Andrew has given me a job as his housekeeper. I clean and cook for him. He has hired a teacher for me, and now I can read and write. I am glad Mister Tyler is here, and I can write you to tell you how I am.

    Being married to Joseph has been so great. We now have a beautiful baby daughter named Elizabeth.

    I thank God every day for all you did for me. You made it all possible. I pray for your safety and hope you are all right.

    Your friend,

    Sarah

She looked up and smiled at Tyler. "Thank you for this." She giggled. "I know I'm grinning like a silly girl, but this is the best gift. Thank you. I wish I could have seen her. She really is doing well?"

"Extremely well." He smiled. "Baby Elizabeth is so beautiful. She wears your name well."

"I couldn't have asked for a greater honor."

They rested in each other's arms under the tree for a while longer, enjoying the peacefulness and aloneness neither of them had felt in a long time.

After a while, they got up and went back to the house. They made plans to go to Rev. Adams' parsonage after supper for the ceremony. Eli went to the parson to arrange the evening. Charley Tyler and Kate, Maggie, Hannah, and Bartholomew would all come.

Just before supper, Mimi came to the house looking for Lizzy.

"Miss Lizzy," she said shyly, "we all heard 'bout yo weddin' tonight, an' we'd like to celebrate with ya. We'd like ta throw ya a celebration when ya get home, ifn' that's all right."

Lizzy glowed. She loved these people, and they loved her. They had all become friends over the past three years. She looked to Tyler, who smiled and said, "We would love that. Thank you so much, ma'am. Is there anything we can do to help?"

Mimi blushed. She'd never been called ma'am by a white man before. "No, suh," she replied. "Jes leave it t' us. We be ready in da barn when ya get home."

"Thanks, Mimi. We look forward to it," Lizzy said, then turned to Tyler after Mimi left the house. "Thank you, Tyler."

"Anything for you, dear," he said. "I know this isn't the big wedding girls want, so I want you to have whatever you desire."

Lizzy giggled. "I don't want a big wedding. I just want you. And I promise you'll enjoy the party tonight. They throw amazing parties down at the workers' village."

"I look forward to it," Tyler said.

Supper was full of laughter and excitement for the upcoming wedding. Lizzy had been nervous that Maggie would feel left out as the only one unmarried after tonight.

Maggie pulled her aside before dinner. "I want you to know that I am so happy for you. You and Tyler deserve each other. You have been through so much and have done so much for so many people. I am bursting with happiness for you."

"Thank you," Lizzy said, still unsure.

"Please, believe me," Maggie said. "I can tell you're nervous about my reaction. I don't mind not being married yet. God has plans for me. If he wants me to marry, he'll bring the right one. It's just not the right time now. Please don't change plans for me."

Lizzy hugged her best friend. "You are so wonderful. Thank you."

The wedding was simple but memorable. The bride was dressed in a simple, white evening dress, while Tyler dressed in one of Lizzy's father's good suits. No cheek was dry during the ceremony. The groom held on a little longer during the kiss and made everyone giggle. After profusely thanking Rev. Adams for performing a beautiful ceremony on such short notice, the entourage left for home and the party at the workers' village.

When they arrived to the village, everyone was in the barn with music already playing. The party was held in the storage side of the barn. The floor was swept. Everything was put in place and stored away to make room for the festivities. As the guests of honor entered, everyone cheered for the newlyweds.

"Welcome, Mr. and Mrs. Parker!" everyone shouted.

"Oh no you don't!" Lizzy laughed. "I do like the sound of my new name, but it's bad enough that you call me Miss Lizzy. I won't have it any more formal than that!"

"Nor will I." Tyler grinned. "Tyler is just fine for me."

"All right, Missuh Tyler." Bartholomew grinned. Tyler rolled his eyes.

Kate and Charley made the same request, making everyone relax.

The party was full of laughter, singing, and dancing. Lizzy and Maggie introduced Tyler, Charley, and Kate to everyone. The workers were a little shy of the newcomers to begin with, but, seeing the ease with which Lizzy and Maggie interacted with them, they all soon became more comfortable.

The food was excellent. All three girls were passed around, with the husbands' permission, to dance with the other men. Everyone had a great time.

"How did you come up with such a great party on such short notice?" Lizzy asked Mimi.

"Well," Mimi answered, "we been wantin to have a party to thank ya and Miss Maggie fo all ya done fo us. We jes didn' know when."

"This is so wonderful," Lizzy exclaimed. "I couldn't have asked for a better wedding party. I especially couldn't have planned a better one. Thank you so much."

"'Scuse me, 'scuse me," Eli announced. "Iffn' the guests of honor, all five of ya, would please come sit right here. We's got somethin' fo' ya."

They all looked curiously at each other but obeyed. They followed Eli to a bench at one end of the barn.

"Miss Lizzy and Miss Maggie," Eli began, "you's been so good t' us in so many ways. We's been want'n to do somfin fo' ya. We knew ya were hopin' and prayin' for Missuh Charley and Missuh Tyler to come home. We was hopin' right 'long wit' ya and plannin' a little somfin special for when dey's come. We gots somfin for ya'all. Fellas, bring it on here."

Some of the men came and set gifts in front of each of them. In front of Charley, they placed a straight-backed chair, intricately carved with ivy. They placed a matching one in front of Tyler. For Lizzy, they gave a rocking chair with rose vines carved in it.

"These are beautiful," they all exclaimed.

"Eli," Lizzy said, "I knew you were teaching some of the men to make furniture, but who did the carving?"

Josiah shyly stepped forward. "I did, Miss Lizzy."

Tears welled in Lizzy's eyes as she looked at the carvings and at his hands, still showing the effects of the burns. She realized how painful the carving must have been for him. She went to him, taking his hands in hers, and kissed him on the check. "The carving is stunning, Josiah," she said. "Thank you so much.

He stepped back, blushing at the praise.

Kate received a carved wooden piece with a painting of the willow tree by the river. Maggie had been helping some of the women learn to paint and draw. "This is gorgeous!" she exclaimed. "Thank y' so much. But how did ya know I'd be here to give it to me?"

Ida stepped forward. "We didn't know, ma'am. We jes wanted to have somfin in case Missuh Charley had foun' someone."

Lizzy and Maggie exchanged glances, not surprised that this woman would believe Charley would come home with a wife.

"Thank ya so much," Kate said.

Maggie received two carved wooden pieces. One had a painting of a deer next to the willow tree by the river. On this one was carefully written, "As the hart panteth after the water brooks, so panteth my soul after thee, O God. Psalm 42:1." The other was a painting of the field with the words, "But let all those that put their trust in thee rejoice, let them ever shout for joy. Psalm 5:11."

Maggie looked up with tears in her eyes. She had been working so hard teaching them to read and write. This was the most precious gift she could have received. "Thank you so much," she choked.

Everyone gave hugs all around.

"Now, fo' de weddin' present," Eli announced.

Five women came forward carrying a quilt for Tyler and Lizzy.

"A weddin' quilt fo' ya,'" Ida said, smiling, as they handed it to them.

They took it with astonishment. It was striking in every detail. "How did you do this?" Lizzy asked. "Surely you didn't do it today. How did you know?" She wasn't really surprised that Ida would know, but she was amazed anew at the woman's gifts.

"You been talkin' 'bout yo' man comin' back," Ida said slyly. "We wanted to have somfin fo' ya' when it happened." She smiled. "All de pieces come from scraps from de cloth you gave us fo' clothes an' things."

"Thank you so much," Tyler said. "This is really lovely."

All the women blushed at the admiration.

"An' finally," Eli announced, "we have a show fo' ya."

They sat back in eager anticipation of the performance. Several of the men women and children got up and stood in front of the group.

"In honor of the weddin,'" Eli began, "and as tribute t' our teacher," he nodded to Maggie, who smiled, "we'd like to read ya somefin."

Each pulled out a Bible. Lizzy had made sure each person received one early on in her status as mistress of the plantation. They began to read from 1 Corinthians 13. Lizzy especially began to weep silent tears when one read: "Charity beareth all things, believeth all things, hopeth all things, endureth all things." They certainly had hoped and endured many trials during this time. Love had kept them going—God's love and love for each other. How fitting was this reading!

Maggie cried through the entire reading, not as much at the words, but at the fact that they were reading. She knew it was illegal to teach them to read. She believed so much in their right to read and gain knowledge that she ignored the law every day and taught classes for them. They had all improved so much during the two years she had taught them. This was the greatest present a teacher could receive.

When it was finished, the audience all jumped up in an excited standing ovation. Lizzy and Maggie ran forward to embrace them all. Effusive thanks and praise was shared all around.

The evening continued with dancing, singing, and storytelling. It was well past midnight when people started showing signs of tiring. Slowly, everyone gave thanks again, cleaned up, and turned in to bed.

On the walk back to the house, Tyler hugged Lizzy and said, "I am so proud of you, honey. You have done so much for these people."

She started to shake her head in modesty. He stopped her.

"No, Lizzy," he said. "You really have. Charley and I had gone down there several times before to try to talk to them and let them know we didn't view them as slaves. Edward especially was so oppressive, we couldn't say anything. When we saw them, they were undernourished, underclothed, demoralized, and broken. No one would get near us. Not one even looked up at us.

"Now, honey, they're healthy, happy, and joyful. Not one looked down when I talked to them. They all looked me straight in the eye as equals. They have been treated like the people they are, and they believe they are worth it now. They have been given so much materially as well and also the ability to read and write. That's amazing! You and Maggie have done wonders. I'm so proud of you. I'm so proud to be your husband."

Lizzy simply hugged him in response, too overwhelmed by his acclamation and love. He had always complimented her in the past, but this was different. She felt more than accepted for who she was and what she stood for. After living without the praise of her father for her whole life and in fear of unacceptance and physical harm for three years, she was unable to voice a reaction.

CHAPTER 19

The rest of the week passed with fun, laughter, and peace. They all played games, shared stories, and even took the horses out for a run in the field. For a few days, it felt like nothing had changed; no one had ever left and everything was the same, with the new well-fitting addition of Kate. The days were enjoyed with smiles all around.

Their joy was not even marred when Sheriff Jones arrived at the door to inform them of Aaron Thomas's recovery. The sheriff said Aaron was recovering slowly with Dr. Ryan, though he continued to rant and rave about Lizzy. He also said that Aaron had a constant guardian, in case he had some strange idea to leave the doctor's place. Everyone was thankful for the sheriff's report and glad Aaron had a guardian.

About a week after the wedding, everyone had settled in for the night. Lizzy awoke from a deep, peaceful sleep to the sound of crashing in the foyer. She stiffened and listened. Then, she heard drunken shouting among a string of curses.

"Where are you? If you're in your bedroom, all the better. I'm gonna come finish what I started!"

Lizzy began to panic. She scrambled to reach for her pistol she kept under her pillow. It wasn't there. Terror seized her. A hand reached out to grab her. She began to scream but was immediately calmed by Tyler's voice. In her deep sleep, she had forgotten he was there.

"Stay here," he said. "Keep the door shut. I'll go out there."

She silently agreed, immensely grateful for his protection.

Tyler grabbed his gun and slipped out the door. He met Charley in the hallway. They silently crept to the top of the stairs. Aaron was still bumping around in the foyer, trying to find the stairs. He continued to scream threats and curses at Lizzy.

Tyler and Charley took posts behind the walls at the top of the stairs. Each one had Aaron in his sights. Each one had a loaded gun, though neither wanted to actually use it. They waited to see what Aaron would do.

Lizzy's door opened, and Maggie and Kate rushed in. None of the girls wanted to be alone.

"Shut the door," Tyler and Charley hissed together.

The girls huddled together, listening behind the door in fear for their men.

Charley began. "Aaron, what do you want?" he demanded angrily.

Aaron stopped for a moment, confused at hearing Charley's voice. He didn't know Charley and Tyler had returned. His anger flared again, and he continued to the stairs, his bad leg and drunkenness making it extremely difficult. "Stay out of this, Charles," he hissed. "This ain't your business."

"It involves my sister," Charley replied, "and you're on my property. I'd say it's very much my business."

"Your sister belongs to me," Aaron slurred. "I'm here to take her."

"My sister's already taken," Charley announced defiantly.

Aaron stopped at the bottom of the stairs. "What are you talkin' about?"

"My sister is married," Charley informed.

"That ain't possible," Aaron sneered. "Edward and I—"

"Edward's dead," Tyler said. "Even if he wasn't, he had no authority over my wife."

"Who's that?" Aaron demanded.

"My sister's husband," Charley announced, "Tyler Parker."

Aaron had never liked Tyler. His family hated the Parkers for freeing their slaves. He hated Tyler for his friendship with Lizzy. The information that he was now Lizzy's husband enraged him all the more. "Well, you won't be for long," he growled as he attempted to climb the stairs.

"Aaron," Tyler said, "I know what you tried to do to my wife."

Aaron sneered, "She was willing."

"You'd better watch how you disrepute my wife. I know she wasn't willing. I'm warning you, you'd better leave now. I won't be aiming for your knee if you come near her again."

"I'm coming for you first, Parker, then I'll take Elizabeth how I want to." He reached in his pocket and awkwardly pulled out a gun. He was using a crutch with the other hand. That, coupled with his drunken state, made the hand holding the gun extremely unsteady.

Tyler and Charley were battle hardened veterans. They were used to being under fire but never from a drunken man boiling with rage. Aaron was so unsteady on his good foot that they had to step from their hiding places to see him and try to get a good shot. Neither wanted to actually kill him, but it was difficult to get any kind of aim. Their injuries didn't help either. Charley leaned against the wall to steady himself and free his hands. Tyler had only the one working arm to hold the gun.

Aaron caught sight of them, swore at Tyler, and attempted to take aim. His gun went off wildly, shooting the wall above their heads, then a second shot was fired, and Aaron went down.

Tyler and Charley looked at each other wondering who had fired; neither had. Then they looked to the front door, which stood wide open. Sheriff Jones was standing in the doorway holding a smoking gun.

Lizzy, Maggie, and Kate couldn't handle the fear any more. They'd heard the gunshots and the silence which followed. They rushed out to see if their men were all right. Seeing them still standing, they stopped in their tracks and stared at the front door.

Maggie found her voice first, "What happened?" she squeaked.

Sheriff Jones answered, his gun still trained on Aaron. "Dr. Ryan was called out on an emergency. Before my deputy was in place to guard him, Mr. Thomas escaped. My deputy ran to me when he found the bed empty. I knew there was only one place he would go."

"How did he get here?" Tyler asked.

"Seth Patterson helped him," the sheriff said.

Lizzy went white. Maggie held on to her friend. "Is Seth still here?" Lizzy asked shakily, knowing her danger was not over.

"He's being held on the porch," Sheriff Jones said distractedly.

At that moment, there was a loud commotion on the front porch, and Seth rushed in the house. He took one look at Aaron's body and fumed. "Who did this?" He didn't wait for anyone to answer. In a fury, he began grabbing things in the foyer and smashing them. He threw a vase at the mirror hanging on the wall. The vase splintered into tiny shards of glass as the mirror shattered, and the frame crashed to the floor.

The deputy in charge of holding Seth ran into the foyer, his face bleeding from the blow Seth had given him to get out of his grasp.

Then Seth caught sight of Lizzy. He stopped and glowered at her. "You denied my friend his pleasure. I'm gonna get mine outta you!" he shouted as he lunged for the stairs to get to her.

Sheriff Jones reacted faster than the others and shot Seth as he flew through the air. His body dropped down on top of Aaron's.

Everything went still. They were all too horrified to even scream.

After a few moments, Sheriff Jones and the deputy checked the bodies to make sure they were dead. Then they silently carried them outside. The foyer was a mess of blood. Lizzy stared at it in revulsion, knowing that was the blood of her attackers.

Kate and Maggie gently turned her away from the gruesome sight and led her to the upstairs sitting room. Soon Hannah joined them. Kate built a fire. Hannah brought hot coffee.

Meanwhile, Tyler and Charley made arrangements for Sheriff Jones to take one of their wagons to transport the bodies.

Tyler and Charley thanked him sincerely for saving everyone's lives.

"*That's* my job," Sheriff Jones said sadly. The emphasis on his words let them know he did not enjoy the killing part of his job. He quietly left the house.

As Tyler and Charley ascended the stairs, they looked down to see the women from the workers' village diligently cleaning the gore from the foyer. Even in the shock of the night, they were amazed at the dedication the women had for Lizzy and Maggie.

Once they reached the sitting room where the women were, they enveloped all three women in protective, loving hugs.

"I'm so sorry," Tyler said. "I can't imagine the fear you must have lived with knowing they were out there. We lived with the fear of attacks by other units, but that was always against our units—nothing personal. I don't even understand the personal vengeance they had against you, let alone how you lived with it."

"It was that fear that nearly broke me," Lizzy said, remembering her dark days.

Lizzy and Maggie let the tears fall, knowing the reason for the fear they'd lived with for so long had now vanished. Their tears were for the seemingly endless nights of terror they'd experienced and now the freedom from that fear.

CHAPTER 20

"Tyler, Charles, how good to see you!" Dr. Ryan exclaimed as he entered the house for his weekly visit. "Meet my wife, Anna."

"Wonderful to meet you," Charley said. "Meet my wife, Kate."

Everyone shook hands as the old friends were reacquainted.

"We've heard of the great things you've been doing here and how you've helped Lizzy and Maggie. Thank you so much," Tyler said.

"It's been a pleasure," Dr. Ryan said meaningfully.

"It's been great to see all they have done here and how they have helped so many people," Anna said.

"We're so proud of them," Tyler said as he kissed Lizzy's forehead. "We're so excited about the work you've done with Maggie as well. She looks great!"

Maggie blushed at the attention. Her leg had been healing. It was a painful but rewarding process. The months of therapy had turned her foot almost straight. Her pronounced limp was now only slight. She held her head higher as well, though Lizzy wasn't sure if that was due to the therapy or her pride in teaching the workers.

"She's a great patient," Dr. Ryan said. "I'm so glad to be of help in all areas. I don't know if they told you, but I was not the most willing helper in the beginning."

Tyler and Charley smiled. The girls had told them about his reluctance.

"Anna helped them with changing my mind, and I am so glad they did. I have been extremely blessed by these people."

"As we all have been blessed by you both," Maggie said.

"Well, do you have anyone for me to check?"

They did have a group of three men in the secret room. Lizzy let Tyler go with the doctor and his wife to see to the needs of the refugees, glad to let Tyler be the head of the house now.

When they returned, Hannah had coffee and cookies for the guests in the parlor. They all sat around the fire enjoying the company.

"I'm sorry about the events of two weeks ago," Dr. Ryan said. "I feel terrible about allowing Aaron to escape."

"It's not your fault," Lizzy said. "You were called away on an emergency."

"That emergency turned out to be fake."

"What?" they all exclaimed.

"When I got to the house the messenger sent me to, no one was there," Dr. Ryan explained. "I believe it was a rouse by Seth Patterson so he could get Aaron out and away from me."

They all sat in contemplative silence for a few moments.

"Well, whatever happened, it's all over now," Charley said.

"Thank goodness," Lizzy said, shuddering.

One day in early February, the five friends were relaxing in the parlor. The conversation turned, as it had quite often since they were reunited, to whether or not they should free the slaves.

"There's so much to think about with this," Lizzy said. "I hate being a slave owner as much as you all do. I feel like a hypocrite. However, I know that if they're set free and word gets out, someone will come kidnap them and sell them back into slavery."

"That is a possibility," Tyler replied, "but what happens if and when the Union troops come here, which I think is inevitable."

"Do you really think it will come to that?" Maggie asked.

Tyler and Charley nodded. "If the North is going to win," Charley answered, "they're going to have to cut deep into the South. I don't think it's a matter of 'if' but of 'when' are they going to get here. I want to be as far away from slave ownership as possible when that happens."

"What do you think will happen?" Lizzy asked.

"If we are still slave owners when the Northern armies get here," Charley explained, "they will throw us out of the house and take everything from us. I mean everything. They will say they're here to set the slaves free, but they won't give them anything to help them on when they are free."

"Really?" Maggie asked.

"Really. The army has the right idea with setting the slaves free, but they don't have a good plan for their lives post-slavery. We'll be separated from them and won't be allowed back on the property to get near them to help. We won't have any way to help them either because everything we have will be taken from us. If we set them free, we have a much better chance of convincing the soldiers where our loyalties lie and staying together."

"But if we set them free," Lizzy countered, "and the Northern armies don't come, and we're found out, then we'll be attacked as traitors to the Confederacy, lose everything, and, again, our people will be kidnapped and sold into slavery."

"That's all contingent on the North not coming, which we think they will," Tyler argued, "and word getting out that they're free. If we make it absolutely clear that they not tell anyone, I really believe they'll keep it quiet. They are extremely thankful and loyal to you two. You've done so much for them over the past years. I don't think any of them want that jeopardized. I really think they won't say anything."

They fell silent, each pondering what exactly to do. They had prayed over this many times together and separately. Each wanted to do what was right. None wanted to put anyone in danger.

"If we do set them free now," Lizzy asked, "will they think I'm a hypocrite for not setting them free earlier?" The question was directed at Hannah and Bartholomew who had just entered the parlor.

"No," Bartholomew said. "We all respect you. You's never lied to us. We knows dat. You tell dem de truth, dey do what you say. No one's gonna say anythin.' Besides, we's de one's tol' you not to do it in de firs' place."

Lizzy smiled. She trusted Bartholomew. She thought a few moments more. Everyone remained silent, sensing she was coming to a decision. "All right," she said strongly. "Let's sign the papers."

Everyone smiled and let out a collective breath. This was a momentous decision. It did put them in danger, but it was a giant weight off of everyone's shoulders. The manumission papers were found in Major Wyley's desk. Everyone gathered around as the papers were presented and the quills dipped in ink.

Excitement filled the air. Each paper was brought out with each worker's name on it. Lizzy and Charley signed their names setting each person free—giving them the life to which they were entitled to.

When the last signature was written and the ink set drying, the conversation turned to money. As free people, they needed to be able to handle their own money. Maggie had been teaching them to count and understand money, as well as read. She felt confident they would be responsible with it.

"They can't go into town with money," Kate brought up. "If they're seen with any kind o' money, someone will know they're not slaves."

The excitement died down. How were they going to solve this problem?

"Maggie, what if you held on to the money, sort of like a bank? They would trust you with that, wouldn't they? You could show them how much they had. They could come to you with purchases they needed, and we could go get it for them," Tyler suggested.

They looked to Hannah and Bartholomew. "I think dat would be a great idea." Hannah smiled. "It be basically what you doin' already, only it be dere—our—money now."

Everything was agreed upon. All the papers were signed.

"Hannah and Bartholomew, would you go to the village to bring everyone to the big house?" Lizzy asked.

They excitedly agreed and returned quickly with the twenty-seven workers and the eight children.

With everyone gathered around, Lizzy proudly announced their decision. She told them both sides of the conflict and why they decided to go ahead with the plan. She also made it very clear the dangers they would face if anyone else found out. Everyone agreed to keep quiet.

They also agreed to have Maggie bank their money. After the papers were passed out and the money ledgers explained, the newly freed men and women profusely thanked their employers.

Lizzy watched as everyone milled around the room talking before they went back to their houses. Since the building of the new houses, she had thought they were happy people. Now, though, they were truly joyful. They held their heads even higher than before. She knew she had done the right thing. She refused to worry about "what ifs" and was determined to be contented in winning the battle she had fought since the beginning of the war.

The next few months were peaceful for everyone on Riverridge Plantation. Everyone was happy and genuinely enjoyed each other's company. Lizzy and Maggie enjoyed welcoming Kate into the family and getting to know her. She fit in very well. It was an adjustment for everyone to be back together after having been separated for three years, but they all made it work and eventually fell into an easy routine. The freed men and women quickly adjusted to their new role, having felt free since Lizzy came in charge.

Spring came and, along with it, planting time. Eli and Bartholomew surprised Charley with a specially fashioned shoe to fit his leg with the missing foot. It fit amazingly well, and Charley was able to help with the planting better than he had hoped for. Tyler helped as well and was unexpectedly quick with the planting, in spite of his stationary arm. Working the fields became therapeutic for both men. They enjoyed working to create a finished product instead of working to destroy, as they had in the army.

Lizzy and Maggie continued to help the few runaways who came to seek refuge at the house. No one knew how much longer they would be working the Underground. They'd all heard rumors that the

Union army was advancing south. Atlanta had become an important city to the Confederates. They were under no illusions that, should the Union army advance as far as Atlanta, they would not punish the Southerners immensely. Lizzy hoped that their involvement in the Underground might prove their loyalty to the Union, though there was no assurance of that.

CHAPTER 21

One night in early May, Lizzy and Maggie crossed the river to take some runaways to Mr. Brown's station. The girls led a young couple while Maggie carried their sick four-year-old daughter. All was going well. They were traversing the well-known path through the dense woods, when they heard footsteps.

"Stop where you are!"

Scared, the young girl nearly jumped out of Maggie's arms to reach her mother. The quick movement startled Maggie and threw her off balance. She tripped on an exposed tree root twisting the ankle she had worked so many months in therapy trying to fix. They quickly halted the family traveling with them. Everyone stood silently still. Maggie bit her lip to keep from crying out at the pain and disappointment at possibly having ruined Dr. Ryan's work.

Lizzy's heart stopped. After three years of nearly no detection, were they now discovered? Was their involvement finally at an end? What would happen to them now? God help us! They all sent up a silent prayer. No one said anything.

"I know you're there," the voice said. "It's no use running. Come out of hiding. Raise your hands, and drop any weapons you might have."

The voice was distinctly northern. Lizzy calmed slightly at the thought. Perhaps this was an ally. She crept forward, motioning for the others to remain behind. Maggie refused and hobbled forward with her.

They were as surprised as their captor when they met face-to-face. Not only was the accent northern, but the uniform was as well. The soldier was obviously startled at having caught two women.

He lowered his gun slightly and gave them a curious look. "What are you doing?" he asked. The girls didn't answer. "Why are you out here so late?" Again, no answer. He became slightly agitated. "Look, ladies, if you don't answer, I'll be forced to assume you're spies and take you in to my commanding officer as prisoners. I'll ask one more time. What are you doing?"

Maggie spoke first, "We're not spies."

"How do I know that?" He decided to change his tactic, wanting to trust them. "Where do your loyalties lie?"

"You answer the question first," Lizzy said, trying not to get trapped.

"Isn't it obvious by my uniform?"

"Unless you're a spy," Maggie said.

"I can see we're going to go around in circles here." He smiled wryly. "Well, I'll start. I'm Lt. Jack Wallace of the United States Army. My loyalties lie with the President, Abraham Lincoln."

The girls relaxed a little, wanting to believe him. "Our loyalties lie with the Union as well," Maggie said.

They eyed each other a few more moments, then relaxed slightly.

"I must say, I'm quite surprised to meet any loyalists this far south," Lt. Wallace said. "I'm even more surprised to meet two women in the woods well after midnight. What are you doing?" He took in a quick breath. "You're part of the Underground Railroad, aren't you?" he whispered.

His excitement was unexpected. They weren't sure how to handle it.

"Do you have runaways with you?" he asked.

They were still wary of him and didn't want to give anything away, when a sneeze blew their cover.

Lt. Wallace smiled a friendly smile. "You can all come out now. I won't hurt you. You're with the Union army now; you're free."

The family stayed hidden. "Why would you say that?" Lizzy questioned.

"President Lincoln emancipated the slaves. Once they're with the Union army, they're free. They don't need to run any more. We'll help them. They can even stay with us and work for pay."

Another sneeze broke the silence of the night. The father brought out his family, cradling his sick daughter, the one sneezing. His look was one mixed with hope and fear. He wanted this man's words to be true, but he knew the possibility of a trap. There was no use hiding, though, since his daughter's sneezes were giving them away.

Lt. Wallace smiled at the family. "Please, come with me. I'll give you something to eat. We'll talk with my commanding officer. You ladies may go now. I'll see to their safety. Or you may come with me. You look as if you might need medical attention," he said to Maggie.

Lizzy and Maggie were not about to see their charges trapped. They followed. Lt. Wallace didn't argue. They reached the army camp a few minutes later. It looked as if they had just arrived. Men were milling about, setting up tents and fires. They looked as if they planned to stay for a while.

The girls hung back as they watched Lt. Wallace take the family to his commander. The commander welcomed the family and gave them a place to sleep for the night, as well as food. Lizzy now felt comfortable that Lt. Wallace was not a spy. Apparently, he felt the same about them as well. He came back, bringing two tin mugs of coffee and a medic.

The medic checked Maggie's ankle and found the bone was bruised. He wrapped the ankle and left.

"Again, I must say, I'm surprised to find loyalists this far south," Lt. Wallace said when the medic left. "Are there more?"

"Just our family, that we know of," Lizzy said. "It's not really something to be announced down here."

Lt. Wallace smiled in understanding. "Well, it is nice to know we have at least some allies here."

They fell silent for a few minutes. The girls realized they'd been gone long enough, and the family would begin to worry soon. They thanked their host and accepted his escort back to the woods. Thanking him again, they continued their journey to the river alone. Silently, they returned home and reported the night's events.

"Did you give him your names?" Charley asked. He was irritated they had gone with the man and had given him the information they had.

"No," Lizzy answered.

"We need to be very careful now," Tyler said. "Who knows what reconnaissance they might do. We could get in some serious trouble if he goes poking around asking for loyalists."

Lizzy and Maggie remained quiet. Surely a lieutenant in the Union army would be smarter than to go around house to house asking for loyalists. They weren't too afraid.

A week later, Eli came to the backdoor looking for Lizzy.

"Dey's someone here to see ya," he said, intentionally not using her name. Lizzy picked up on that. She was startled when he presented Lt. Wallace.

"Thank you," she said. "Would you please go get—"

"Dey's on de way," Eli answered before she finished. He'd already sent someone to get Charley and Tyler.

"Thanks, we'll be in the parlor." She guided Lt. Wallace to the parlor, where Maggie and Kate were sitting with their mending. Maggie was startled as well.

"Lt. Wallace," she said, "what brings you here?"

"Reconnaissance," he answered.

They all became a little nervous at the word. Who else was traipsing around their property? Where else had he been before he found them? They decided to wait until Charley and Tyler arrived to ask their questions. Thankfully, they didn't have to wait long. When Charley and Tyler heard about their visitor in a blue uniform, they dropped their work in the field and came running. They were suspicious of anyone who came to the house, especially since visitors were rare.

They came silently in and sat down—Charley next to Kate on the love seat and Tyler in between Lizzy and Maggie on the sofa. Lt. Wallace did not miss the protectiveness of their seating arrangement or the looks of suspicion on their faces. Nor did he miss the fact that still no one gave their names; he found that amusing given the fact he had been able to find out other important information about them.

"First," he began, "I want you to know that I come peacefully. I believe you to be Union sympathizers. I'm sure we can both use the allies." No one responded. "I've come to help and ask for help in return."

"What kind of help?" Tyler asked skeptically.

Lt. Wallace took a deep breath, "I need some information. Not much," he rushed on at their surprised faces, "but some information. I could get it myself, but that would take time, and I believe, if you help me, my commanding officer might pass you by in upcoming events."

"What upcoming events?" Charley asked.

"I don't know exactly," he replied. "Even if I did, surely you know I couldn't tell you details."

"Yet, you're asking details from us," Charley countered.

"Different details," Lt. Wallace said. "All I know is that the general wants to end this war quickly, at the expense of the Confederates."

"Who is your general?" Tyler asked.

"General William Tecumseh Sherman."

Tyler and Charley exchanged glances.

"I see you've heard of him," Lt. Wallace said.

"Everyone in the Union army has heard of him," Charley answered, "and of his dislike for all things Confederate."

"I thought so," Lt. Wallace said. "Am I to assume correctly that you served in the Union army?" he asked both Charley and Tyler.

"Yes," they answered.

Lt. Wallace asked about their unit and some of their experiences. Tyler and Charley gave some information but tried to keep it brief. They weren't sure how much to trust this man.

"Like I said," the lieutenant continued, "I'd like to help you. Would you be willing to help me?"

"What details do you want to know?" Tyler asked. "What help would you be willing to give us?"

"Like I said, it's not much that I couldn't find out on my own. It would just be much quicker to learn it from you, if you already knew it; just a few military targets in town, perhaps some names as well. This would be in exchange for protection. I could all but guarantee our troops would pass by you in upcoming battles, if they knew beyond a doubt you were allies."

"You ask a great risk of my family, sir," Charley said. "You give no guarantees."

"You're absolutely right," Lt. Wallace answered. "But, with all due respect, sir, this is war. With war comes great risk and little guarantee. I can give you my word I will do my best."

"Well, as of right now, your word means nothing to us," Charley said. "We know nothing of you," he paused. "Our family has already been faced with danger. We've already paid great prices for the risks we've taken. I'm not sure I want to gamble much more."

"I don't expect an answer right now," Lt. Wallace said. "Please think about it. I'll return in a day or two. We can talk more then." He stood to leave. No one stood with him. He wordlessly turned to walk out the way he had come.

"Lieutenant," Maggie called. He turned to look at her. "Come back tomorrow. We'll have an answer for you then." He nodded and walked away.

Charley and Tyler gave short, bitter laughs. "He'll be wasting his time when he comes back," Charley said. "There's no way I'll risk our family anymore. We'll be fine without his so-called protection."

"I disagree," came Kate's quiet but firm opinion.

Thankful she spoke, Lizzy and Maggie agreed.

"What do you mean?" Charley asked incredulously.

They had all quickly learned that when Kate gave an opinion, it was an opinion worth listening to. She had proved herself to be a quiet, reflective person. When her opinion was given, it was not without much personal deliberation and thought. Therefore, her opinions carried much weight. Lizzy and Maggie decided to let her continue the conversation.

"I believe we need t' take a stand," she explained. "We've stood aside here, hoping to remain out o' the situation; hoping they'll leave us alone. Well, it looks pretty clear t' me that we're gonna be in it, no matter what. We've got t' take a stand and say which side we're on."

Charley looked patronizingly at his wife. "Honey, I believe we've already done that. They've got to believe we're on their side."

"I think you're wrong. I don't believe there's anything we've done or been a part of that they can't find folly with," she said matter-of-factly.

Charley was becoming a bit flustered. "If you're talking about just saying that we're Union loyalists, I can agree with you. They could simply think we're lying. But what about Tyler and me fighting for the Union?"

"How are they t' know you weren't spies?" Kate countered.

Charley was taken aback at his wife's frank opposition. "What about freeing the slaves?" he questioned.

"How are they t' know ya didn't just do it now for the protection?"

He was getting frustrated. "What about Lizzy and Maggie's involvement in the Underground Railroad?" He thought he had her now.

Lizzy answered this one. "There's no proof."

Tyler gaped at her. "What do you mean?"

"Being part of the Underground Railroad requires ultimate secrecy. You don't know the people involved. You don't keep any record or any proof that you're part of it. All precautions are taken so no one can implicate you in illegal activities. There is no proof."

Tyler and Charley were stunned. They didn't expect this opposition from their wives. They were the heads of this household. Their wives were supposed to submit to them. They were doing this for their good. They didn't want their wives to risk any more danger. They were trying to protect them. Charley was frustrated enough to tell them just that.

"We're trying to protect you," he said. "We're the heads of the household. We're trying to do what's best for our family. We don't want anyone to do anything too risky. Surely we can survive this without sacrificing what we believe. He's basically asking us to be spies. That's wrong."

Lizzy loved her brother, but sometimes he could become a little too heavy-handed, and she wasn't about to take it. "You may be the head of the household now," she said, "but Maggie and I defended this house for three years without you. We made it work. We protected everyone here and did a fine job of it. We did have to do some things we're not proud of, but it was all for the greater good. I'm not going to sit here and let you be oppressive with us. We'd like to make this decision together, but you've got to decide what's right. Are we going to take our stand with the side we've fought with for three and a half years, or are we going to sit aside and let them think we're the enemy?"

Charley and Tyler were too stunned to answer.

Maggie cut in gently, "If we don't take a stand with the Union, they'll think we're Confederates and fight us just the same. The Confederates will eventually find out which side you fought on and what we did with the slaves. They'll treat us as they treat the Yankees. If we join with the Union now, at least we'll have their protection, no matter what happens."

"If the Union loses though, we'll be left at the mercy of the Confederates," Charley argued defeatedly.

"That's if the Union loses," Kate answered. "If they do, we'll just pack up and leave with them. We'll still have their protection though."

Charley and Tyler considered all sides. Their wives were right.

Tyler took a deep breath and squeezed Lizzy's hand. "All right, we'll do it. May God protect us."

CHAPTER 22

The next afternoon, Lt. Wallace arrived as he had left—through the back door. He waited until Tyler and Charley could be found before entering the house. The three men met the women in the front parlor. Charley began the discussion.

"We have talked about your proposal at length," he said seriously. "We have looked at it from all sides—discussing the good and the bad for helping you and remaining as we are. The main point for us is protection and safety for this family. In some capacity or another, we have all been protecting this family for the past three and a half years."

"By family," Lizzy said, "we don't just mean those of us in this room. We mean everyone living on this property—those working in this house and in the fields; living in the workers' village."

Lt. Wallace nodded in understanding.

Gesturing at Lizzy and Maggie, Tyler said, "My wife and friend had been the sole protectors of everyone here for three years before we returned from the war. Everyone's safety is extremely important to us."

Lt. Wallace nodded again.

"With all that said," Tyler continued, "we want to take you at your word when you say you'll do your best to keep us safe. Therefore, we accept your offer and are willing to help."

Lt. Wallace visibly relaxed. He had been nervous for their sake that they would not accept. "I'm pleased to hear it," he said.

Charley stepped in, gesturing to the others as he spoke. "We have done all we can to help the Union cause so far. My brother-in-law, Tyler, and I fought for the Union for three years. We were wounded for the Union. My wife, Kate, was a nurse for the Union army. My sister, Elizabeth, and our friend, Margaret, continue to be a part of the Underground Railroad. We have set our slaves free. However, we understand how it all can be refuted. We want no questions as to where our loyalties lie."

"You're right," Lt. Wallace replied. "Someone could refute your past involvements. I'm glad you've decided to help. I think it will be near impossible to refute your loyalty now."

After a momentary silence, Maggie asked, "What do you want to know, Lieutenant?"

He jumped right in with questions about military targets and supply areas. Maggie and Lizzy were surprised at how much they could answer. When they had gone to town, they had lingered a little longer when they were around soldiers, listening in on conversations in case they learned valuable information—which they had.

When it was finished, moods were mixed. They were relaxed and tense at the same time. It was finished, their ultimate treason to the Confederacy complete; their loyalty to the Union hopefully irrefutable.

Maggie broke the silence, "Why did you want to help us so much, Lieutenant?"

"Please, call me Jack," he said. "When I met you two the other night, I was reminded of my home. My mother and sisters are heavily involved in the Underground Railroad. I helped before I enlisted. Their involvement is at great peril to themselves. My father is deceased. My grandparents live with my family now. My grandparents are from the South. They completely disagree with the Underground Railroad and would turn my family in, if they knew. My mother and sisters are the strongest women I know. You two reminded me of them. I guess I felt that protecting you might be akin to protecting my family."

"Thank ya for yer protection, Jack," Kate said.

"I think it will be my pleasure." Jack smiled. "I should be getting back to my unit to report the news. I appreciate the help you gave me. It was more than I'd dared hope for." He stood to leave. He turned to Tyler and Charley. "On a personal note," he began shakily, "if she consents, of course, I would like your permission, as the heads of the household, to return and call on Miss Margaret."

Maggie looked down and blushed in obvious pleasure. Tyler and Charley looked at each other and grinned. Lizzy and Kate shared a smile of knowing.

Tyler knew Maggie well and knew the smile she gave was one of hope for consent. He answered, "You have our permission, given all propriety be considered."

"I wouldn't have it any other way." Jack grinned, grateful. "I will return soon with news from my superiors."

The next day, Jack surprised them with his return. This time, he went to the field to talk with Tyler and Charley first and then, with their permission, went to the big house to tell the women. The women were all in the dining room cleaning up from breakfast when Hannah brought the lieutenant in to see them.

"Good morning, ladies," Jack said with a smile.

They returned his greeting and invited him to sit at the table with them and finish what was left over. He graciously accepted, having eaten only army issued rations for so long.

"What brings ya back so soon?" Kate asked.

"Well," he answered between mouthfuls, "last night, I immediately went to my superiors with the information you were so kind to give me. They were eternally grateful and insisted that you all be protected immediately. They dispatched ten of us to be the guardians of this property and everyone on it. We are stationed in the woods across the river. The entire army has been spread out along the river, so we aren't very conspicuous."

"That's wonderful!" the women cried, relieved to have their espionage finished and Jack able to keep his word.

"Tyler and Charles have given their permission for me to survey the grounds, so we may know best how to defend it," Jack said. "Miss Margaret, I wonder if you might be interested in joining me? I will need a guide for this task."

Maggie smiled and agreed. Lizzy and Kate knew this would be a good time to finish clearing the table. They got up and finished their task as Maggie talked with Jack about the grounds.

"What do you think?" Lizzy asked Kate when they were in the kitchen.

"I think she could do much worse." Kate smiled.

"I think he'd be great for her," Lizzy said. "He seems like a strong man who could really take care of her. She needs that."

"And he's already proven he can stand up to our men," Kate laughed. Lizzy laughed with her. They knew that any man who came to take Maggie away would need to be able to stand his own with Tyler and Charley.

"How's your ankle?" Jack asked as they left the house.

"It's fine," Maggie answered. "A little bruised. Our doctor will come tomorrow to look at it."

"You're still limping."

Maggie looked down. "I've always limped," she confessed. "I was born with it."

He stopped and waited for her to look at him. "I don't mind a limp," he said, looking straight into her eyes.

She visibly relaxed. No man had ever showed this much interest in her knowing she limped.

They kept walking, and Maggie gave him a tour of the land. He wanted to know every hill, field, and building on the property, so as to know how best to defend it. He came back every day, and they walked the grounds together. Each day, he brought one of the ten soldiers dispatched to defend the land. When the tour was over, he would send the soldier back, and he stayed at the house a few hours more getting to know the family. They all really enjoyed his company and secretly agreed that he would be a nice addition. Maggie glowed every time she saw him, which was enough for Kate and Lizzy.

"You've suffered a bad sprain, Margaret," Dr. Ryan said the next day during his visit. "This will set you back a ways in your therapy."

A tear fell down Maggie's cheek. She had worked so hard.

Jack put his hand on her shoulder. He was thankful she allowed him to be in on this appointment. "Remember, I don't mind the limp," he whispered in her ear.

She squeezed his hand, relishing the feeling of a man focusing just on her.

"I'll do whatever I need to, Doctor."

He placed one of the earlier splints back on her leg, and she began her therapy again.

One day in early June, Eli came to the house with news of a visitor. "Dey's in gray uniforms," he told Lizzy. "I's already sent someone to fetch Charley and Tyler. Dey be here any minute."

"Thank you, Eli," Lizzy said. She didn't attempt to hide her fear. She had no idea of the reason for a visit from Confederate soldiers. Their secrets could have been found out. She forced herself to remain calm as she found Maggie and Kate. Thankfully, Tyler and Charley arrived to the house before the soldiers did. They stood on the porch, waiting for the soldiers to arrive, not wanting to invite them to the house.

"Afternoon," the captain said pleasantly as he strode to the foot of the porch.

"Afternoon," Charley replied, standing at the top of the stairs on the porch. "What brings you out here?"

"Well, sir, as I'm sure you know, Union troops have been amassing across the river planning to attack at some point in time. We're dispatching our soldiers across from them, ready to defend our town."

"Yes, sir, we knew that," Charley said.

"Well," the captain continued he squinted into the sun looking up at Charley, "your property lines up with the river. We'd like to dispatch soldiers along the edge to complete the line of defense."

Charley paused for a moment, as if considering the request. Then he answered, "I'm sorry, Captain, I can't give my permission."

The captain looked shocked. He had not planned for any resistance. His eyes narrowed, and his cordiality took a hard tone. "Why not?" he asked.

"Well, as you can see, our house is very close to the river, as are many other buildings on our property," Charley purposefully refused to call the houses "slave row" and didn't want to raise more suspicion by calling them the "workers' village." "I'm afraid having soldiers this close to our house would be distressing for the women."

"But we would be there in protection of the women," the captain said.

"Sir, I know how soldiers think," Charley replied. "I can say for sure, I do not want my family in that close quarters with soldiers who have been away from their women for a long time."

The captain was speechless. He had come expecting full cooperation and instead was receiving a decided no. "Are you sure we can't change your mind?" he asked. "It would greatly help the Confederate cause and the defense of our town."

"I understand your point of view, sir, but my first defense has to be that of my family. Thank you." Charley pointedly dismissed the soldiers, who turned in confusion and left the property.

They waited on the porch until the last soldier was out of sight. "Do you think that worked?" Lizzy asked.

"I sure hope so," Charley answered. "I'm sure they're suspicious, but who can fault us wanting to protect our women?" He smiled at them, gave Kate a hug, and he and Tyler walked back to the field.

"You'll have to tell Jack when he comes today," Lizzy said to Maggie.

"I will," Maggie said and blushed.

"Ya like him, don't ya?" Kate asked.

"Very much," Maggie said, smiling.

The girls went back into the house giggling, thankful to have this pleasant distraction.

CHAPTER 23

"Something strange is going on at that house."

"I know, but there's nothing we can prove. They're well within their rights to not accept soldiers on their land, especially with their women in mind."

"It's not just that. My son was on to something a long time ago. If they hadn't killed him, I bet he would have found something."

"He was stupid and went after the girl."

"Yours wasn't any smarter," came the terse reply.

"Mine had a legitimate claim on the Wyley girl before the war."

"Well, she ain't the Wyley girl anymore now, is she? She's married to that abolitionist's boy," Oliver Patterson cursed. He was bitter about his son's death and blamed Lizzy and Maggie for it. The sheriff couldn't convince him that his son was at fault. Judge Thomas was equally as outraged at his son's death, not caring to listen to the sheriff's explanation. Both men blamed Lizzy and Maggie and wanted revenge.

"There's got to be something we can do," Judge Thomas said, gulping the brandy in one swallow.

"If we go there now, we're going to get the same fate our sons did, and we'll have our wives to answer to."

A sly smile came across Oliver Patterson's face. "I know," he said, refilling their two glasses, "a battle's inevitable. Let's just wait until then, take our own men to Riverridge and take care of it then."

Judge Thomas thought about it for a moment. He wanted all legal ramifications thought of before anything occurred. If they could make it look like just another skirmish in upcoming battles …He downed the second glass of brandy. An evil grin spread across his face. "Get what information you can out of the soldiers. I want a well-coordinated attack. Gather your best men."

Oliver agreed. They shook hands and parted company.

"I don't know, honey. I just don't think it's a good idea."

"It's th' best way we can help."

"It's the most obvious way we can help."

"I think th' ten soldiers protectin' our land will be obvious enough." Kate and Charley had had this conversation many times, to the same end. Kate was now pacing the study in frustration.

"Honey, come sit down," Charley urged.

"I'm too restless t' sit down. This is th' way I can help. It's what I do. I'm good at it. I'm wastin' my God-given talent sittin' 'ere. Why won't ya let me help?"

"I'm trying to protect you." He felt as if he were constantly butting heads with his family. It wasn't that he actually disagreed with them or wanted something different. He just wanted to protect them.

"This is war, Charley. Protection comes at a price. I'm willin' t' pay that price t' help the others."

They stared at each other for a few moments, gauging whether or not the other would back down.

Finally, Kate pulled her last card. "You've been there, Charley. Ya know that to a wounded man, every second counts. Askin' the men t' take th' wounded across th' open river, not knowin' 'ow th' water will be, is askin' them to take some o' th' men t' their deaths." She paused for effect before she made her last plea. "If th' hospital was much farther away at Gettysburg, we would have lost Tyler."

Charley gaped at her, trying to see if she was telling the truth. He knew his wife never lied to him. He was thankful for all the doctors and nurses had done for his best friend. How could he now not give that same possibility to another soldier?

He gazed out the window at the birds chasing each other. How he envied them. They had no idea a war was waging. All they worried about was getting food for their families. How he longed for those days.

"All right." He sighed. "We'll tell Jack tomorrow. But I don't want anyone moving anything here until the battles start. I don't want to make obvious our loyalties until we absolutely have to."

Kate wrapped her husband in a hug. They were going to offer part of their land as a field hospital for the Union army. She was going to get to nurse again.

"We want to help." Lizzy and Maggie burst through the door, followed by Tyler.

Charley gritted his teeth. He wasn't surprised that others were listening in to their conversation, but he was getting annoyed with not having space of his own. "As I know there is no way to stop you, you heartily have my blessing."

Laughing, Tyler slapped his friend on the back, seeing that he was finally coming around to understanding that the women were going to do what they wanted to do.

Tyler had understood much faster than Charley that Lizzy and Maggie were used to making their own decisions. It would be a hard habit for them to break. Tyler didn't really want to break that habit. He came to value his wife's opinion and decisions. She had been through much here without him, and he didn't want to devalue that. If it was something he absolutely disagreed with, he'd say something, but so far that hadn't happened.

The next few weeks were tense for everyone. General Sherman's forces were tenaciously cutting their way through Georgia on their way to Atlanta. Both sides were suffering many casualties, but Sherman continued on. War on their home front was inevitable.

Everyone at Riverridge was doing what they could to prepare. With Dr. Ryan's help, Kate taught Lizzy, Maggie, and many of the women workers what she could about nursing, so they could help in at least a small capacity. Tyler and Charley, along with the men workers, helped Jack and the soldiers with figuring out the defenses of the plantation and getting things ready to set up for the field hospital.

On July 20, 1864, Union troops reached Peachtree Creek, about three miles north of Atlanta. Newly appointed Confederate General John B. Hood attacked Union General George H. Thomas after the Union forces crossed the creek. The Confederates nearly overran the Union soldiers during the ensuing battle. However, Union forces held, forcing the Confederates back. The Union troops advanced. For the next month and a half, Atlanta and surrounding areas would be under siege with near constant battles raging; the Union forces aim to cut railroad supply lines to the major Confederate hub.

During this time, Riverridge was used as a field hospital for many wounded Union soldiers. All of the residents of the plantation were constantly busy helping. The plantation remained safe from major battles.

One night in mid August, during a lull in fighting, Lizzy and her family were out helping bring water to the wounded. A gunshot ripped through the air. Lizzy and Maggie dropped to the ground and hid behind a near by tree. Tyler was at their side in an instant.

"Elizabeth Wyley!" came a menacing voice. "Where are you? You're a traitor to the Confederacy. We've come to make sure you get what you deserve!"

"Who is that?" Kate whispered. She and Charley had found their way to the tree.

Lizzy and Maggie looked at each other in fear. They knew the voice.

"It's Oliver Patterson," Lizzy stammered.

Tyler and Charley looked at each other in a mix of fear and determination. There was no way they were going to let this man harm their wives.

Jack found them and crouched by the tree.

"There are seven of them," he informed. "They've all got rifles. They're hiding in that grove of trees." He pointed to the trees. "I've got my men circling around behind them. Are you armed?"

"Always," Charley answered. He and Tyler showed their weapons.

"Good," Jack said. "Come with me."

Tyler looked back at Lizzy, who nodded her support.

"We'll stay here," she said.

The men ran to another hiding spot with a better vantage point.

Shouting ensued. Lizzy and Maggie recognized the voice of Judge Thomas as well. Now they were really scared. Both men had vengeance against them. They prayed for the safety of their men and themselves. Shots rang out. Men screamed.

"We've got to get the men away from the wounded soldiers," Lizzy said.

"We've got t' stay here," Kate hissed. She agreed with Lizzy but knew her sister-in-law would put others' safety in front of her own.

"Kate's right, Lizzy," Maggie pleaded. "These men are out for us. We've got to stay where we are."

"If we move just to that tree over there, there will be less danger to the wounded soldiers," Lizzy argued.

"No," the others snapped.

"It's not that far away," Lizzy said, "just a little that way. We'll still have the cover of these trees." She pointed as she spoke, rising up slightly from her hiding point. In that instant, another shot rang out. Lizzy's body snapped back, slamming against a tree trunk. Maggie screamed. Kate rushed to her side. Lizzy was gasping for air. The bullet had ripped through her collarbone.

Kate fought panic as she tried to save her sister-in-law's life. Where was her bag when she needed it?

Tyler ran through the trees, dodging bullets to reach his wife. He was frantic with worry. "Help her! Help her!" he yelled at Kate.

Kate tried to ignore him, knowing he was just a worried husband. "Maggie, go get my bag and a doctor."

In shock, Maggie dumbly obeyed, crawling behind them through the trees. Thankfully, Kate's bag was close. One of the army doctors was already on his way after hearing the initial shots.

Kate was putting pressure on the wound to try to stop the bleeding. "Tyler," Kate shouted over his wails. She waited until he looked at her. "Go help Charley and Jack."

"But," he tried to protest.

"Go," Kate shouted again. "She needs your protection."

This seemed to snap him out of his fear. His face turned to stony hatred. He grabbed his weapon and ran off.

The doctor and Kate worked on Lizzy. The pain was so intense, Lizzy had passed out. Maggie helped hold her as the doctor worked.

Maggie marveled at the steadiness of the doctor's hands, then noticed that Kate was steady as well. Maggie was shaking like a leaf. She prayed harder than she could ever remember praying. Shots and shouts rang out around her. Lizzy was pale. She seemed to be losing a lot of blood. Fear gripped Maggie to the point she was unable to think.

What seemed like an eternity later, all was quiet around them. The doctor continued working. Charley and Tyler ran up to them. In a manner that left no room for argument, Kate motioned for them to be still. Everyone held their collective breaths. Finally, the doctor relaxed. He pulled the bullet out. He and Kate began to stitch Lizzy's shoulder.

When they finished, he turned to Tyler, who had only just begun to allow himself to hope. The doctor smiled. "Your wife will make it, Mr. Parker."

In relief, Tyler sat on the ground next to his wife, tears openly flowing down his face.

Maggie finally came to. She looked around, wondering where Jack was. Fear gripped her anew. "Where's Jack?" she asked.

Charley answered. "He's with his men. Two were wounded in the fight."

Maggie relaxed. "What happened?" she asked.

Tyler raised up and put his good arm around his friend. "They were outnumbered, drunk, and outexperienced," he said. "You won't have anything to worry about from them anymore. Some of the doctors are helping clean up and take the bodies away."

"Bodies?" Maggie asked shakily.

"They're dead," Tyler clarified.

The fear-based adrenaline stopped flowing, and Maggie gave into the raging tears.

CHAPTER 24

More fighting occurred through the end of August. Kate and Maggie served the wounded soldiers that continued to arrive at their field hospital. Lizzy remained inside. Tyler tended her recovery. Charley helped Jack and his men with the continued defense of Riverridge. With the defeat of Oliver Patterson and his men, the threat to the plantation had lessened. Using the grounds as a field hospital had placed unspoken protection over Riverridge. Plus, word had spread of the attack on the women and the valiant protection.

On the evening of September 1, 1864, Jack came in to the dining room as the others were eating supper. "Union troops have cut through Confederate lines. The Confederates are retreating to Lovejoy's Station."

Everyone was relieved. The fighting should soon be over. Life could resume a somewhat natural pace. They ate their supper in peaceful silence as they contemplated what this could mean.

Suddenly, a knock sounded on the door. Hannah brought in one of Jack's men.

"Excuse me, Lieutenant," the soldier said. "I think you should come see this."

Jack got up, without question, and followed him. The others did the same. Once outside, the soldier handed Jack his looking glass and pointed him toward the city. A bright red glow was hovering over parts of the city.

"What is it?" Charley asked.

"The Confederates are burning anything essential to their cause. They're retreating," the soldier answered.

Flames flickered on the horizon. No one could look away. "At least it's just military material," Charley said. "I hope nothing else catches fire."

They stood and watched the flames in a mixture of sadness and relief. They were relieved that the Union would be in control now but sad that parts of the city were in flames. They watched until the flames died down and went to turn in for the night. No one could guess what the next few days would bring.

The next day, Union troops occupied Atlanta. Sherman had won. He asked for the evacuation of the city, wanting to be rid of Confederates. By September 4, most of the city had evacuated. Sherman decided to continue his march through Georgia. On his way out, he left a wake of destruction.

"What the—" Tyler jumped from his seat in the parlor and ran out the front door. The others followed, leaving their quiet evening. They could not have been prepared for what they saw, nor would they ever forget the sight. Red-gold flames lit up the night sky.

"The city's on fire!" Lizzy exclaimed.

"What's happening?" Maggie asked.

One of Jack's soldiers came galloping up on his horse. He didn't bother to dismount. "Lieutenant!" he shouted. "Sherman's destroying the city!" He spurred his horse on to inform others.

"Stay here!" Jack ordered the others. "I'll go see what I can find out."

They stood transfixed, unable to tear their eyes away from the gruesome sight. The entire town seemed to be engulfed in flames. Kate ran inside for the looking glass. She handed it to Charley, who stared through it in horror. He reluctantly passed it to Tyler who did the same.

"What do you see?" Lizzy demanded.

Tyler didn't answer. He simply dropped his arm to his side, his mouth gaping open. Lizzy snatched the glass from him to look for herself.

It seemed as if every building was in flames. Red-gold tongues licked every part of the city, leaving devastation in its wake. Lizzy wanted to scream. She wanted to run to the town and make it stop. This was their home. It was their city. They didn't agree with everything it stood for, but it was home. How could the Union soldiers do this? They were supposed to be the moral ones in this war. How could they leave behind such ruin? The sobering thought made her sick.

Unable to look away, they remained staring at the ruination of their city as the fire devoured everything it touched. No one said anything—thankful they were far enough away from the carnage that they were undamaged, yet disgusted at what the side they had fought so hard for had done.

Jack had returned with the confirmation that Sherman wanted the city destroyed as he left. It wasn't enough simply to win the battles and evacuate the city. He needed to break the spirit of the people who remained by devastating what they had left.

The next day was filled with silence. No one had words to say. Jack took some of his men along with Charley and Tyler to the city to see what could be salvaged. They came back more discouraged than before. Fires still raged through parts of the city. It was worse than they thought.

"Only the nicest houses are left standing," Tyler said absently. "The soldiers kept those for their housing. A few of the churches are still standing, thanks to Father O'Reilly of the Catholic Church. Most machinery is destroyed. The railroads are cut off; bodies litter the streets. We didn't see any civilians left. We were told there were a few, but mainly soldiers remain. Dead animals are strewn about. There's so much carnage, it will take weeks or months to clean it up. It's horrible. Please, Lizzy, don't ask me to take you down there. It's not a fit place for you to be."

She was curious, but the look in his eyes told her to squelch that curiosity for her own good. She wrapped her good arm around her husband and agreed.

The next few months would be filled with attempts to come to grips with what had transpired during the war. The war was not over yet, but, for Lizzy and her family, it was time to begin rebuilding. Their plantation had survived. The wounded had been transported to hospitals as needed. What was left of the cotton had been harvested, though no railroads were working yet to transport the goods. Lizzy resigned herself to the fact that this crop would be wasted. Tyler and Charley helped Jack and the other soldiers who remained for occupation with whatever clean up was occurring for the city, though by December, destruction and ruin was still prominent.

The bright spot in these months came with Maggie's relationship with Jack. They continued seeing each other and were married the week before Christmas by Jack's army chaplain. Their group was finally complete with six. Jack moved into the spacious plantation mansion, not wanting to subject his new bride to soldiers. Though this made for a full house, the family was whole. The support was needed for each member.

The new year turned and, with that, a hope for an end to the war.

CHAPTER 25

"Maggie, there's a letter here for ya," Kate said.

"A letter? Mail is coming through now?" Maggie asked.

"Yes," Jack answered. "Now that Atlanta is part of the Union, communication lines have opened up. They're still working on the supply lines, but communication is starting to trickle through."

Maggie read the envelope. "It's from my mother!" she exclaimed. She had not heard from her family since they moved, with the communication lines down. Tearing into the envelope, she pulled out the letter and poured over the contents.

"Oh no!" she exclaimed.

"What?" Jack asked.

"It's my father," she said tearfully. "He passed away six months ago."

"Oh my goodness." Kate empathized. "What happened?"

"Heart attack," she answered sadly.

"I'm so sorry, honey," Jack said he put his arm around her.

She cried for a few minutes, then read the rest of the letter.

"My mother said she has decided to remain with my grandmother. She's not returning to Atlanta." Maggie felt abandoned. She hadn't been extremely close to her father, but she was close to her mother. Now knowing her mother wouldn't return and not knowing when she would see her next left a bitter taste in her mouth.

"I'm so sorry," Jack repeated, not knowing what to say to comfort his new wife.

Maggie snuggled into her husband's arm as she cried.

Kate left them together to let the others know of the news.

Maggie confided her feelings in her new husband. "I feel abandoned," she said into his shoulder.

"Honey," he said, moving her so he could see her face. "You are not abandoned. We are all here for you. We love you. We are your family. I understand the hurt you must feel, but please know that you will never be abandoned."

Maggie sniffed. "Thank you," she said, amazed again at the love this man showed for her.

The next day, the family held a small memorial service for Maggie's father. She felt so blessed by the family she had here. They all knew they were not alone in anything that came their way. They had endured so much more than any of them would have ever imagined—so much loss, so much fear. They were able to make it through and remain sane due to the help of each person in their little band and due to the strength each member drew from their heavenly Father.

"Can we talk with you for a moment?" One afternoon in March, Charley, Tyler, and Jack entered the parlor, where their wives were working on a baby quilt for one of the workers.

The women put aside their work and gave their husbands their full attention.

"We've been talking," Charley began. "We've noticed that, though things are peaceful around here, there's still a restless air hanging around, especially around you three."

The women started to protest. "We know you," Tyler interrupted. "With the Underground Railroad no longer needed, we can tell that you're struggling with," he paused, not wanting to hurt their feelings, "feelings of uselessness."

Lizzy smiled. "You do know us very well."

Maggie and Kate agreed.

"Well," Charley continued. "We came up with an idea."

"It was Charley's idea," Tyler insisted, wanting to give credit where it was due. "We just agreed with him," Jack added.

Charley smiled. "Anyway, we noticed how much you enjoy working with the freed men and women, especially teaching them. You all practically glow when you are working. Well, what would you think about opening up a school for more freed men and women than just the ones working for us? You could teach them reading, writing, Bible, even nursing. Then Jack, Tyler, and I could teach them business. They could also help out with the crops and household chores as payment, along with a small wage."

"Charley, that's a wonderful idea," Kate exclaimed. "I really did enjoy teachin' nursin.' There will be many people coming back t' th' city who will have no schoolin' or trainin' or anythin.' What a great idea." She beamed at her husband.

"It really is a great idea," Maggie agreed excitedly. "I have the most fun teaching them. It will be great to incorporate more people with this."

Lizzy agreed. "I like it. We have so much timber around here, we could put together a log schoolhouse. I like the idea of them helping around the plantation too. They'll be getting something in return for their work, most of them for the first time in their lives."

Everyone was excited. They made plans for the men to cut down trees and make a log schoolhouse, while the women gathered whatever materials they had to help teach the people. Hannah and Mimi had already been telling them about the freed men and women returning and having nothing with them. This would be a great way to help them get started.

Lizzy, Maggie, and Kate had been feeling a little useless of late. They weren't allowed to help with the clean up of the town since it was so dangerous. Lizzy's shoulder had healed, but it had taken a long time. She was just recently able to do the repetitive motions of sewing with little pain.

Preparations were made, and everyone set out to work. The workers loved the idea and pitched in to help wherever they could. When the soldiers were not working, they helped with the log schoolhouse. Teaching materials were not readily available since the railroad tracks were still being worked on, so the women were innovative in coming up with supplies. With everyone working, they thought their school should be able to open by the end of April.

On April 10, 1865, Jack came galloping up to the plantation. He had been in town. He found everyone working at the schoolhouse site. "Lee surrendered!" he shouted, out of breath.

Everyone stopped working. "What?" Charley asked.

Jack jumped off his horse and accepted the water Eli handed him. After catching his breath, he began excitedly. "Confederate General Lee surrendered to General Grant yesterday in Virginia. The war is ending!"

After a brief moment of stunned silence, Charley and Tyler began the celebration with whoops and cries of joy. Everyone else entered in. They took the rest of the day off from work and celebrated the nearing end of the long and terrible war. They celebrated with abandon. Musicians brought out their instruments. Everyone danced. A bonfire was set up. Food was prepared in between dances. Everyone was overjoyed.

The next few days, the work seemed lighter. Smiles spread across faces. People sang as they worked. They continued to celebrate the surrender in small ways each day.

On Saturday, April 15, after having reverently observed Good Friday the night before, shocking news reached the plantation. One of Jack's soldiers came riding up to give him the news. After receiving the news, he soberly returned to the dining room where everyone was eating lunch.

"President Lincoln was assassinated," he announced.

Everyone was too stunned to answer. No one had any more appetite. They simply stared at their food as it grew cold on their plates. Each silently excused themselves from the table to grieve over their fallen leader.

"Lord, I don't understand," Lizzy prayed. "This man wanted what was right for your people. He wanted to preserve the Union, the country founded on Your principles. He sacrificed so much for this. Plus, he knew no man should ever own another. He went against so much in this country to fight for what was right. How could such a tragedy happen to such a good man?"

The next day was Easter. They attended services with the soldiers. Their group had not been completely welcomed back by the few townspeople who had remained and since returned. The news of their loyalty to the Union had spread. They simply chose to remain close to the soldiers and the freed men and women until attitudes could be changed, if ever they were.

The Easter services were simple and somber, given the news of their fallen leader. How odd it was, Lizzy thought, to be celebrating the resurrection of their Spiritual Leader while mourning the death of their country's leader. The chaplain held a simple funeral for their fallen commander the next day, not wanting to interfere with the Easter celebration.

The shock of President Lincoln's death soon waned as life on the plantation went on as normal. On April 27, they heard the news of another Confederate surrender the day before. This surrender was not celebrated as much as the first one, since they knew there were more forces needing to surrender.

On May 1, their school opened. Thirty new freed men and women attended, agreeing to help with the work on the plantation in exchange for wages and schooling. It proved to be an incredible experience. After having been denied their basic rights, even for education for so long, everyone in attendance was extremely hungry for knowledge. Nothing fulfilled Kate, Maggie, and Lizzy like their times working at the school.

Tyler and Charley thoroughly enjoyed the new workers in the field. They sang as they worked, and the people were extremely grateful to their new employers.

May 5 brought news of more Confederate surrenders. However, everyone was so busy and excited about the school that no one paused to take notice.

News of more importance arrived on May 12. Confederate President Jefferson Davis was captured near Georgia. The faltering attempt at a country was coming to an end.

"I think it's time for us to move," Maggie said one evening, when she and Jack were getting ready for bed.

"Move where?" he inquired.

"I think just to my parents' house, down the river."

"Are you sure?" He was ready to move and have his own house, but he hadn't wanted to suggest the idea to his wife, knowing the bond she had with those they were living with.

"I am ready," she said she and hugged him. "Thank you for staying here. I know it hasn't been easy. I know you've wanted to be alone and start our own life together. It's been wonderful to have the bonds with this family. I think I'm ready to start our own family though. My parents' house has stood empty for nearly four years. It will take a while to clean up, but I think I'm ready to start our lives together, alone."

He smiled and kissed her.

"We've actually discussed the same thing," Charley said, when Maggie and Jack shared their news at breakfast the next morning.

"What, you're ready to get rid of us?" Jack asked joking.

"Well…" Kate teased.

"No." Charley smiled. "Kate and I have discussed wanting our own place. We don't want to leave the plantation, but we think our own space would be nice. We actually thought we'd like to live in the guest house."

"Are you sure?" Lizzy asked. "It's so much smaller than the big house."

"We know," Kate said. "I'm not used t' livin' in such fancy quarters. I come from humble background and actually prefer the small house."

"As much as we've loved living here with everyone," Charley said. "We're ready for our own place. Perhaps someday we'll build a bigger house. As I said though, we don't want to leave the plantation. This will keep us close to everything but in our own place."

Lizzy and Tyler looked at each other in relief.

"Does that look mean you are relieved to have us close or relieved to have us gone?" Charley asked.

"Both," Lizzy giggled. "It has been so wonderful to have everyone here, but four families under one roof is a little much, even if the house does have room to accommodate us all. We each need to start our own lives. You men need to be the heads of your own families, not the shared head of many families. Maggie's house is close enough that they can still come and help with the school. The guest house is close enough that you can still be leader of the plantation. Bartholomew and Hannah will still be here. Do you mind if we stay here?"

"Of course not," Charley said. "I think I will prefer the guest house. I'm glad you want to stay here."

Lizzy was happy. She didn't care as much for the fancy trimmings of the house, but she wanted to remain close to Hannah and Bartholomew.

The move date was set for three days later. The couples enjoyed each other's company for the last nights under one roof. They played games and laughed heartily. They even invited the workers up for a party in the sorely neglected ballroom.

The houses were cleaned during these days to get ready for the move. Once the houses were ready, each couple moved their respective things to start their new lives.

"It sure is quiet," Lizzy said, after everyone had finally moved.

They stood in the doorway of the kitchen and watched as Charley and Kate carried the last of their belongings to the guest house.

Tyler stood behind her and wrapped his arm around her waist. "Is that so bad?" he asked, with a hint of teasing in his voice.

"I guess not," Lizzy sighed. "It's just that this house has been the home to so many people, especially in the past four years, I kind of got used to the noise. It seems somewhat empty now."

"Think of it this way," Tyler consoled, "now we are free to be our own family. And I am free to pamper my wife and protect her. I am also free to take the burden of head of the house off of her and carry it on my large shoulders." He gave her a squeeze, which she returned.

"I like the sound of that."

May 27, 1865, brought the most relieving news of all. The last Confederate troops had surrendered the day before. The Confederacy was no more. The Union had won. The United States of America was united again.

After being told the news, tears freely flowed from the eyes of men and women alike on Riverridge Plantation. They had fought long and hard to this end. It had been a difficult and, at times, horrific road, but they had endured and came out stronger than before. Their faith had been challenged, but God saw them through and held on when they wanted to let go.

At the schoolhouse, Lizzy looked at the people around her—some with light skin and some with dark skin, but all she considered family. "This is what God intended," she said as Tyler came to put his arm around her.

"In His eyes, there are no slave, no free, no black, and no white," he agreed as he kissed the top of her head.

Lizzy turned to embrace her husband. She had waited until the most opportune time to share her news. She whispered in his ear, "Now we can raise our child in a truly free country."

She laughed at the surprise on his face.